PANGS OF LOVE

PANGS OF LOVE

STORIES BY

David Wong Louie

ALFRED A. KNOPF

New York 1991

THIS IS A BORZOI BOOK
PUBLISHED BY ALFRED A. KNOPF, INC.

Some of the stories in this volume originally appeared in somewhat
different form in the following publications: *Agni Review*: "Birthday."
Colorado State Review: "Disturbing the Universe." *The Iowa Review*:
"Bottles of Beaujolais," "One Man's Hysteria—Real and Imagined—
in the Twentieth Century." *Kansas Quarterly*: "Warming Trends."
Mid-American Review: "The Movers." *Ploughshares*: "Displacement."
Quarry West: "Love on the Rocks."

  "Social Science" first appeared in *An Illuminated History of the Future.*

  "Displacement" was reprinted in *The Best American Short Stories
1989.*

Grateful acknowledgment is made to New Directions Publishing Corporation for permission to reprint a poem by Tu Fu from *100 Poems
from the Chinese*, translated by Kenneth Rexroth. Copyright © 1971
by Kenneth Rexroth.

LIBRARY OF CONGRESS CATALOGING-IN-PUBLICATION DATA

Louie, David Wong.
  Pangs of love / David Wong Louie.—1st ed.
    p.   cm.
  ISBN 0-394-58957-2
  1. Asian Americans—Fiction.   I. Title.
PS3562.O818P36   1991
813'.54—dc20   90-53544
                                                   CIP

Manufactured in the United States of America
First Edition

In memory of my father

Contents

PANGS OF LOVE

Birthday

There's a man outside the door. He pounds away at it with his fists, and that whole side of the room shakes. He can pound until the house falls. I don't care, it's his house; he can do with it what he pleases.

He talks to me through the door. His talk is nothing like his knock. His voice is gentle, soothing, contrite. I might even be tempted to say it's sweet, only he's a man, and the man that he is.

I came to see the boy. It's true I have no rights except those that come with love. And if I paid any attention to what the court says, I wouldn't be here. The court says the boy belongs to the man, the boy's father. This has been hard to take. After all, the boy calls us both by our first names, and as far as I'm concerned that means we're equals.

It's the boy's birthday, and back in the days when the world was cold and rainy and sane, back in the days when we still lived together, I had promised we'd go for an afternoon of baseball—sunshine, pop, hotdogs. I told the man I was coming. I kept calling his number, but no one answered. I left plenty of messages on his machine, detailing what I had planned for my date with the boy. No response. When the boy first moved into this house, I tried phoning him every couple of weeks. I just wanted to hear him say my name again, Wallace Wong—the clearest three syllables in his vocabulary when his mother introduced us. But all I ever got for my troubles was the man's recorded voice—until yesterday, that is, when he interrupted the message I was leaving to say, "Wong, why don't you leave us alone?"

I just hung up on him. I couldn't talk to someone who used that tone of voice.

The boy's mother is gone from the picture. She's in New York; I say New York because that's where she's from originally, but she might be in Topeka for all I know. Losing the boy almost killed her. All those days in court for nothing. What did that black robe know about the weave of our three hearts? The man won custody. Perhaps he bribed the judge; it's happened before. More likely it's because he's making money now writing movies, and in this town that's everything. He had written a script based on their marriage and breakup, which was made into a film and did well at the box office, so now he's in big demand.

One day I came home from the shop, and she was gone. No note then, and not a word from her since. But I'm confident she'll come home once her heart's on the mend. Her disappearance wasn't a complete surprise. She's a quirky one. I've learned to expect such behavior. When we first started going out, she wanted me to prove that I really loved her. She was still recovering from the marriage then and didn't trust what anyone said about anything, especially love. So she said she needed proof. I told her okay, but for weeks she couldn't decide what she wanted me to do. Then one day while we were having lunch at a restaurant, she said, "This is it."

"What?"

"Steal his radio." She pointed across the street.

"You crazy?"

The radio went into a health club with a man built like a heavyweight boxer.

I crossed the street, and as I followed the radio into the building, I imagined the possible headline for tomorrow's paper: CHINESE ROMEO BITES GYM FLOOR. Having accepted the possibility of severe bodily injury, I found the actual theft of the radio surprisingly easy. I just hung around the locker room, watching him strip and flex, and when he got up to relieve himself, I snatched up the radio left sitting on the bench.

She met me on the street in front of the gym. "Keep it," she said. "A present from me to you."

This I didn't appreciate. I reminded her the size of that man's fist was bigger than my entire head.

"Frank," she said, laughing in a mean sort of way, "wouldn't hurt anyone he wasn't married to."

That's Frank out there, punching the door.

'm sitting on a kiddie chair. My knees are pressed against the bottom of a table that's under two feet tall. It's as if I'm crammed in a crate. In front of me I have a drawing pad and eight thick crayons. Sooner or later, the man will find the key to the lock or poke his fist through the door. Before that happens, I want to leave the boy a note, just to let him know I didn't forget his birthday. But unless he's learned to read in the past few months, words will be useless. So I have to say my piece with pictures, and I'm not much when it comes to pictures.

I take up the red crayon and draw a circle; then I put in some eyes. I'm trying for a self-portrait but it's sizing up more feline than *Homo sapien*. Soon I admit defeat and finish off the cat with a pair of triangles for ears.

The man calls my name. "Don't do anything funny while I'm away," he says. His footsteps go down the stairs.

I hurry to the window. The man's walking up the front path. He goes about halfway, turns, and looks back at the house. He catches my eyes and gestures with his hand, like an umpire thumbing a guy out.

I try a yellow crayon. I make another circle, but now I'm distracted by the man's absence. Can't draw with him there, can't draw without him. I go to the window. He's standing at the curb, waiting for the boy, or maybe he's called the police.

Back at the table again, I give my drawing some teeth, big yellow squares. My creation reminds me of my father, though no one else would make the connection.

"What good's a son that doesn't know who his own father is?" That's what my father said when I told my parents about the boy and how the three of us planned to set up housekeeping. He didn't care for the idea of his only son adopting a used family. He gritted his false teeth, which he does when he's mad, and said, "Wallace" (he never uses my American name), "don't be such a jerk. There are millions of available Chinese girls. And I'll tell you a secret. The basic anatomy's the same no matter where it comes from. Just say yes, and we'll go to China and find you a nice girl."

My mother nodded, her hair jet black from a beautician's bottle. She said, "Love between lions and sheep has but one consequence." She talks in aphorisms. I don't know if they're the real thing or if she makes them up.

My parents had their hearts set on Connie Chung. "Marry your mother a girl she can talk to without having to use her hands," said my father.

"What makes you think Connie Chung can even speak Chinese?" I said.

"Because she's smart; otherwise, she wouldn't be on TV," said my father.

My mother said, "Only a fool whistles into the wind." At this, even my father shot her a funny look.

On the drive over here I heard a story on the radio about California condors going extinct. I tried to imagine myself as a condor at the dead end of evolution. In my veins I felt the primordial soup bubbling, and my whole entropic bulk quaked as I gazed at the last females of my species. I knew I was supposed to mate, but I wasn't sure how. Yeah, I'd probably have to start by picking a partner. But which one? I looked them over, the last three in creation; she'd need to have good genes. Finally, after careful consideration, I chose—her, the bird with the blond tail feathers. Then I heard my father's voice: "No, not that one, that one."

I wonder if he might be right. Maybe I'd be wise to pack a few suitcases full of Maybelline and soft Italian shoes and go over to China. Plenty of women there in that lipstick-free society. Seduce them with bourgeois decadence, and they'll gladly surrender their governmentally mandated 1.2 children to me.

This morning I taped a sign on the door for my customers, saying that I had to attend a funeral. Even though Saturdays show my best profit, for the boy's birthday I didn't bother to open the shop. I operate an Italian-style café. I traffic in slow death: buttery eggs, pinguid coffee, and sweets on top of sweets. At first business was slow. People didn't believe a Chinaman could produce a decent cappuccino. I could hardly blame them. I'd shy away, too, from moo shu pork from a Sicilian's pan. But I do all right now, and take off when the need comes up.

So I drove over to the man's house, and when I first caught sight of it I was surprised by its size, its thick Greek columns, its funereal cypresses, its imposing terra-cotta roof.

Seated on a white cast-iron love seat by the front door, the man was hunched over a book in which he appeared to be writing. I walked up the long front path, flanked on both sides by enormous expanses of chipped white stone where there should've been grass. He acted as if I weren't there. He just kept on scribbling. This reminded me of his courtroom manner: done up in a pinstriped suit, he sat at his table, writing feverishly on a yellow legal pad, as if he were an agent of the law.

I hated that time. The boy and his mother stayed downtown in a hotel to be near the court building. Each night my father would call to ask who was winning. Of course he was rooting against us. My mother wanted to know if I was eating rice again, now that the girl was gone. I got so confused talking to them that I moved out of the house just to avoid their calls. I set up a cot in the café storeroom and slept next to egg cartons, milk crates, and hot exhaust from the refrigerator fan. Those nights I fell asleep listening to talk shows on the radio.

They were good company. So much misery on the airwaves, it was a comfort. I heard this one guy complaining about his chronic indigestion, and the radio doctor, without so much as laying a stethoscope on him, diagnosed that the caller had cancer. I listened to too many women with a similar story. The husband's a hitter, they'd say, and in the morning she's ready to hit back, but by then the bum's gone off somewhere, so she smacks the kids instead, and wants to know why she doesn't feel sorry for doing so. We were all half-crazed insomniacs, one big aching family.

I even called a radio psychologist the night of the day the boy's mother left me. The second I got through to the station I realized how desperate I was, and felt pretty silly. But I didn't hang up. I had a conversation with the show's producer. He said my story was too complex. He wanted me to simplify it. He advised me that if I wanted the listeners' sympathy I should consider dropping the "Chinese stuff." Before I listened to another word, I told him that I hoped one day he'd be lonesome and heartbroken in the back roads of China, thousands of miles from Western ears, and the nearest ones carved from stone.

"I've been expecting you," said the man. He motioned for me to sit next to him on the love seat. I held my ground. He crossed his legs and reopened his book to a page marked with a greeting card. "You like poetry?" he asked, then bowed his head and finished copying a poem from the book onto the card. "I read this one back in high school, so I guess it must be good." He handed me the card when he was through. His handwriting looked like ants set end to end, painfully tiny words crawling all over the place.

I said, "Would you mind calling the boy?"

"We should talk," he said, taking back the card and slipping it into a hot-pink envelope. "I don't know you from the Gang of Four, and here you are asking for Welby."

I had braced myself for that. Welby. I can hardly say it. Named the poor kid after a TV doctor. The boy's mother swears it was all the man's doing. When she comes home, and we're settled, we'll go to court and have his name changed.

"It's his birthday," I said. "We have plans. The ball game, remember?"

"And don't think he hasn't talked about seeing you," the man said.

"Well then, let's not disappoint the boy." I took a step forward and reached for the doorbell.

"That's not necessary," said the man, rising from his seat. "We're talking now."

He pushed back the cuff of his long-sleeved shirt and checked his watch. "Can you spare me a few minutes?" he said and, with a sweep of his hand, invited me to sit again. This time I did.

"The scene opens in a supermarket," he began. "Rows of fruits and vegetables. People, carts fill the aisle. Close-up on Welby; he's about eighteen months old, sitting in the kiddie seat. I go squeeze avocados. Reverse angle: Welby watches as I join the swarm of shoppers. Pan of aisle, finally zeroing in on a nice-looking lady, who parks her cart next to mine. Zoom in: she's talking to her own kid, who's too big for the kiddie seat and looks awkward and clumsy in it. His head's bowed, eyes dim and sad. His mother says, 'Here's another little boy,' and she disappears among the shoppers. Zoom in on me in the crowd. I look over at Welby. Cut back to kids. Welby's leaning across the cart and pats the new boy, nothing rough, just finding out what the other kid feels like. Twin shot: big boy freezes, letting Welby do his thing, the way people let mean dogs sniff all they want, instead of trying to get away. I return to the cart. See the kid's crying, no noise, just these tears on his cheeks. Mom comes back. I apologize. Close-up on Mom: she's eating a candy bar right in front of her kid's face. You know something's wrong with the picture, but you can't figure out what. It takes a few seconds, but then you realize the kid's blind. Fade out."

"Scene from a new movie?" I asked.

"No, from real life."

"Oh. Look, we have to get going." I stood up and stepped away from the door. "So what's your point?"

He looked at his watch again. "Look, she left me, she

left you. On that score, we're dead even." He came up behind me and put his hand on my shoulder. "Say, what kind of car you driving?" He gave me the gentlest push, and we started walking up the front path. "You know what Welby thought when he came to live here? He thought he was being punished for breaking up our marriage. How do you think that made me feel? We all do things we don't mean, and end up hurting people. I hurt her, she hurt me; now you're hurt."

We were still walking toward the curb. The man nudged me whenever my feet slowed down.

"Frank, look, thanks for the talk."

"Sure," he said. "It's about time we had a man-to-man." He touched me on the shoulder again.

"But you're forgetting something—where's Welby? We really should hit the road. I promised him batting practice."

"Say, that reminds me, what kind of tickets you buy? I'll reimburse you for them."

We reached the curb. He opened the driver-side door and rolled down the window. "The ballpark express," he said, sweeping his hand past the opening, like a model on a game show showing off a prize.

I slid in behind the wheel. "Okay. Now call Welby."

He shut the door and crouched, his big forearms resting against the bottom of the window. "Listen to me," Frank said. "To Welby, you're big time. You're like a living, breathing video game. There've been times I couldn't stand being around him. He'd tell stories: 'One day me and Wallace Wong' did this, did that. I'm never in any of his stories." The man looked into the side-view mirror and fixed his hair. "But I'm his father, right? Come on, give me a chance. Leave us alone, okay? He's starting to get used to me."

It was obvious he wasn't going to hand the boy over.

So I proposed a trade: I'd do what he wanted, but in exchange I'd get the boy for the afternoon. We'd have so much fun, the man would need all of geologic time to chase those nine innings from the boy's memory.

He drummed his fingers against the door and looked at his watch. "It's late," he said. "You better get rolling." He reached across my body and pointed at the ignition switch.

My equal and opposite reaction: I leaned on the horn. I got in two long blasts before he stopped my hand. "The people in this neighborhood are still sleeping," he said. "Now listen up, friend, I'm telling you for your own good—you don't want to be here."

"So get the boy," I said. I brought my fist down on the dashboard to show I meant business. The glove compartment flew open. Things spilled onto the passenger seat.

"Hey, my radio," said the man.

"Your what? What do you mean, your radio?" I had brought it along so we could listen to the play-by-play in the stands.

"That's her. Zenith eight transistor with a crack in back where the battery goes."

I shook my head.

"Don't be that way," he said. "I know all about it. Sylvie told me she made you steal it."

"She what?"

"Sylvie always was a touch *loco en la cabeza*." He tapped his finger against his temple. "She always had funny ideas, don't you think so?"

"Here," I said, "take the radio."

"No, you keep her."

"I don't want it. I never did."

"No, keep her," he said. "Must feel like she belongs to you now anyway."

He stood up from his crouch and checked the time. "We need to stop fooling around. I have an appointment in a few minutes with someone. So, if you don't mind—"

"You mean like a date, Frank? You have a girlfriend?" He didn't answer.

"Well, don't let me stand in the way of romance. Just call the boy, and we'll be off. Think of me as his sitter. Then you two will have the whole afternoon free to yourselves."

The man put his hands on his hips and arched his back. "Nothing's clicking with you, is it? Come with me," he said. "I have something to show you."

We walked up the front path, and I followed him into the kitchen. "Smell that?" he said. "Welby's birthday cake. My first ever, and I'm doing it from scratch. Fudge swirl topped with chocolate mousse frosting." He caught my eye and grinned. He was proud of his achievement. The place was a mess—bowls, spoons, measuring cups, cookbook, batter, eggshells, flour scattered and smeared everywhere. The cake layers were cooling on racks. "I'm trying my best," he said.

I was standing in an archway that separated the kitchen from the dining area. Past the round glass table, the wall of glass bricks, the giant earthenware horse, just to the left of the dwarf lemon tree, I spotted the staircase to the second floor. I had a clear path, an easy dash, and I'd be upstairs where the boy was waiting for me.

"Say, you cook in a restaurant," he said, picking the cookbook off the counter. "Maybe you can help. What do they mean by fold egg mixture into the chocolate?" he asked. "Am I supposed to pour the whole thing out and fold it with my hands?" He had his nose in the book and reread the passage.

I didn't hang around to give my expert advice.

The boy's room was the second off the hallway. I locked the door. Why there was a lock on the boy's door, I'll never know. But I was glad it was there. At first, I thought I had the wrong room. It didn't look like a child's room. At least not one the boy's age. The walls were covered with posters of TV starlets. So much cleavage and bare thigh couldn't be good for someone that young. I wondered what a social worker would think if I sent one up here.

The man knocked on the door. "Can't you see," he said, "Welby's not home? I sent him to a friend's for the night so I can bake his cake. It's a surprise."

It was my surprise. "He has to come home sometime," I said.

"Get out of there!" he shouted. "You can still make the game if you leave now."

I didn't answer. The man then started to pound on the door. I went over and inspected the boy's toy shelves. I couldn't tell if the boy had chosen the toys or, like the posters, they were a reflection of the man's tastes. There was such an emphasis on angles, gadgetry, and intimidation. Very high-tech stuff. Mostly robots, rockets, and spaceguns. So much plastic and chrome. Do kids instinctively gravitate to these materials? Whatever happened to animal love, the considerate petting of fur? I searched for the stuffed rabbit I had given him back in the good times. It was nowhere in sight. I wanted to believe it had accompanied him on the overnight but knew that wasn't likely. Then I tried to imagine the boy playing with these contraptions. I tried to hear the accompanying narrative as he sailed the toys through outer space. But I couldn't remember his voice. It was lost to me, just as my own boyhood voice is forever gone, tumbling across light-years and, like radio signals, bouncing off the four corners of the universe.

watch the man coming toward the house. I hear him climb the stairs. He goes past my room. Then, a few minutes later, he knocks at my door. "You're in there now," he says. "So stay put. Got it?" He hurries downstairs. I go to the window. He's in a sports coat now, as he jogs to the curb. In one hand is a bunch of flowers wrapped in pink paper, in the other the greeting card. I don't know what to think. First killer robots and now poetry and roses?

The man runs off the curb. He surveys the sun-washed street, checks his watch once more, and then looks back at me.

Soon a car pulls up behind mine. I look for the boy in the backseat. If I do seventy all the way, we can still catch the first pitch.

The driver gets out: a woman with coral-red hair, cropped close to her scalp, earrings like a set of handcuffs, and miles of doodads around her neck. She's wearing a sleeveless purple jumpsuit that shifts like leather. I try my best to see into the car. But there's no sign of life.

The woman adjusts her sunglasses and throws her arms around the man. He crushes the flowers against the small of her back. I had forgotten about her coming. Quite a change from the boy's mother. But that's none of my business.

I return to the little table and look at what I've drawn. I wish I had some talent. At least a bit of imagination. On the page is a flock of animals, ones the boy used to ask me to draw. "How about a horse," he'd say, handing me a crayon. And no matter how the drawing turned out, I'd say, "That's a horse," and he'd generously say, "That's a horse."

I don't know if he'll still be so generous, now that he's abandoned rabbits for ray guns, but he'll know who did the drawings. It troubles me, though, that I haven't said what I want to say, that no matter how hard I try, I'm stuck doing the same old things in the same old ways. What have I accomplished but a page full of nouns—a camel, a dog, a cat, a cow, a bird, and my famous horse. Sure, I can try adopting a new vocabulary, sketch in a rocket ship, a rectangle, and a few well-placed triangles. That shouldn't be too hard. But that's not how he knows me. Ours was a simpler world. He must be a different boy now. The universe he knows has expanded, just as his palette broadened during our time together. This is inevitable. But in this expansion have I been eclipsed? Am I like a rattle, once a favorite toy, then—not so much discarded, but neglected with the discovery of blocks and things with wheels? I wish there was some way for me to know what he's up to, the way my father came home one day from Sears with a bat and ball and glove for me. There he was, son of China's great famines, who knew nothing of earned-run averages or the number of homers Mantle hit in '56, but somehow he anticipated my next step. With the boy, I didn't know what to think. Will the drawings delight him? That's what I mean—I should know.

I look out at the street. The trunk of the woman's car is open, and there's a ton of luggage stacked on the sidewalk. She must be here on an extended visit or else she's moving in. None of that's my business either, but she better not think she can take the boy's mother's place.

The woman goes over to my car. It's just an old VW square-back, but she's really checking it over. She does a lap around it, then sticks her head in the driver's window. She holds the radio up in her hand. The man's saying things that don't seem to please her. She spins away from him and starts up the front path. The man points at the house. She flips up her sunglasses. She sees me; I see her, too. I've waited a long time for this day. But it isn't how I've imagined it would feel when Sylvie finally came home.

The man catches her halfway up the front walk. They argue, but I can't hear them. About a minute later, they move slowly toward the street, turn at her luggage, and keep walking until they're gone from sight. It's plain they're giving me a chance to leave.

I go downstairs. The house is still sweet with baking.

I reach the foyer but then make a U-turn and go to the kitchen. The layers of cake have cooled nicely.

What else is there for me to do? It is his birthday.

I crack an egg and separate the yolk from the whites. I repeat this three more times. I add sugar to the yolks and beat them with a whisk. This feels good. Then I heat up a pan of water and melt the chocolate in a second pan. In the meantime I beat the egg whites. I'm not thinking now. The whites hold their peaks perfectly. I mix the chocolate with the sugar and the yolks. Then I fold in the whipped whites.

I work briskly. And for the first time in a long time, perhaps for the first time ever, I feel at peace. I'm not familiar with this recipe, but I know what I need to do.

I spread the mousse on the layers of cake. I spread it on thick. This, I know, the boy will like.

Displacement

Mrs. Chow heard the widow. She tried reading faster but kept stumbling over the same lines. She thought perhaps she was misreading them: "There comes, then, finally, the prospect of atomic war. If the war is ever to be carried to China, common sense tells us only atomic weapons could promise maximum loss with minimum damage."

When she heard the widow's wheelchair, she tossed the copy of *Life* down on the couch, afraid she might be found out. The year was 1952.

Outside the kitchen, Chow was lathering the windows. He worked a soft brush in a circular motion. Inside, the widow was accusing Mrs. Chow of stealing her cookies. The widow had a handful of them clutched to her chest and brought one down hard against the table. She was counting. Chow waved, but Mrs. Chow only shook her head. He soaped up the last pane and disappeared.

Standing accused, Mrs. Chow wondered if this was what it was like when her parents faced the liberators who had come to reclaim her family's property in the name of the People. She imagined her mother's response to them: "What people? All of my servants are clothed and decently fed."

The widow swept the cookies off the table as if they were a canasta trick won. She started counting again. Mrs. Chow and the widow had played out this scene many times before. As on other occasions, she didn't give the old woman the satisfaction of a plea, guilty or otherwise.

Mrs. Chow ignored the widow's busy blue hands. She fixed her gaze on the woman's milky eyes instead. Sight resided at the peripheries. Mornings, before she prepared the tub, emptied the piss pot, or fried the breakfast meat, Mrs. Chow cradled the widow's oily scalp and applied the yellow drops that preserved what vision was left in the cold, heaven-directed eyes.

"Is she watching?" said the widow. She tilted her big gray head sideways; a few degrees in any direction Mrs. Chow became a blur. In happier days, Mrs. Chow might have positioned herself just right or left of center, neatly within a line of sight.

Mrs. Chow was thirty-five years old. After a decade-long separation from her husband, she finally had entered the United States in 1950 under the joint auspices of the War Brides and Refugee Relief acts. She would agree she was a bride, but not a refugee, even though the Red Army had confiscated her home and turned it into a technical school. During the trouble, she was away safely studying in Hong Kong. Her parents, with all their wealth, could've easily escaped, but they were confident a few well-placed bribes among the Red hooligans would put an end to the foolishness. Mrs. Chow assumed her parents now were dead. She had seen pictures in *Life* of minor landlords tried and executed for lesser crimes against the People.

The widow's fondness for calling Mrs. Chow a thief

began soon after the old woman broke her hip. At first, Mrs. Chow blamed the widow's madness on pain displacement. She had read in a textbook that a malady in one part of the body could show up as a pain in another locale—sick kidneys, for instance, might surface as a mouthful of sore gums. The bad hip had weakened the widow's brain function. Mrs. Chow wanted to believe the crazy spells weren't the widow's fault, just as a baby soiling its diapers can't be blamed. But even a mother grows weary of changing them.

"I live with a thief under my roof," the widow said to the kitchen. "I could tell her to stop, but why waste my breath? She's too dumb to understand me anyway."

When the widow was released from the hospital, she returned to the house with a live-in nurse. Soon afterward her daughter paid a visit, and the widow told her she didn't want the nurse around anymore. "She can do me," the widow said, pointing in Mrs. Chow's direction. "She won't cost a cent. Besides, I don't like being touched that way by a person who knows what she's touching," she said of the nurse.

Nobody, not even her husband, knew, but Mrs. Chow spoke a passable though highly accented English she had learned in British schools. Her teachers in Hong Kong always said that if she had the language when she came to the States, she'd be treated better than other immigrants. Chow couldn't have agreed more. Once she arrived, he started to teach her everything he knew in English. But that amounted to very little, considering he had been here for more than ten years. And what he had mastered came out crudely and strangely twisted. His phrases, built from a vocabulary of deference and accommodation, irritated Mrs. Chow for the way they resembled the obsequious blabber of her servants back home.

The Chows had been hired ostensibly to drive the widow to her canasta club, to clean the house, to do the shopping, and, since the bad hip, to oversee her personal hygiene. In return they lived rent-free upstairs in the rooms where the widow's children grew up, three tiny bedrooms and a large bath. Plenty of space, it would seem, except the widow wouldn't allow them to clear out her children's old furniture and toys and things that pressed up against their new life together.

On weekends and Tuesday afternoons, Chow borrowed the widow's tools and gardened for spending money. Friday nights, after they dropped the widow off at the canasta club, the Chows dined at Ming's and then went to the amusement park at the beach boardwalk. First and last, they got in line to ride the Milky Way. On the day the Immigration authorities finally let Mrs. Chow go, before she even saw her new home, Chow took his bride to the boardwalk. He wanted to impress her with her new country. All that machinery, brainwork, and labor done for the sake of fun. He never tried the roller coaster before she arrived; he saved it for her. After that very first time he realized he was much happier with his feet on the ground. But not Mrs. Chow. Oh, this speed, this thrust at the sky, this UP! Oh, this raging, clattering, pushy country! So big! And since that first ride she looked forward to Friday nights and the wind whipping through her hair, stinging her eyes, blowing away the top layers of dailiness. On the longest, most dangerous descent, her dry mouth would open to a silent O and she would thrust up her arms as if she could fly away.

Some nights as the Chows waited in line, a gang of toughs out on a strut, trussed in denim and combs, would stop and visit: MacArthur, they said, will drain the Pacific; the H-bomb will wipe Korea clean of Commies; the

Chows were to blame for Pearl Harbor; the Chows, they claimed, were Red Chinese spies. On occasion, overextending his skimpy English, Chow mounted a defense: he had served in the U.S. Army; his citizenship was blessed by the Department of War; he was a member of the American Legion. The toughs would laugh at the way he talked. Mrs. Chow cringed at his habit of addressing them as "sirs."

"Get out, get out!" the widow said. She brought her fist down on the table. Cookies broke, fell to the floor.

"Yes, missus," said Mrs. Chow, thinking how she'd have to clean up the mess.

The widow, whose great-great-great-grandfather had been a central figure within the faction advocating Washington's coronation, was eighty-six years old. Each day, Mrs. Chow dispensed medications that kept her alive. At times, though, Mrs. Chow wondered if the widow would notice if she were handed an extra blue pill or one less red.

Mrs. Chow filled an enamel-coated washbasin with warm water from the tap. "What's she doing?" said the widow. "Stealing my water now, is she?" Ever since Mrs. Chow first came into her service, the widow, with the exception of her hip, had avoided serious illness. But how she had aged: her ears were enlarged; the opalescence in her eyes had spread; her hands worked as if they were chipped from glass. Some nights, as she and her husband lay awake in their twin-size bed, Mrs. Chow would imagine old age as green liquid that seeped into a person's tissues, where it coagulated and, with time, crumbled, caving in the cheeks and the breasts it had once supported. In the dark she fretted that fluids from the widow's old body had taken refuge in her youthful cells. On such nights she reached for Chow, touched him through the cool top sheet, and was comforted by the fit of her fingers in the shallows between his ribs.

Mrs. Chow knelt at the foot of the wheelchair and set the washbasin on the floor. The widow laughed. "Where did my little thief go?" She laughed again, her eyes closing, her head dropping to her shoulder. "Now she's after my water. Better see if the tap's still there." Mrs. Chow abruptly swung aside the wheelchair's footrests and slipped off the widow's matted cloth slippers and dunked her puffy blue feet into the water. It was the widow's naptime, and her physician had prescribed a warm footbath to stimulate circulation before she could be put to bed; otherwise, in her sleep, her blood might settle comfortably in her toes.

Chow was talking long distance to the widow's daughter in Texas. Earlier, the widow had told the daughter that the Chows were threatening again to leave. She apologized for her mother's latest spell of wildness. "Humor her," the daughter said. "She must've had another one of her little strokes."

Later, Mrs. Chow told her husband she wanted to leave the widow. "My fingers," she said, snapping off the rubber gloves the magazine ads claimed would guarantee her beautiful hands into the next century. "I wasn't made for such work."

When she was a girl, her parents had sent her to a Christian school in Hong Kong for training in Western-style art. The authorities agreed she was talented. As expected, she excelled there. Her portrait of the King was chosen to hang in the school cafeteria. When the colonial Minister of Education on a tour of the school saw her painting, he requested a sitting with the gifted young artist.

A date was set. The rumors said a successful sitting would bring her the ultimate fame: a trip to London to paint the royal family. But a month before the great day she refused to do the Minister's portrait. She gave no reason; in fact, she stopped talking. The school administration was embarrassed, and her parents were furious. It was a great scandal; a mere child from a country at the edge of revolution but medieval in its affection for authority had snubbed the mighty British colonizers. She was sent home. Her parents first appealed to family pride; then they scolded and threatened her. She hid from them in a wardrobe, where her mother found her holding her fingers over lighted matches.

The great day came and went, no more momentous than the hundreds that had preceded it. That night her father apologized to the world for raising such a child. With a bamboo cane he struck her outstretched hand—heaven help her if she let it fall one inch—and as her bones were young and still pliant, they didn't fracture or break, thus multiplying the blows she had to endure.

"Who'd want you now?" her mother said. Her parents sent her to live with a servant family. She could return to her parents' home when she was invited. On those rare occasions, she refused to go. Many years passed before she met Chow, who had come on the grounds of their estate seeking work. They were married on the condition he take her far away. He left for America, promising to send for her when he had saved enough money for her passage. She returned to Hong Kong and worked as a secretary. Later she studied at the university.

Now as she talked about leaving the widow, it wasn't the chores or the old woman that she gave as the reason, though in the past she had complained the widow was a nuisance, an infantile brat born of an unwelcomed union. This time she said she had a project in mind, a great canvas of a yet undetermined subject. But that would come. Her imagination would return, she said, once she was away from that house.

It was the morning of a late-spring day. A silvery light filtered through the wall of eucalyptus and warmed the dew on the widow's roof, striking the plums and acacia, irises and lilies, in such a way that, blended with the heavy air and the noise of a thousand birds, one sensed the universe wasn't so vast, so cold, or so angry, and even Mrs. Chow suspected that it might be a loving thing.

Mrs. Chow had finished her morning chores. She was in the bathroom rinsing the smell of bacon from her hands. She couldn't wash deep enough, however, to rid her fingertips of perfumes from the widow's lotions and creams, which, over the course of months, had seeped indelibly into the whorls. But today her failure was less maddening. Today she was confident the odors would eventually fade. She could afford to be patient. They were going to interview for an apartment of their very own.

"Is that new?" Chow asked, pointing to the camisole his wife had on. He adjusted his necktie against the starched collar of a white short-sleeved shirt, which billowed out from baggy, seersucker slacks. His hair was slicked back with fragrant pomade.

"I think it's the daughter's," said Mrs. Chow. "She won't miss it." Mrs. Chow smoothed the silk undershirt against her stomach. She guessed the shirt was as old as she was; the daughter probably had worn it in her teens. Narrow at the hips and the bust, it fit Mrs. Chow nicely. Such a slight figure, she believed, wasn't fit for labor.

Chow saw no reason to leave the widow's estate. He had found his wife what he thought was the ideal home, certainly not as grand as her parents' place, but one she'd feel comfortable in. Why move, he argued, when there were no approaching armies, no floods, no one telling them to go? Mrs. Chow understood. It was just that he was very Chinese, and very peasant. Sometimes she would tease him. If the early Chinese sojourners who came to America were all Chows, she would say, the railroad wouldn't have been constructed, and Ohio would be all we know of California.

The Chows were riding in the widow's green Buick. As they approached the apartment building, Mrs. Chow reapplied lipstick to her mouth.

It was a modern two-story stucco building, painted pink, surrounded by asphalt, with aluminum windows and a flat roof that met the sky like an engineer's level. Because friends of theirs lived in the apartment in question, the Chows were already familiar with its layout. They went to the manager's house at the rear of the property. Here the grounds were also asphalt. Very contemporary, no greenery anywhere. The closest things to trees were the clothesline's posts and crossbars.

The manager's house was a tiny replica of the main building. Chow knocked at the screen door. A radio was on and the smell of baking rushed through the wire mesh. An orange-colored cat came to the door, followed by a girl. "I'm Velvet," she said. "This is High Noon." She gave the cat's tail a tug. "My mother did this to me," said Velvet, picking at clomps of her hair, ragged as tossed salad; someone apparently had cut it while the girl was in motion. She had gray, almost colorless eyes, which, taken with her hair, gave her the appearance of agitated smoke. She threw a wicked look at the room behind her.

A large woman emerged from the back room carrying a basket of laundry. She wasn't fat, but large in the way horses are large. Her face was round and pink, with fierce little eyes and hair the color of olive oil and dripping wet. Her arms were thick and white, like soft tusks of ivory.

"It's the people from China," Velvet said.

The big woman nodded. "Open her up," she told the girl. "It's okay."

The front room was a mess, littered with evidence of frantic living. This was, perhaps, entropy in its final stages. The Chows sat on the couch. From all around her Mrs. Chow sensed a slow creep: the low ceiling seemed to be sinking, cat hairs clung to clothing, a fine spray from the fish tank moistened her bare arm.

No one said anything. It was as if they were sitting in a hospital waiting room. The girl watched the Chows. The large woman stared at a green radio at her elbow broadcasting news about the war in Korea. Every so often she looked suspiciously up at the Chows. "You know me," she said abruptly. "I'm Remora Cass."

On her left, suspended in a swing, was the biggest, ugliest baby Mrs. Chow had ever seen. It was dozing, arms dangling, great melon head flung so far back that it appeared to be all nostrils and chins. "A pig-boy," Mrs. Chow said in Chinese. Velvet jabbed two fingers into the baby's rubbery cheeks. Then she sprang back from the swing and executed a feral dance, all elbows and knees. She seemed incapable of holding her body still.

She caught Mrs. Chow's eye. "This is Ed," she said. "He has no hair."

Mrs. Chow nodded.

"Quit," said Remora Cass, swatting at the girl as if she were a fly. Then the big woman looked Mrs. Chow in the eyes and said, "I know what you're thinking, and you're right. There's not a baby in the state bigger than Ed; eight pounds, twelve ounces at birth and he doubled that inside a month." She stopped, bringing her palms heavily down on her knees, and shook her wet head. "You don't understand me, do you?"

Mrs. Chow was watching Velvet.

"Quit that!" Remora Cass slapped the girl's hand away from the baby's face.

"Times like this I'd say it's a blessing my Aunt Eleanor's deaf," said Remora Cass. "I've gotten pretty good with sign language." From her overstuffed chair she repeated in pantomime what she had said about the baby.

Velvet mimicked her mother's generous, sweeping movements. When Remora Cass caught sight of her, she added a left jab at the girl's head to her repertoire of gestures. Velvet slipped the punch with practiced ease. But the blow struck the swing set. Everyone tensed. Ed flapped his arms and went on sleeping. "Leave us alone," said Remora Cass, "before I really get mad."

The girl chased down the cat and skipped toward the door. "I'm bored anyway," she said.

Remora Cass asked the Chows questions, first about jobs and pets. Then she moved on to matters of politics and patriotism. "What's your feeling about the Red Chinese in Korea?"

A standard question. "Terrible," said Chow, giving his standard answer. "I'm sorry. Too much trouble."

Mrs. Chow sat by quietly. She admired Chow's effort. She had studied the language, but he did the talking; she wanted to move, but he had to plead their case; it was his kin back home who benefited from the new regime, but he had to bad-mouth it.

Remora Cass asked about children.

"No, no, no," Chow said, answering as his friend Bok had coached him. His face was slightly flushed from the question. Chow wanted children, many children. But whenever he discussed the matter with his wife, she answered that she already had one, meaning the old woman, of course, and that was enough.

"Tell your wife later," the manager said, "what I'm about to tell you now. I don't care what jobs you do, just so long as you have them. What I say goes for the landlady. I'm willing to take a risk on you. Be nice to have nice quiet folks up there like Rikki and Bok. Rent paid up, I can live with anyone. Besides, I'm real partial to Chinese take-out. I know we'll do just right."

The baby moaned, rolling its head from side to side. His mother stared at him as if in all the world there were just the two of them.

Velvet came in holding a beach ball. She returned to her place beside the swing and started to hop, alternating legs, with the beach ball held to her head. "She must be in some kind of pain," Mrs. Chow said to her husband.

The girl mimicked the Chinese she heard. Mrs. Chow glared at Velvet as if she were the widow during one of her spells. The look froze the girl, standing on one leg. Then she said, "Can Ed come out to play?"

Chow took hold of his wife's hand and squeezed it the way he did to brace himself before the roller coaster's forward plunge. Then in a single, well-rehearsed motion, Remora Cass swept off her slipper and punched at the girl. Velvet masterfully sidestepped the slipper and let the beach ball fly. The slipper caught the swing set; the beach ball bounced off Ed's lap.

The collisions released charged particles into the air that seemed to hold everyone in a momentary state of paralysis. The baby's eyes peeled open, and he blinked at the ceiling. Soon his distended belly started rippling. He cried until he turned purple, then devoted his energy to maintaining that hue. Mrs. Chow had never heard anything as harrowing. She visualized his cry as large cubes forcing their way into her ears.

Remora Cass picked Ed up and bounced on the balls of

her feet. "You better start running," she said to Velvet, who was already on her way out the door.

Remora Cass half smiled at the Chows over the baby's shoulder. "He'll quiet down sooner or later," she said.

Growing up, Mrs. Chow had been the youngest of five girls. She'd had to endure the mothering of her sisters, who, at an early age, were already in training for their future roles. Each married in her teens, plucked in turn by a Portuguese, a German, a Brit, and a New Yorker. They had many babies. But Mrs. Chow thought little of her sisters' example. Even when her parents made life unbearable, she never indulged in the hope that a man—foreign or domestic—or a child could save her from her unhappiness.

From the kitchen Remora Cass called Mrs. Chow. The big woman was busy with her baking. The baby was slung over her shoulder. "Let's try something," she said as she transferred the screaming Ed into Mrs. Chow's arms.

Ed was a difficult package. Not only was he heavy and hot and sweaty but he spat and squirmed like a sack of kittens. She tried to think of how it was done. She tried to think of how a baby was held. She remembered Romanesque Madonnas cradling their gentlemanly babies in art history textbooks. If she could get his head up by hers, that would be a start.

Remora Cass told Mrs. Chow to try bouncing and showed her what she meant. "Makes him think he's still inside," she said. Ed emitted a long, sustained wail, then settled into a bout of hiccups. "You have a nice touch with him. He won't do that for just anyone."

As the baby quieted, a pain rolled from the heel of Mrs. Chow's brain, down through her pelvis, to a southern terminus at the backs of her knees. She couldn't blame the baby entirely for her discomfort. He wanted only to escape; animal instinct told him to leap from danger.

She was the one better equipped to escape. She imagined invading soldiers murdering livestock and planting flags in the soil of her ancestral estate, as if it were itself a little nation; they make history by the slaughter of generations of her family; they discover her in the wardrobe, striking matches; they ask where she has hidden her children, and she tells them there are none; they say, good, they'll save ammunition, but also too bad, so young and never to know the pleasure of children (even if they'd have to murder them). Perhaps this would be the subject of her painting, a non-representational canvas that hinted at a world without light. Perhaps—

Ed interrupted her thought. He had developed a new trick. "Woop, woop, woop," he went, thrusting his pelvis against her sternum in the manner of an adult male in the act of mating. She called for Chow.

Remora Cass slid a cookie sheet into the oven and swept Ed off Mrs. Chow's shoulder and then stuck a bottle of baby formula into his mouth. He drained it instantly. "You do have a way with him," said Remora Cass.

They walked into the front room. The baby was sleepy and dripping curds on his mother's shoulder. Under the swing High Noon, the cat, was licking the nipple of an abandoned bottle. "Scat!" she said. "Now where's my wash gone to?" she asked the room. "What's she up to now?" She scanned the little room, big feet planted in the deep brown shag carpet, hands on her beefy hips, baby slung over her shoulder like a pelt. "Velvet—" she started. That was all. Her jaw locked, her gums gleamed, her eyes rolled into her skull. Her head flopped backward as if at the back of her neck there was a great hinge. Then she yawned, and the walls seemed to shake.

Remora Cass rubbed her eyes. "I'm bushed," she said.

Mrs. Chow went over to the screen door. Chow and the girl were at the clothesline. Except for their hands and legs, they were hidden behind a bed sheet. The girl's feet were in constant motion. From the basket her hands picked up pieces of laundry that Chow's hands then clipped to the line.

"Her daddy's hardly ever here," Remora Cass said. "Works all hours, he does. Has to." She patted Ed on the back, then rubbed her eyes again. "Looks like Velvet's found a friend. She won't do that with anyone. You two are naturals with my two. You should get you some of your own." She looked over at Mrs. Chow and laughed. "Maybe it's best you didn't get that. Here." She set the baby on Mrs. Chow's shoulder. "This is what it's like when they're sleeping."

Before leaving, the Chows went to look at Rikki and Bok's apartment. They climbed up the stairs. No one was home. Rikki and Bok had barely started to pack. Bok's naked man, surrounded by an assortment of spears and arrows, was still hanging on the living-room wall. Bok had paid good money for the photograph: an aboriginal gent stares into the camera; he's smiling, his teeth are good and large, and in his palms he's holding his sex out like a prize eel.

Mrs. Chow looked at the photograph for as long as it was discreetly possible before she averted her eyes and made her usual remark about Bok's tastes. Beyond the building's edge she saw the manager's cottage, bleached white in the sun. Outside the front door Remora Cass sat in a folding chair, her eyes shut, her pie-tin face turned up to catch the rays, while Velvet, her feet anchored to the asphalt, rolled her mother's hair in pink curlers. Between the big woman's legs the baby lay in a wicker basket. He was quietly rocking from side to side. Remora Cass's chest rose and fell in the rhythm of sleep.

Driving home, they passed the boardwalk, and Mrs. Chow asked if they might stop.

Chow refused to ride the roller coaster in the daytime, no matter how much Mrs. Chow teased. It was hard enough at night, when the heights from which the cars fell were lit by a few rows of bulbs. As he handed her an orange ticket, Chow said, "A drunk doesn't look in mirrors."

The Milky Way clattered into the terminus. After she boarded the ride, she watched Chow, who had wandered from the loading platform and was standing beside a popcorn wagon, looking up at a billboard. His hands were deep in the pockets of his trousers, his legs crossed at the shins. That had been his pose, the brim of his hat low on his brow, as he waited for her finally to pass through the gates of Immigration.

"Go on," an old woman said. "You'll be glad you did." The old woman nudged her young charge toward the empty seat in Mrs. Chow's car. "Go on, she won't bite." The girl looked back at the old woman. "Grand-muth-ther!" she said, and then reluctantly climbed in beside Mrs. Chow.

Once the attendant strapped the girl in, she turned from her grandmother and stared at her new companion. The machine jerked away from the platform. They were climbing the first ascent when Mrs. Chow snuck a look at the girl. She was met by the clearest eyes she had ever known, eyes that didn't shy from the encounter. The girl's pupils, despite the bright sun, were fully dilated, stretched with fear. Now that she had Mrs. Chow's attention, she turned her gaze slowly toward the vertical track ahead. Mrs. Chow looked beyond the summit to the empty blue sky.

Within seconds they tumbled through that plane and plunged downward, the cars flung suddenly left and right, centrifugal force throwing Mrs. Chow against the girl's rigid body. She was surprised by Chow's absence.

It's gravity that makes the stomach fly, that causes the liver to flutter; it's the body catching up with the speed of falling. Until today, she had never known such sensations. Today there was a weightiness at her core, like a hard, concentrated pull inward, as if an incision has been made and a fist-sized magnet embedded.

Her arms flew up, two weak wings cutting the rush of wind. But it wasn't the old sensation this time, not the familiar embrace of the whole fleeting continent, but a grasp at something once there, now lost.

Chow had moved into position to see the riders' faces as they careened down the steepest stretch of track. Whenever he was up there with her, his eyes were clenched and his scream so wild and his grip on his life so tenuous that he never noticed her expression. At the top of the rise the cars seemed to stop momentarily, but then up and over, tumbling down, at what appeared, from his safe vantage point, a surprisingly slow speed. Arms shot up, the machine whooshed past him, preceded a split second earlier by the riders' collective scream. And for the first time Chow thought he heard her, she who loved this torture so, scream too.

As she was whipped skyward once more, her arms were wrapped around the little girl. Not in flight, not soaring, but anchored by another's being, as her parents stood against the liberators to protect their land.

Some curves, a gentle dip, one last sharp bend, and the ride rumbled to rest. The girl's breath was warm against

Mrs. Chow's neck. For a moment longer she held on to the girl, whose small ribs were as thin as paintbrushes.

The Chows walked to the edge of the platform. He looked up at the billboard he had noticed earlier. It was a picture of an American woman with bright red hair, large red lips, and a slightly upturned nose; a fur was draped around her neck, pearls cut across her throat.

"What do you suppose they're selling?" he asked.

His wife pointed at the billboard. She read aloud what was printed there: "No other home permanent wave looks, feels, behaves so much like naturally curly hair."

She then gave a quick translation and asked what he thought of her curling her hair.

He made no reply. For some time now he couldn't lift his eyes from her.

"I won't do it," she said, "but what do you say?"

She turned away from him and stared a long time at the face on the billboard and then at the beach on the other side of the boardwalk and at the ocean, the Pacific Ocean, and at the horizon where all lines of sight converge, before she realized the land on the other side wouldn't come into view.

Bottles
of Beaujolais

I will move storms . . .
—A Midsummer Night's Dream

It was a little after eight one morning in late November. Fog, fat with brine, snailed uptown. Bits of the wayward cloud beaded between my lashes, crept into the creases of my clothing, and infiltrated my every pore, seeping a dank chill throughout my body. On the radio the man said the fog had set a new record for low visibility. Later, as the taxi pulled in front of the sashimi bar where I worked, the cabbie said that by nightfall the city would be covered with snow.

Unlocking the door to the sashimi bar, I watched Mushimono in the show window standing upright on his hindquarters. He was thick and cylindrical, a furry fireplug. The otter, whose love for fish had inspired my employer to install him as a sales gimmick to lure other fish connoisseurs to the shop, seemed baffled by the fog. From his home—an exact replica of the otter's natural habitat that stretched twelve feet long, reached as high as the ceiling, and jutted six feet into the shop—Mushimono snapped his anvil-like head from side to side, like a blind man lost, following the sounds of traffic he could not see. Mushimono was one of those peculiar creatures evolution had thrown together like a zoological mulligan stew; he had a duck's webbed feet, the whiskered snout and licorice disc eyes of a seal, a cat's quickness, and fishlike maneuverability in water. His fur was a rich burnt-coffee color and it grew thicker with each shrinking day of the year.

Mr. Tanaka, the sashimi master, met me at the door. He had the appearance of a box. The bib of his apron cut across his throat, exaggerating his dearth of neck. An imaginary line that extended up from his thin black necktie and past his purplish lips met his mustache at a perfect perpendicular, reinforcing this illusion of squareness. Above this plane sat two tiny eyes that shimmered like black roe.

Without ceremony Mr. Tanaka told me to make fog. "It not good this way," he said. "Fog outside and no fog inside make Mushimono crazy." He sliced each syllable from his lips with the precision of one of his knives.

The otter stood frozen, as if a mortal enemy were perched nearby. Yet, in spite of this stasis, I saw movement. Perhaps it was the eerie quality of the fog-sifted light or some strange trick of the eye that caused the twin curves of Mushimono's belly and spine to run congruously before tapering together at the S of his thick, sibilant tail. Silken motion where there was none at all. Strong but delicate lines. My thoughts drifted off to a moving figure of another sort: Luna, and the gentle crook of her neck, the soft slope of her shoulders, the slight downward turn of the corners of her mouth.

"Don't forget, only fresh fish for Mushimono," Mr. Tanaka warned.

"I know, I know."

"Sluggishness no substitute for nature," he said, clasping his hands behind his back as he paced the length of the trout-spawning tank. "For Mushimono a fish dead even if it look alive to you. If eyes not clear like—"

"Saki—"

"Their center dark like—"

"Obsidian. Then—"

"They dead," Mr. Tanaka said, completing a favorite adage.

"You mean good as dead."

The sashimi master furrowed his brow, stroked an imaginary beard, and stared at me with those two lightless eyes before he headed for the sashimi bar.

When I was first hired, Mr. Tanaka had promised to teach me the art of sushi and sashimi. In fact, during my interview he had said, "Good mind," a reference to the fact I had graduated cum laude, "make for steady hand." But as the weeks passed, so did my hopes of ever learning how to wield the razor-sharp knives that could turn chunks of tuna into exquisite paper-thin slices. My primary task, as it turned out, was to be Mushimono's keeper. The food fishes and shellfishes were off limits to me. Even when I offered to help scale and shuck, he said, "This operation too delicate a matter for my business, for my sashimi, and for the fish himself for me to permit this ever." I was unhappy at first, but Mr. Tanaka managed to keep me with a more than generous salary. And the job had its share of benefits—all the fish I could eat and Luna's daily stroll past the shop.

I netted three speckled trout from the spawning tank and put them in a pail. All the way to Mushimono's, they nibbled the water's surface and sounded like castanets. As I released the trout into the murky pond in the show window, which extended deep into the basement of the shop, Mushimono regarded me with uncharacteristic calm, undisturbed by my intrusion into his world. I wondered if the odd atmospheric conditions were to blame.

Mushimono's world was an exact reproduction of the lakeshore environment of southern Maine from which he came. Mr. Tanaka had hired experts in the fields of ecology, zoology, and horticulture to duplicate the appropriate balance of vegetation, animals, and micro-organisms found in the wild.

But I made the weather. From an aluminum-plated console attached to the otter chamber, replete with blinking amber lights and grave black knobs, I was the north wind, the cumulonimbus, the offshore breeze, the ozone layer. I was the catalyst of photosynthesis. I was the warm front that collided with my own cold front—I let it rain, I held it up. I greened the grasses, swelled the summer mosses, sweetened the air, and then plucked bare the trees. I was responsible for the death of all summer's children. In time I would freeze the pond. Yes, I had the aid of refrigerators, barometers, thermometers, hydrographs, heaters, humidifiers, sunlamps, and fans. But I threw the switches. I possessed nature's secret formulas. What were all those transistors, tubes, wires, and coils without me? I made the weather. I was night and day. It was no illusion. I turned the seasons. I manipulated metabolism. I made things grow.

Humidifier set high. Saturation point. Dew point. Refrigerated air. Steamy wisps of white rose from the pond—an immense caldron of meteorological soup—and evaporated the further they curled from the water. In no time the show window was filled with fog as dense as surgical gauze. By increments, Mushimono disappeared.

There was a clock inside me. Its alarm—my accelerated pulse, my shortened breaths—went off each day at the same time. I crouched at the foot of the show window beside the weather console, and anticipated Luna's imminent arrival. I fancied there was something organic between us: a chemical bond, a pheromone she emitted that only I could sniff from the air that telegraphed her approach to the shop. Or perhaps it was something mystical, perhaps our souls had been linked in former lifetimes. Or was it some strange configuration of the ions in the atmosphere that drew us together? From the hundreds of feet that shuffled past the sashimi bar each morning, I always knew which belonged to Luna, for hers were like distant fingers snapping. When she walked, there was music on the pavement.

No. It was not some cosmic magnetism that pulled us together, and our molecules were not aligned in any extra-physical way. This was plain, pedestrian infatuation.

Luna's lacquered nails tapped the glass pane. She stopped each day at the same hour to see Mushimono and lavish her attentions on a creature insensitive to her charms. My stomach gurgled in anticipation. I heard a splash of water as the otter dived into his pond. Unable to see Luna through the fog, I pricked up my ears and listened for her. Past the fog and the layers of glass I heard the wet suckling noise, like a child nursing, that she was making with her lips, those succulent, baby shrimp. As always, her kisses were not meant for me.

I longed to see her and I could have satisfied my longing

simply by flicking on the sunlamps and burning off the fog. I had the power but not the nerve. Mushimono's welfare was my first priority, my second was to stay employed, and sadly the yearnings of the heart could do no better than a distant third.

Luna tapped once more. Through the fog her red beret was a muted shade of plum. She was no more than a shadow whose substance fluctuated with her proximity to the glass. The fog hid Luna; it caressed her, as Zeus, disguised as a cloud, once caressed Io. And since this cloud was mine, then I was Zeus to Luna's Io.

After several minutes, when Mushimono failed to materialize from the pond, Luna's impatient ghost vanished in the mist.

B y the lunch hour the fog outside had worsened. For the very first time, Luna entered the shop. She had a parcel tucked under her arm. Our first meeting without glass. Even sopping wet, she was beautiful. Water droplets sparkled in her hair. Her eyes were as blue as lapis. Her voice was unexpectedly deep. But even more of a surprise was the narrow gap between her two front teeth, a gap so dark and rare and suggestive of the mysteries that draw men to women.

"These are for the weasel," she said as she handed me the parcel. "I hope it likes Nova." She adored Mushimono, Luna explained, and was concerned when he failed to make an appearance that morning. I assured her of his good health. Luna lit a cigarette. Smoke rose and slowly curled up and formed a jagged halo in the damp air around her head. She seemed distracted, gazing at the rear of the shop where Mr. Tanaka's customers lunched at the sushi counter and the Italian-café tables. I leaned my elbow on the weather console and explained—I might have bragged a little, but how could I resist?—that I had made the fog that obscured her view of Mushimono.

"Give me summer," she said, her voice as raspy as July sparklers.

"I'm afraid snow's predicted for tonight."

"Snow, fog, what's the difference?" She drew more smoke into her lungs. "It's a mess any way you slice it. In a month the winter solstice, and your Mistermomo will hibernate for the duration. It's a waste and a shame. I mean it. That weasel makes my day; a little life in all this concrete." She exhaled a long agonized breath. "I'm getting depressed just talking about it." Luna removed her beret and shook off the water. "I think I was a Californian in a former life." She dragged on the cigarette and then added as an afterthought, "Hey, if you're the weather wiz, why don't you do something about this fog?"

I told her that a sudden change in barometric pressure in Mushimono's tank might cause him grave discomfort. This wasn't the total truth but she trusted me at my word. She got ready to leave and said she would stop in on her way home from work if the fog cleared by then. She wanted to make sure Mushimono was in good health. I told her if it was snowing out when she arrived, I would demonstrate how I made snow. She sighed. "All morning long, all I hear is talk of the bottom line; everything with those brokers is the bottom line." Luna crushed her cigarette under the sole of her snakeskin pump. "I come here to get away from all that, to see my Mistermomo, but I don't get weasel. You give me snow. Snow, snow, snow. It's so depressing."

She knotted her belt and turned up the collar of her raincoat. She spun on her heel and started to leave. As she reached for the door, she turned suddenly and apologized for the outburst. "See you later." Here she grinned. "By the way, my name's Peg." Peg! I thought. *Peg?* One hangs coats on pegs. How could my Luna be this monosyllable? This Peg?

B y afternoon the fog had lifted, and I burned off the fog from the otter chamber. Mushimono was indifferent to the change in weather, surfacing only for quick breaths before returning to his underwater lair. At three Mr. Tanaka left for the day. I closed shop. In anticipation of Luna's visit, I went shopping and returned with candles and bottles of wine. I lit the candles and waited for Luna. When finally she tapped at the front door, it was already dark and the candles had burned to half their original length.

We had barely said hello, and I was still holding the door open, when she handed me her Burberry and whisked past me, losing me in her perfume. She sped to the little café table I had set up, with its dancing flames and breathing wine. She did not even ask after Mushimono.

Luna took the bottle in her hands, cradling the neck up like the delicate head of a baby. "Beaujolais!" she shrieked. "I can't believe it! How fortuitous. I think I might cry." She sniffed the bottle. "This is the wine of summer, the picnic wine." She lit a cigarette and puffed anxiously. "This is the wine for lovers. Oh, you don't understand, do you? I just had the best summer of my life."

I poured equal amounts of the ruby-red liquid into porcelain saki bowls. The color of her fingertips matched the beaujolais. We lifted our bowls and, after a moment of deliberation, she offered a toast: "To Mistermomo and Édouard Manet. Or is it Monet? No, Manet." We drank the bittersweet juice of love. As I sipped, I watched Luna over the rim of my bowl. Her skin glowed as if lit from within.

"Those guys in Manet's, or maybe it is Monet's, 'Déjeuner,'" she said, putting emphasis on the middle syllable, which she pronounced "June," "were crazy for beaujolais. They drank it by the gallon. Honestly. I read it in an art magazine." Her cheeks were flushed from the wine. I admired her cameo earrings. Luna said the Impressionists were her favorite painters, and they and the wine reminded her of summer.

"Baudelaire—" I began, having recalled his immortal line, *One should always be drunk*.

"No, no, it's pronounced 'beaujolais,'" Luna said. "See here? Beaujolais." She pointed a finger at the wine label.

"Of course," I said. "My French is terrible." I refilled the bowls.

I never cared for the smell of burning tobacco, but the smoke rings rising from her pursed lips seemed fragrant, almost sweet, as if her body had purified the smoke. Then Luna let out a terrible cough. "Bronchitis," she muttered as she raised the bowl up to her mouth.

"You should take care of yourself," I said. "You ever think what those cigarettes are doing to you? Maybe you can try something athletic, like skating or skiing."

She narrowed her eyes and fixed me with a stare. "What's with you and snow?" And as if that had not already chilled my blood, she said the one thing a lover hates to hear from his beloved: "You sound like my mother."

I apologized. Then she apologized.

"It's me," she said. "The bum lungs, the cigarettes are part of the package. You can say I live life on the edge. I mean van Gogh called it quits before he was forty." She coughed. "This sounds crazy," she said, "but each time I have an attack I feel that much closer to the inner me."

Luna drained her bowl and then replenished it with the dregs from the bottle of beaujolais.

I went behind the sashimi bar to prepare a snack for us. I selected a long shiny knife from Mr. Tanaka's impressive collection. I was surprised by how light it felt in my hand. I removed a block of yellowfin from the refrigerated case and started cutting the fish into crude cubes. The steel seemed to melt through the flesh. At first, I was tentative in my approach to the fish, but soon, caught up in the sensuality of slicing, in the thrill of moving through flesh, I was imitating the sashimi master's speedy hands, approximating his flashy blade act. Where was the mystery of his art? It was mine already. I looked over at Luna and smiled while my busy hands whittled away at the shrinking hunk of fish. I imagined how I might one day audition for Mr. Tanaka, with Luna there for inspiration, and dazzle him with my newfound skills. I glanced down to admire my handiwork. My hand was a bloody mess.

"I fancy myself a burgundy," Luna said.

I clenched my fist, sticky with red pearls of trouble. I felt dizzy but worked hard to hold myself together.

"But, you know," she said, "people like to classify me in the sauterne family."

I wanted to be brave, but every man has his limits, especially when he is watching his blood run from his body.

"I'm bleeding," I said.

"Oh. You say you're a burgundy too?"

"No, I'm bleeding, like a pig!" I flicked my wrist, spattering the pristine countertop with bright red beads.

"Put some mercury on it," she said.

"Some what?"

"Grab ahold of that tuna. It's full of mercury. I read it in—"

"You mean Mercurochrome. That's not the same as—Ah, forget it." I tightened my fist, hoping to staunch the flow. I saw my evening with Luna slipping away.

"Call it what you want, it's probably in the tuna anyway."

I ran cold tap water over my hand. My blood turned a rust color in the stainless-steel sink. There were three major cuts—on the thumb, the heel, and the meaty tip of the middle finger—and numerous nicks. Moments later I bandaged my aching hand in a linen napkin.

Luna sipped her beaujolais and then offered me a taste. I drank. She marked the spot where my lips had come in contact with the bowl and drank the final swallow with her mouth positioned on the very same spot. I retrieved the second bottle of wine, a chablis, from the refrigerator. I had to ask Luna to uncork it.

"To me, you are a burgundy," I said. Each syllable echoed in my ears long after it had left my lips. My face burned but my extremities felt cold. "There's nothing remotely sauterne about you. You're not even blond." The wines raced through my veins, their friction swelled my wounded hand. I could have sworn my lungs had shrunk—there seemed to be much less air to breathe. "I won't hear another word about you and sauternes. You're definitely burgundy, Luna."

"What did you call me?"

"Burgundy, Luna."

"Peg. I'm Peg."

"You don't have to test me. You're burgundy all the way."

"Yes. Burgundy. Simple and elegant—"

"Rich and full-bodied, Luna."

"Peg!"

"But burgundy—"

"Yes. Earthy, robust, and generous."

"Soft-eyed, soft-lipped, Luna-Peg."

Fires smoldered under my lids. My jaw dropped. My skin drooped from sore bones. And in their core the marrow had hardened.

"Drinking burgundy is an event," she said.

"I adore a fine burgundy."

We drank our wine by the mouthful.

"I don't get it," she said. "Sauternes are such flippant, insignificant wines. Silly vacuous fruit juice—"

"But, Luna, you're not silly or vacant."

"And you, sir, are—let me see—yes, a mature port. I mean it. You have those superior powers of discernment that are the trademark of all good ports." She raised her bowl to my lips. "Drink," she said softly. "You must mend your blood." I gulped her offering, obeying her angelic voice. She refilled her bowl and drank.

I rested my wounded hand on my thigh. The napkin was badly stained. I needed to rest. My heart pounded like the surf, and when the sea receded, I baked under the hot suns beneath my lids until the tide washed over me once more. My head kept time with my pulse, rocking back and forth, from shoulder to shoulder. I unwrapped my hand and dipped the hot digits in the chilled wine. The wounds gaped, the skin around them twitching. The wine rusted. Luna lifted my hand from the bowl and kissed each finger, alternating the kisses with puffs off a cigarette.

"Beaujolais," Luna lamented, staring longingly at the empty bottle. "All gone. The end of summer. No more Monet, Manet—oh, hell. No more of all that crazy light and sun and heat and color; the boys and girls at play. The boys on the beaches and wonderful beaujolais."

I closed my eyes. They had outgrown their sockets. As I dozed in and out of sleep, I slipped to the borderlines of consciousness where the heres and theres overlap. I sat on my spine with Luna here beside me. But when sleep swept me under, dreams became the intimate here while the things defined by time and space were the distant theres. Luna, repainting her lips as I opened my eyes—here. Then she was there, untouchable, a shadow in my fuzzy dreams. In this place her words turned to music.

"Give me the summer any day of the week," she sang.

I skinned back my lids and was blessed by the sight of her sad cool blues staring at me.

"Luna," I said, smiling. "Burgundy Luna." I took her by the wrist, as big around as a sparrow's breast, and directed her eyes to Mushimono's lakeshore. "Consider it summer again," I said languorously. "Your wish is my command."

"Don't tease," Luna said. "You're two months too late and five months too early."

Her words were lyrics to a love song. What did it matter what they meant? After all, who made the weather? I said, "Who is day and night? Who turns the seasons? Who makes things grow?"

"You sick or what?" She checked my temperature. "You're hot."

I blew out the candles and watched the complex spirals of smoke twist to the ceiling. "Suddenly, it's no more," I said. "Like that, I'll rid us of winter. Summer will be yours again, my dear Luna."

"It's Peg. My name is Peg. You're not well, are you?"

Then the tide inside me ebbed; my body flowed into the chair like a Dali watch. Luna, I thought, is Helen of Troy and Raphael's Madonnas rolled up in one. Luna is Penelope at the loom. Eurydice in Hades. Luna is Mozart at seven. Shirley Temple at eight. Luna is that side of the moon we see, and all we imagine the invisible half to be. Luna is Titania kissing Bottom. Io snatched by Zeus. Marilyn married to DiMaggio. "Luna is Peg," I said out loud, "a lovely mystery, a mysterious loveliness."

"God, if you feel that way, call me Luna. Call me Lunatic. I mean it. Burgundy Luna. I sort of like that."

"I can make summer come and go." My words trickled off my shoulder and down the front of my shirt. "We'll picnic," I said, "picnic."

She sat up excitedly, then slumped back into her seat. "It won't be the same," she said. "How can we have a picnic without the right wine?"

I suggested saki.

"Oh, saki is so— Ceremonial. Let's face facts. Chardonnay goes with fish, cabernet goes with meat, but beaujolais is the stuff of picnics."

I grabbed the empty beaujolais bottle and funneled some saki into it.

"That's indecent," she said. "That stunt might work on a two-year-old but not on me." She joined me behind the sashimi bar and held the bottle up to the light. "I guess an emergency's an emergency, but the color's all wrong."

Suddenly, she reached for one of Mr. Tanaka's special knives. Silver flashed between us. Luna's eyes were the sky. In them I soared. Back on earth I was trembling. The cold steel parted the earlier, now crusted cuts. Thin red lines appeared across my fingers and palm. She took my hand and smiled mischievously. She squeezed it over the funnel until blood streaked from palm to heel, where droplets hung like lizard tongues. The blood rolled slowly through the funnel and splashed thickly in the saki. In time, we had translated the saki into a bottle of beaujolais.

"I know we could've pretended," she said as she pressed my hand to her lips. "But why exhaust our imaginations?" The tip of her tongue traced the wounds, splitting, stinging, and soothing them all in the same lick. "You're wonderfully strong port." She squeezed my hand over the funnel once more. The heavy droplets pinged the saki's surface faster and faster until she achieved the coloration she desired. It resembled an orange rosé. Pleased with her work, Luna raised my hand and smeared my blood over her lips. I took the bottle by the neck and intoned, "To Luna."

"To summer," she said, clasping her hand over mine.

Outside the lakeshore, Luna worked the controls of the weather console as I gave her instructions. I was too dizzy and weak to perform the magic myself.

Luna poured beaujolais into a bowl. "Drink," she beckoned, "wine mends blood." I drank from the bowl she held to my lips. The wine was warm and unpleasantly salty. I felt hot, then cold, then hot again. I closed my eyes. The lids seemed lined with sand. I dreamed of Luna, naked as the otter, standing in the street outside the lakeshore, tapping at the window. Then I woke and saw her at the controls, and this seemed like an equally implausible dream.

The sunlamps burned at noontime intensity. Though the fans were idle, convection stirred a gentle breeze in the lakeshore that rustled the dead leaves along the ground. Soon, because of the contrast between the heat inside and the relative cold outside, dew started to form on the chamber's four glass walls.

"Eighty-two degrees and climbing," Luna sang out. The otter suddenly sprang out of the pond. He scurried up the muddy embankment and darted from one end of the compartment to the other. He pawed the glass, but Luna, fixed on her work at the weather console, did not notice.

"Humidity, let's see, is up to sixty-eight percent," she said. "Barometric pressure reads thirty-point-two-three and rising."

Mushimono stood erect on his haunches and stared devotedly at her, as if he were kneeling, waiting to receive Communion.

W e entered the lakeshore. The otter dived into the torpid water. Luna spread her plaid blanket on the ground. I basked under the brilliant suns, whose healing rays sealed my wounds. Beside me Luna arranged a still life of bowls, lox, and the beaujolais.

"This is great," Luna said as she untied the laces of my shoes. "They won't believe me tomorrow at work."

"Lovely day, if you don't mind me saying so myself." Thick dew clung to the window, blocking any view of the world beyond.

"This is really great. Better than Bermuda. I mean it. Summer in winter, day at night." Luna turned her back to me and rolled her stockings off her ankles. "There's money in this operation. I'll tell the brokers about it. They'll probably flip but they'll know what to do." She stretched out alongside me, undoing the third and fourth buttons of her silky blouse, hiking her skirt past her thighs. She poured a bowl of the new beaujolais and made me drink. "You remind me of someone. It's your eyes. So big and round and black." She scratched her head for the answer. She picked up the lox. "I see it now," she said, "Mistermomo! You and that sweet weasel."

Luna knelt by the lake and floated the slices of lox, orange-pink rafts, one by one, on the stagnant water. "Oh, Mistermomo," she called, "I have a treat for you." She made her suckling sound, so odd and wet.

"Where's that weasel?"

"He likes fish, not filets."

"Filets," she said, "are fish."

"Mushimono likes his fish with gills and fins."

Luna clenched her teeth, perfect white shells, tightening the skin around her mouth. She glared at me as if I were mad. Tucking the hem of her skirt into the waistband, she waded knee-deep into the lake.

"Jesus, it's freezing!"

With her next step she suddenly plunged into thigh-deep water, stirring a turbulence that sucked the lilylike filets toward her. When the ripples subsided, one filet was clinging to the front of a bare thigh. Rather than removing it, she smoothed the lox against her skin with caresses and pats that produced sounds like those of lovers' stomachs pressed together. The lake, she discovered, was too deep. As she emerged from it, Luna shivered and coughed. She unhitched her algae-blotched skirt and let it fall in a pile at her feet. She seemed frail and small. She gestured for the beaujolais. I picked up a bowl and was horrified by what I saw. The contents had been retranslated by the suns. The blood had coagulated into a cinnamon crust, sealing in the saki underneath. "I need some wine," she said, "my lovely summery beaujolais. I'm freezing."

I started to feel the ache in my hand. My head throbbed from the alcohol. "It's gone," I said as I stared at the bowl, the hardened blood, the obscene saki. The sunlamps stung my eyes.

'm cold," she said. She reached across me for the bowl, and when she glimpsed the cruel scab bobbing on the dirty saki, she dropped the bowl, and it cracked against a rock. The fire was gone from her eyes and skin. Beads of pond water seemed frozen upon her arms. She trembled.

Her pale face was the leaden-gray of cod steak and filled with the indecisiveness of a three-quarters moon. "It's a nightmare," she said.

I wiped a portion of the window clear of dew. No moon in the sky, but snow, lots of snow, just as the cabbie had forecast. Flakes fell in bunches. I shook my sore hand. I heard her pick her raincoat up off the ground, overturning the bowls, the bottle, and all the picnic things that had been resting upon it. I followed the flight of several flakes from the lamplight's nimbus to the white street below. She tiptoed from the show window. A gust of cool air shot in from the shop. Not a soul was on the street. Absolutely quiet, as it must have been at the beginning of time. I could hear my hand throb. In the pond the lox was being semi-poached by the sunlamps, and gave off a rank smell. Not far away I detected the gentle hiss of nylons inching over her legs. Then the rustle of raincoat, the click of her pumps, and the squeak of the front door opening. She crossed the street. Her collar brushed up alongside her ears; each flake seemed to make her flinch and shrink deeper into her coat, like a tortoise into its shell. She struggled, small, shivering, solitary, against the storm.

Peg, I thought. I wiped away some dew. The snowfall was spectacular. "Peg," I whispered. She slipped from sight.

I ran outdoors, following the pair of unbroken footprints leading from the sashimi bar to where she stood on the avenue hailing a cab. "Peg!" I shouted as the cab pulled up to the curb. I began to run. "Peg!" I glided like a cross-country skier in the narrow lane she had cut in the wet snow. "Peg!" There on the sidewalk I saw a salmon filet. "Peg." I was my own echo. Then I became aware of a strange sound coming from behind. Imagine mah-jongg tiles tossed together in a tin can. I took a quick look back, but saw nothing. "Peg." She was climbing into the cab.

I ran harder and with my increased speed the mah-jongg tiles grew louder, more urgent. "Peg." My eyes fixed on the amber lamp shining at her shins through the balls of exhaust at the foot of the open car door.

I slid in next to her and slammed the door. Immediately I heard a metallic scratching. I opened the door and there, illuminated by the footlamp, I saw the otter, upright on his hind legs. He was panting, out of breath. "What is it, a dog?" Peg asked. She clutched my arm as she peeked over my shoulder at Mushimono.

"Don't be afraid," I said as the otter flopped into the compartment with us. "He seems very gentle tonight." I closed the door gingerly behind him.

"You've got to take him back," she said, sliding into a corner, away from the otter.

No, I thought, no. Not this night, with my happily aching hand and Peg so near. We were warm and cozy in the cab. She nestled close to me; the otter, stretched to its full length over half of the backseat, seemed to purr; the wheels of our taxi hummed as snow beneath them turned to slush.

I tapped the glass that divided the cab into two compartments. "Central Park," I told the cabbie. "To the lake where you rent those boats in the summer, you know, where the ducks live."

The otter first. Before my hand, before Peg's wet clothes. Before whatever might pass between us next. It was my duty—the otter's care.

The cab swerved uptown. Snow kept falling. It covered the city, softening edges, blurring lines. But I had never seen things any clearer than I did that night. Blizzard-force gusts made our journey difficult. I told the cabbie not to rush. We could not outrace the storm. There would be snow, plenty of snow. I knew by daybreak the snow would turn to rain and by noon it would all be forgotten.

Social Science

From the second story of the house, Henry watches Mrs. Steiner climb from the backseat of a hired '67 Eldorado, and before its tail fins completely slip from view, a second car pulls up to take its place alongside the curb. A tall, bare-legged woman in white pops out of the cherry-red Porsche and shakes Mrs. Steiner's hand. They turn as one and face the house. The old woman points at the date palm on the front lawn, diverting the other's attention away from the house and its flaking coats of paint. More than once he has overheard Mrs. Steiner rave about the exquisite sweetness of the palm's sad inedible fruit.

The women go through the first floor, discussing square footage, carpeting, plumbing, and interest rates. They open every door they pass. On the second floor it's more of the same. When they discover Henry lying shirtless in his hot study, Mrs. Steiner apologizes to her well-tanned companion: "Henry's my tenant. His wife used to live here with him, but she's gone. Henry doesn't need all this space now, so there's no need to be sorry for him."

After the Porsche drives off, Mrs. Steiner returns to Henry, still half-naked in his study, and says, "I wouldn't sell the holes in the walls to that one. Belongs to one of those cults, I bet. Got more things hanging from her ears than decorations on a Christmas tree." Mrs. Steiner shakes her head, and her bluish hair bobs and weaves.

She takes her leave and goes outside to wait for her cab. Henry eyes her tidying the patch of grass that surrounds the FOR SALE sign. She picks up broken palm fronds and plucks weeds, working with the fastidious devotion of one on a visit to the family plot. Henry feels a twinge in his stomach. This happens whenever the

FOR SALE
By Owner
No Appointment Necessary

sign crosses his line of vision. It's as if his body were trying to tell him something's wrong, the way a toothache calls attention to invisible decay. When Mrs. Steiner first put the house on the market, she and Henry struck a deal. In exchange for a reduction in rent, he has agreed to show the house to anyone who wishes to see it. But doing so leaves him feeling like a condemned man advising his executioner on the best way to do him in. He hates the thought of moving, hates equally living in renter's limbo, never knowing, from day to day, if he'll have a home. At times, he wonders whether Mrs. Steiner is deliberately delaying the sale just to torment him. She has certainly fielded several credible bids, but in every instance she has invented excuses for prolonging the process. She turned away one guy because of his turquoise ostrich-skin cowboy boots, another because he wanted to put a hot tub in the yard; there was the couple with the McGovern sticker on their car, and the black man she suspected was a professional athlete of some kind.

Henry relaxes a little the instant he hears Mrs. Steiner's cab pull away. He is lying on the maroon couch by his desk where, prior to the interruption, he had just finished grading a composition by his favorite student, Agnes. Trained in grad school to penetrate the surface of literary texts, Henry rereads the paper, analyzing the pellucid symbolism and the quivering tropes that riddle the paper she calls "How to Make Melon Balls." The subtext is obvious, her message to Henry clear—she has a crush on him—but the problem of making the proper response is, from a professional standpoint, a tricky one. He imagines combing the essay for grammatical flaws—this isn't as simple as it sounds, since she's an exceptional writer—or, failing that, fabricating a few; next he might invite her to his office to discuss, let's say, dangling modifiers; the minutes fly by, and he awes her with his mastery of the rules of grammar, she's swooning as he fleshes out subordination; and just as this scene, playing in his head, swiftly moves to its inevitable and well-deserved climax, Henry hears a strange voice out in the hallway, putting an end to the private lesson. Someone knocks. The door swings open. "I'm Dave Brinkley," says the man stepping into the study. "Nice place you have here."

With his head pillowed comfortably on his arms, Henry tells the stranger that he's too busy to show the house. He can go look for himself. Henry closes his eyes, hoping to find Agnes there under his lids. But Dave Brinkley, awash in cologne, steps deeper into the study, apologizing for the intrusion. He explains how he had seen the sign and thought the place deserted. He's standing within an arm's reach of Henry and sees the stack of essays on the desk. He says that he too is an "educator," an assistant professor of psychology at the state college across town. Having established this professional bond between them, Dave Brinkley pulls the chair away from the desk and parks it at the end of the couch where Henry's resting his head. He sits down and they engage in faculty-lounge chitchat, covering comparative salaries, course loads, and the quality of the student body at their respective schools. Dave Brinkley then starts to describe his impression of what Henry's mental state must be at that precise moment. "You see me coming between you and this house. To you, I am an interloper, a sexual rival of sorts. If I bought this house, you would feel emasculated, and we might not be friends anymore. That is why we need to talk."

When Dave Brinkley finally leaves, the sun in the smog is the color of iodine. By then Henry has long forgotten Agnes and split infinitives. Dave Brinkley occupies his thoughts. He had come to California to find his estranged wife when he heard she was "doing time in Hollywood." He wanted to buy the house and try to salvage their marriage. "I can see why she loves the West Coast. The sun, the surf—and the air is not all that bad when it is the right color. This is her world. I can never hope to take her away from paradise." He unscrewed the wedding band from his finger, and said, as he handed it to Henry, "I was a fool to think I could keep a girl like her in Ohio." When Henry had some difficulty deciphering the engraved name, Dave Brinkley started to spell it, enunciating each letter with the phony suspense of an emcee reading the winning digits of a lottery number. "C-H-R-I-S-T—"

"You're married—to the model?"

"Good, you are familiar with her work then. How about that cover-girl complexion?"

A few days later Mrs. Steiner phones. "I like that Dave Brinkley fellow. So educated and forthright." After she hangs up, Henry calls the psych department at the state college. The secretary corroborates Dave Brinkley's story but adds a significant twist. His name wasn't Brinkley when he applied for the position. It had been changed only after his arrival in California.

Henry drives to the university library and descends into the stacks. He locates back issues of *People, Glamour, Mademoiselle.* He sees the model in swimsuits, in evening gowns, in every imaginable shade of lipstick. Such teeth, he thinks. Photo after photo she smiles as if she does it for free. Then, in *Self,* in an article entitled "Blondes Are Back and Bare as Ever!" Henry uncovers the vital statistic he has been seeking. In boldface type the caption under the bikini-clad model reads: "One of the most eligible bachelorettes in America, Christie's looking for a man to complement her busy life-style."

In class that day, Henry stares suspiciously at the rows of faces before him and tries to reconcile the names on the registrar's roster with the students who claim them as theirs. To his own dismay, he realizes he even doubts the authenticity of his prized Agnes. When her thin, braceleted arm lolls weak-wristed in the air, waiting to be acknowledged, Henry can only nod in her direction, forsaking the name that once had given him such pleasure to say.

W eeks pass and the FOR SALE sign remains firmly in place. It probably will withstand *the* earthquake. Mrs. Steiner keeps showing prospective buyers the house but can't decide who truly "deserves" it.

Dave Brinkley drops by often. He comes armed with questions about the wiring, the roof, the septic tank, and then hangs around for conversation. At first, these visits annoyed Henry, but gradually Dave Brinkley's persistence won out and Henry started talking to the psychologist about Marybeth, their marriage, and their subsequent divorce in the same quasi-professional way people came to Henry for help with their cover letters.

One night Dave Brinkley knocks at the front door. They shake hands as usual, the psychologist smiling, his facial muscles tensed to the twitching point. "I just want to take some measurements," he says with a giggle, pulling a tape rule from his pocket.

"Not tonight, Dave," Henry says. "It's late and I have papers to grade."

"Me, I have exams at home. But I am too excited. I think the house is mine."

Henry offers his congratulations. He pumps Dave Brinkley's hand once, then abruptly extricates himself from the grip. He excuses himself and goes upstairs and mans his desk. He searches for Agnes's essay, in hopes the sensual loops of her script might relieve, at least temporarily, the uncomfortable pressure building beneath his scalp. But before he can test her penmanship's analgesic worth, Dave Brinkley bursts into the study. He says, "I have a date with her Friday night."

Henry turns in his seat. "With *her*?"

"Yes, yes, with Marybeth."

Henry jumps up from his chair. "Marybeth who?"

The psychologist sits on the couch and crosses his legs and drapes his arm across the backrest. "Marybeth," he says, "your wife, your ex-wife." His eyes fix upon Henry as if he were watching a stranger undress. "You are angry, of course," Dave Brinkley observes. "You are burning up inside, and that is only appropriate. Marybeth has betrayed you, and, to a lesser degree, so have I." He tweaks the tip of his nose. "Relax your fists, Henry, forget the macho stuff, it doesn't suit you. Let us talk. Let your unfiltered feelings out. Express yourself to me." He opens up his arms in an all-embracing gesture of peace.

Henry stalks to the door of the study. He looks across the hallway at the bedroom—or, more precisely, at the spot in front of the mirror where Marybeth lifted her dumbbells in the morning and brushed her hair a hundred times at night. He remembers watching the hem of her nightshirt rise to mid-thigh with each upward sweep of her arm. He tries to visualize her there in front of the mirror but his imagination is weak. At best she is an erasure, barely perceptible, lacking definition. "How'd you find her?" he says to the hallway.

"I did nothing more devious than dial 4-1-1."

"And like that," Henry snaps his fingers, "she agreed to go out with you. You must have the wrong girl."

The psychologist chuckles. "Remember what I taught you? By calling her 'girl,' you reveal to the world a basic hostility toward her. Have I not established that as the root of your marital problems?"

"You're not going out with my Marybeth," Henry says, shaking his finger in a threatening way.

"Now that's better. Let your anger out."

Henry waves his hand in disgust.

"Look, I am not leaving until we talk." Dave Brinkley gets up from the couch and looks around the room. "I just called her and said you and I were good friends. We are good friends." He goes to the center of the floor and says, looking up at the light fixture in the ceiling: "I am new in town. You tell me about this nice girl. What am I supposed to do?" He peeks in the closet. He sits on the edge of the desk, folding his tweedy arms over his chest. "Back in my apartment I already played this scene out. When I took your part, you said some hateful things about me. But now that I am here, you are all but silent. We must be adults and work on this." He claps his hands together. "You be me, and I will be you." He tweaks his nose again.

The sight of the gold band on Dave Brinkley's left hand revives Henry. Like Popeye after spinach, he can feel his inner resources galvanize. In the murky pools of his memory, a school of Christie Brinkleys, toothy and blow-dried, swim to his rescue. While the psychologist—as Henry—twists his face and prepares to deliver a diatribe against himself, the real Henry launches a preemptive strike: "What's become of your model-wife?"

"Good effort. I can hear that nastiness coming through."

Henry repeats the question, and after a few long seconds, the question finds its mark. Dave Brinkley stops talking and lowers his gaze, sweeping the floor with it. For the next few seconds he only exhales. He fidgets clumsily with the things on Henry's desk. The psychologist is sputtering; he's winged, and Henry knows it. But he lets him get away: when Dave Brinkley—he does this innocently, biding his time, trying to catch his breath—picks up the top essay from the stack on the blotter, Henry says, "Put her down."

"What pretty handwriting," the psychologist says as a grin brightens his face. "Do you want to tell me about Agnes? Come, Henry, out with it. How can we be friends otherwise?"

H enry can see her shaking her head like a robin tearing a worm from the ground. She's holding the phone on her hip, collecting her thoughts. The song "Psycho Killer" is playing on the old phono she bought years ago at a yard sale so she could listen to music while she worked in the garage stuffing envelopes. Through the telephone lines, the singer sounds like poultry. "You promised you'd leave town," she finally says into the mouthpiece.

"How do you know I haven't left?"

"Your friend told me."

"What friend?"

"Forget it. I didn't say anything."

"Turn off the record. I can hardly hear you."

"Good."

"What?"

"I said I hope he buys that house. Maybe then you'll leave." Her voice is lean and aggressive. He can picture her mannerisms: raking her hand through her long hair, sniffing her fingertips, shifting her weight, cradling the phone between cheek and shoulder. This was how she ran her direct-mail advertising service out of the garage; stuffing envelopes, licking stamps, while talking to printers and clients over the phone.

Because the house is on her mailing lists, he still receives mail from her almost every week.

"Why'd you think I agreed to meet this Brinkley character? Because he's a chum of yours? Not in a million. I'm gonna see to it he buys that house. If he needs cash, I'll sell part of the business and I'll give him a loan, cheap. Then maybe you'll leave."

They hang up without the conversational equivalent of a concluding paragraph that marks a resolution of conflict. Henry turns to his students' papers for solace. He reads one by a Vietnam vet who, writing about his experience as a POW, tells how he was unable to remember during captivity a single detail of his wife's face.

Mrs. Steiner is standing by the FOR SALE sign. She looks as squat and round as its red letters. A man in madras slacks and green sports coat joins her on the lawn. He is carrying a briefcase. Together they admire the sign.

They enter the house where Henry is sipping coffee in the kitchen. Mrs. Steiner says, "This is Mr. Escrow."

"No, ma'am," the man says, with a chuckle. "I work for the escrow company. My name's Mooney."

"How silly of me."

"Happens all the time, ma'am." The escrow man then reaches his hand out to Henry and says, "And you must be Mr. Brinkley."

"Oh my, no," Mrs. Steiner says, giggling. "Aren't we a pair! This is Henry, my tenant. I would never have imagined anyone confusing Henry with good Mr. Brinkley."

The escrow man sets his briefcase on the table and removes a manila envelope that he hands to Mrs. Steiner, who in turn hands it over to Henry. She says, "You must perform this duty faithfully or not do it at all. Henry, I want you to give this to Mr. Brinkley when he comes here on Sunday."

Henry looks at the escrow man, who shrugs his shoulders and says, "Mr. Brinkley's intrigue, I assure you. This is highly irregular practice for a firm such as ours."

Using a roll of packing tape she pulled from her purse, Mrs. Steiner tapes the envelope to the refrigerator. "So you don't forget," she says. "And so you don't peek and spoil Mr. Brinkley's surprise."

Thursday after class Henry drives to the state college. He arrives too early for Dave Brinkley's office hours. As he waits, he reads the psych professor's door, covered not only by the kinds of cartoons and news clippings academics find amusing but a 200-question true/false personality test, with such items as: (47) I sleep with my clothes off and the lights on. (89) I am as healthy as a blonde. (152) Fashion models adore the touch of tweed.

Henry tires of this excess and tries the door. It isn't locked. The place smells like a bottling plant for cologne.

Henry is stunned by its overall neatness. Papers are in folders and meticulously stacked at the corner of the desk; pens are capped; pencils sharpened; the typewriter wears its dustcover. There's an impressive wall of books, cloth-bound and alphabetized, with stately brown spines. Henry peruses the titles until he uncovers, wedged between Boggs's *Sexual Deviation in the Tropics* and Blumberg's *Blondes: A Subject for Scientific Analysis*, an unusual tome with a wordless spine. It's not a book at all but a picture frame, and under the glass there's a collage of dozens of Christie Brinkleys in tennis togs. Spurred by this discovery, Henry searches the desk drawers and finds, beneath a pile of soiled running clothes, an 8 × 10 glossy of the model's broad lunar face, one rouged cheek adorned with a dedication executed in a loose, flamboyant script: *Dear Dave, Hey, are we related? Thanx for the letters. Luv, Christie.*

Henry's looking through a folder labeled "At the Beach with Christie B.," filled with cutout Christies in swim-wear, when the phone rings. After some consideration, Henry decides to answer. A student in Dave Brinkley's Psych 101 course is on the line pleading for an extension on her paper assignment. Henry grants it.

Once he cradles the phone, he suddenly feels uncom-fortable with his body, as if he were clothed, from head to toe, in a new pair of Levi's. His hand trembles slightly as he turns the pages of the desk calendar. On each leaf CHRISTIE? has been scrawled in the time slots set aside for his office hours. Then the phone rings again. He picks up the receiver but doesn't say anything. "Hello?" a familiar voice says. "Hello? Is this David Brinkley's line?" At first, Henry thinks it's the same student calling again. But as he slowly depresses the clear plastic nib on the cradle, he realizes the person on the other end had been Marybeth. With his finger still on the nib, he stares at the phone's black mantle, trying to see her: hip out, fingers raking her scalp, peeved Henry's friend has slipped her a wrong number. As he expected, the phone rings again, and this time he's prepared. Holding his nose, he pretends he's Dave Brinkley's answering machine: "Hi. I am not in the office at the moment—"

"I hate these stupid machines," says Marybeth. She speaks rapidly, trying to fit her message within the allotted time. "Listen, something's come up. Seven's out of the question. See you at the Dolphin around seven-thirty. And don't bring your answering machine." She slams the phone down, and it pops like a pistol shot in Henry's ear.

That same afternoon a short, bearded man in a white linen suit comes to the house. "I'd like to make you an offer for this property," he says. "I guarantee you won't get a penny more from anyone else."

Henry steps back from the door so the man can enter. "I'll have a look at the interior when we sit down to sign the contract," he says. "I'm well acquainted with this vintage." He hands Henry his business card. "I already own similar units in the neighborhood."

The Golden Dolphin is one of those seafood stops along Route 1 specializing in redwood decks, sea gulls, Cinzano umbrellas, and food served on mango halves. Marybeth was particularly fond of it when she and Henry first came to town. The place is packed with the usual Friday-night crowd of faculty members, students, tourists, and third-rank Hollywood types. Seven o'clock. Henry's sitting at the end of the restaurant bar, near the hostess's station, waiting for Dave Brinkley. He orders beer and nibbles goldfish crackers. Ten after seven. As he had been for his office hours, Dave Brinkley is late again. Perhaps he won't even show up. The mere thought of Marybeth being stood up by the likes of Dave Brinkley upsets him almost as much as the thought of the two of them actually meeting. Perhaps she got her message through to him after all. Perhaps they suspect Henry and have changed their plans accordingly.

Henry goes to see the hostess, a pretty coed he believes he has seen on campus. "Don't you go to the university?"

"Biz Admin," she says, smiling big. Her hair is a shade lighter than her teeth. "You go there too?"

"I . . . I work at Student Services," he says. "I counsel kids on academic probation."

"Guess I'll see you there someday," she says with professional good cheer. "Will you be dining with us tonight?"

"I have a reservation for two."

"Name?" She scans the date book on the hostess stand.

"Brinkley. At seven."

"The Brinkley party. Wow, lucky you showed up. We almost gave your table away." She picks up two menus. "We all here?"

"Not yet, but I'll wait at the table."

She tosses her hair and leads Henry out to the deck. "Voilà, just as you requested, one of our most romantic tables." She hands Henry a menu. "Mr. Brinkley, everything's special tonight."

The cocktail waitress, a starlet in an oversized T-shirt with dolphins riding the silk-screened waves over her breasts, takes his order. After his beer arrives, he sees the hostess winding her way through the crowded dining room, followed closely by Dave Brinkley, who's gesticulating wildly and saying such things at her that diners turn around in their seats to stare. When they finally arrive at tableside, Henry springs to his feet and reaches for the other's hand. "Dave, old pal!" The psychologist's hand is puffy and extremely warm.

"Wow, so you two do know each other," the hostess

says, relieved. "Gawd, I thought I really blew this one. I mean, you both said Brinkley; okay? So I figured, hey, brothers; okay? But he"—she nods at Dave Brinkley—"he said he's expecting a lady friend, so I thought, Wow, Lisa, what a major screwup." She drops her hands on both men's shoulders and exhales dramatically.

"That will be all, miss." The psychologist tries to shoo her away with a flick of his wrist.

"But are you or aren't you expecting a third?" she asks.

The men answer simultaneously. One yes, the other no.

"Now that's really . . . wow!" she exclaims. "Incredible. Like twins." She stares at the two as if they were talking fish.

"By my watch you're twenty-two minutes late," Henry says the instant the hostess leaves.

"Your watch doesn't count here." Dave Brinkley is ready to leap at Henry. A plumb line dropped from his chin would strike the center of the table. The surf tumbles behind him. Smog or clouds obscure the moon. A storm candle casts a rare light that reduces Dave Brinkley's face to a series of simple planes; he has the look of a portrait executed with a paint knife.

"Marybeth can't make it," Henry says. "She called me and said something's come up. Those were her exact words."

"This is delusional fantasy. Why didn't she call me?"

"You're the expert, you figure it out." He peeks at his watch. Seven-thirty. Soon Marybeth will make her appearance. "Dave," he says, "let's go somewhere and talk."

His face buried in his ringless hands, the psychologist appears deep in thought. Perhaps he is paging through the textbooks in his mind for advice in resolving the present conflict. When the waitress comes to the table, he abruptly drops his hands from his face and fixes Henry with a

strange look. "I see no reason to go hunt for another restaurant. We are here. And we have our table."

Henry says, "I know a better place for seafood." He
glances at the waitress, then down at his watch. He scans
the interior dining room for Marybeth. "We used to eat
here a lot. The food's mediocre. She probably chose this
place for sentimental reasons."

The waitress leaves them to make their decision. As she
recedes into the dining room, Henry thinks he spots
Marybeth framed in the crook of the waitress's arm and
the curve of her waist; he's almost certain it's her.

"No, this was my idea. Their Louies are simply—"

"Dave," Henry interrupts, "did I ever show you a picture of Marybeth?"

"No. Nor do I recall hearing you describe her. Which
is odd," he says, reverting to his clinical voice, "because
most people start with a physical description of their ex."

Marybeth wades through the busy dining room, squeezing past chairs, ducking trays, avoiding busboys darting
in her lane.

"Excuse me," Henry says. "Back in a sec. I see a former
student who owes me work on an incomplete from last
quarter. I've been trying to get hold of her."

"Ask the young lady to join us," the psychologist calls
as Henry enters the dining room.

He intercepts her before she can set foot on the deck.
She looks different from his memory of her; her meta-
morphosis is utterly disconcerting. Not only has she picked
up several well-placed pounds, she's tinted her hair a silvery blond and wears it short so her facial bones are more
prominent, attenuating the shape of her face. And her eyes,
could she have had them tinted too? And her skin, is she
tanned or is this Mediterranean complexion hers? "I'm
late," she says, her equanimity incompatible with the sur-

prise of Henry's presence. "Let me pass, Hank." Had she always called him Hank? She steps away in her simple black dress, cinched at the waist with a red patent-leather belt, and a pair of ankle boots. Then she stops, turns, and says, "What are you doing here?"

"Brinkley can't make it. He tried to reach you but you weren't home. So he called me."

"And like a pup you came running." She sweeps her fingers through her new short curls. "Hank, don't be an ass. What are you after?"

"Seafood," he says. "I know a new place not far from here. Come on, the bum stiffed you. Aren't I at least second best?"

"Drop it. The girl said Brinkley's back on the deck. In fact, she said two Brinkleys are out there." She goes out into the salt air. Once there, she appears lost; she must be looking for a table occupied by two men.

The instant Henry catches up to her, Dave Brinkley stands and waves and grins and mouths "Hi." She moves toward him. Although Henry can't see it, he can feel the heat of her smile. "So you are a former student of Henry's," Dave Brinkley says, holding out his hand to Marybeth.

As acid can melt fingerprints, last night's dose of Marybeth has erased that part of Henry's brain that controls forgetting. All Saturday morning she has been unforgiving. She haunts the house, going through her old routines but dressed as she had been the night before. He sees her in the tub, inflated pillow under her neck, her stockinged legs crossed, her feet covered with the same frumpish ankle boots. In the kitchen she licks the lid of an opened can of soup. In the bedroom she lifts her

weights in front of the mirror, her eyes, fierce and an-
thracitic, concentrating on the slip-slide of the dozens of
bracelets on her arms. How easily those same eyes found
Dave Brinkley's last night and softened. Instant friends
they were, linked by a common annoyance. "Dave," she
said, loud enough for Henry to hear, "I know a quiet place
where we won't be disturbed."

Mrs. Steiner phones. She reminds Henry to stay near
the house tomorrow when Mr. Brinkley comes for the
envelope. "Maybe you can put on a suit and look nice for
him. I bet you haven't done that since your wedding day."

Henry climbs the stairs, his legs heavy, as if chim-
panzees were clinging to them. In his study he shuffles
a stack of essays, and miraculously Agnes's rises like
cream to the top. Divine Providence! He picks up the
phone and dials the campus switchboard. The operator
rings Agnes's extension number in the dorm. Without any
pretext he'll ask her to lunch. They'll go to a place where
people in ankle boots aren't served. But after too many
unanswered rings his enthusiasm for the adventure dies,
and for a fleeting instant he thinks Dave Brinkley has way-
laid Agnes too.

Upstairs he reads her essay, a paean to a boy named
Buzz. No camouflaged emotions here. Not a single cryptic
trope. Just unadulterated, unfiltered, irrational goo from
the heart. No matter what methodology he employs in his
reading of the text, one sentiment prevails: "Buzz is best."
Henry puts down his pencil and takes up the red ballpoint
reserved for his other students. Soon her essay resembles
the latticework of arteries and veins on an anatomical chart.
He populates the margins and the tight spaces between
lines with convoluted bloodworms. He maims every sentence, bad or good. Finally, Henry awards a grade: D +.
Then he reconsiders and whites-out the vertical component

of the plus sign. He has seen it happen so many times before—as love grows, writing skills decline.

've come to sweeten the pot," the man in the white linen suit says. "My original bid was very generous but it seems you need more inducement." He plucks a checkbook from his breast pocket. "What'll it take to close the deal? Five hundred dollars?" He steps past Henry into the house. They sit down in the kitchen. "As I said, I'll bump my bid up three G's, and you get this five hundred as soon as we shake hands."

"This sounds like a bribe."

"It's a bribe only if you don't take it. Otherwise, it's called sound business practice." He sets the check down on the middle of the table. Henry studies the check, made out to no one, and he smiles, and then the man smiles.

"I'll take it in cash," Henry says, letting the check fall from his hands.

The man frowns, massages his beard, then whips out his billfold. "Let's see. I only have two hundred and eighty-five dollars on hand. I'll give you a check for the rest. My signature is as good as a gun in a bank."

Henry nods. "Looks like you just bought a house."

"I did? Are you sure?"

Henry shrugs and goes outside. A minute later he returns with the FOR SALE sign. "She's yours if you want her."

The man laughs and pumps Henry's hand. "I like you. You're an odd one." He sits down to write the check. "You just sold me your house and I don't even know your name. Who do I make it out to?"

"Brinkley. Dave Brinkley. But don't give it to me now. Send it to my box in the psych office at the state college."

The man laughs again. "Didn't I say you were odd?"

He slips the checkbook away. He picks the cash up off the table, neatens it into a pile, and presses it into Henry's open palm. They shake hands. The man says his lawyers will contact Henry Monday to work out the details.

The man drives off in his silver coupe.

Henry is sitting on the front steps, replaying the events that have left him $285 richer, when the red sports car, top down, pulls up. The same bare-legged woman, now sporting a big sunbonnet and wraparound shades, strolls up the front walk toward Henry, but then abruptly cuts across the lawn to where the FOR SALE sign once stood. She stares at the hole. "Excuse me," she calls to Henry, "does this mean it's sold?"

He goes over to her at the hole. Her lips are the same red as her car. "I was just driving by and thought I'd take another look. But I guess I'm too late."

"Hasn't Mrs. Steiner contacted you?"

"No, why?"

"Isn't your name—? What did she say again?"

"I'm Dorinne. Dorinne Weiss."

"That's right. Dorinne. And you haven't spoken to Mrs. Steiner? The house is yours. Honest. She told me, 'Henry, take down that sign. I want that lovely Dorinne lady to live here.' "

"I can't believe it. This is a joke, right? I better call Mrs. Steiner."

"No," Henry says. "She's out of town. Went to see her mother."

"Mother? She must be very old."

"That's why she went to see her." He invites Dorinne into the house. For the next forty minutes she examines the rooms, inch by inch.

The house immediately takes on her particular smell. She says, "Henry, come help me celebrate."

"Love to," he says. "But first—" He goes to the kitchen and tears the taped envelope from the refrigerator. Inside the envelope he finds important-looking documents. The title and deed to the property. Suddenly, Henry sees Dave Brinkley's plan. When, as instructed, Henry gives Dave Brinkley the envelope, he will be literally turning the house over to him: "Here, take my home, and all the past lives it holds; here, take Marybeth."

Dorinne points to the documents. "Are those for me?"

He looks up from the papers, startled by her voice. These should be hers, he thinks; this house should be hers. He curses Mrs. Steiner for choosing Dave Brinkley's money, for being such a bad judge of character. If only she had seen past Dorinne's earrings and accepted her bid, then all Henry had to do was to make Dorinne fall in love with him, and he could stay in the house as long as he liked.

"Just paper," he says. "Old stuff. They're not important. One says I was married, the other says I'm divorced."

They go to her car. He opens the driver's door for her. She ties down her hat, knocks off her shoes, adjusts her sunglasses in the rearview mirror. She smiles. Those teeth! So healthy and bright! As she throws the car into gear, Henry wonders how long it'll be before she lets him behind the wheel.

Pangs
of Love

Each night, like most Americans, my mother watches hours of TV. She loves Lucy and Carol Burnett, then switches to cable for the Chinese channel, but always concludes the broadcast day with the local news and Johnny Carson. She doesn't understand what Johnny says, but when the studio audience laughs, she laughs too, as if invisible wires run between her and the set.

My mother has lived in this country for forty years and, through what must be a monumental act of will, has managed not to learn English. This does no one any good, though I suppose when it comes to TV her linguistic shortcomings can't be anything but a positive evolutionary adaptation; dumb to the prattle that fills the airwaves, maybe her brain will wither proportionately less than the average American's.

I am thirty-five years old, and for the past nine months have lived with my mother in a federally subsidized high-rise in the lower reaches of Chinatown. After my father died, my siblings convened a secret meeting during which they unanimously elected me our mother's new apartment mate. They moved her things from Long Island, carpeted her floors, bought prints for the walls, imported me for company, then returned to their lives. I work for a midsize corporation that manufactures synthetic flavors and fragrances. We are the soul of hundreds of household products: the tobacco taste in low-tar cigarettes, the pine forests in aerosol cans, the minty pizzazz of toothpastes. We have sprays that simulate the smell of new cars; in fact, we have honed the olfactory art to a level of sophistication that enables us to distinguish between makes and models. Our mission is to make the chemical world, an otherwise noxious, foul-tasting, polysyllabic ocean of consumer dread, a cozier place for the deserving noses and tastebuds of America.

My mother's in her pajamas, her hair in a net that seems to scar her forehead. I'm sitting up with her, putting in time. I flip through the day's paper, Johnny in the background carrying on a three-way with Ed and Doc, when my mother's laugh starts revving like a siren. I shoot her a look—fat-lipped, pellet-eyed—that says, What business do you have laughing, Mrs. Pang? My mother's a sweet, blockish woman whom people generally like. She's chatty with her friends in her loud Cantonese voice and keeps her cabinets and refrigerator jammed tight with food, turning her kitchen into a mini grocery store—she's prepared for a long famine or a state of siege. Now, feeling the stab of my glare, she holds in her laughter, hand over mouth schoolgirl-style, hiding those gold caps that liven up her smiles, eyes moist and shifty dancing.

I roll my eyes the way Johnny does and return to the paper. The world's going through its usual contortions: bigger wars, emptier stomachs, more roofless lives; so many unhappy, complicated acres. As a responsible citizen of the planet, I slip into my doom swoon, a mild but satisfying funk over the state of the world. But then she starts again. Fist on cheek blocking my view of her gold mine. Her round shoulders quivering with joy. I click my

tongue to let her know she has spoiled my dark mood.
She turns toward me, sees the sour expression hanging on
my face like dough, points at the screen where Johnny's
in a turban the size of a prize pumpkin, then waves me
off, swatting at flies. Ed's "ho-ho-ho" erupts from the box,
the siren in her throat winds up, and all I see is the dark
cave of her mouth.

What I need is a spray that smells of mankind's worst
fears, something on the order of canned Hiroshima, a mist
of organic putrefaction, that I'll spritz whenever the audience laughs. That'll teach her.

I stumble over my own meanness. Some son I am. What
does she know about such things anyway? It's fair to say
she's as innocent as a child. Her mind isn't cluttered with
worries that extend beyond food and family. When she
talks about the Japanese raids on her village back home,
for instance, it's as a personal matter; the larger geopolitical
landscape escapes her. She blinks her weary eyes. She's
fighting sleep, hanging on to Johnny for one more guest
before turning in. Suddenly, I have the urge to wrap my
arms around her solid bulk and protect her, only she'd
think I'm crazy, as I would if she did the same to me. "Go
to bed," I say. "I'm not tired yet," she says. I cup my
hands over my face, my fingers stinking of toilet-tissue
lilacs and roses, and think things that should never enter
a son's mind: a bomb explodes over the Empire State, forty
blocks due north on a straight line from where we are
seated, and glass shatters, and she's thrown back, the net
on her hair, her pajamas, her beaded slippers on fire, and
she hasn't a clue how such a thing can happen in this world.
And I imagine I'll never see her again.

I fetch the newspaper, go to the couch where my mother's seated, and splash-land down beside her. I'm all set to
translate the headlines, to wake her up to the world, when

I stop, my tongue suddenly lead. I don't have the words for this task. Once I went to school, my Chinese vocabulary stopped growing; in conversation with my mother I'm a linguistic dwarf. When I talk Chinese, I'm at best a precocious five-year-old, and what five-year-old chats about the military budget? Still, I'm determined and gather my courage. "What's that?" I ask, pointing at the dim photo on the front page. An Afghan guerrilla, eyes to sky, on the lookout for planes, crouches near the twisted body of a government soldier; in the desolate background there's a tank, busted up in pieces. My mother pulls on the glasses she bought at the drugstore and takes a closer look. "A monkey?" she says. I finger the body. She gives up. "That's a dead person," I say, pulling the paper away. "People are dying everywhere."

"You think I don't know. Your father just died." Her voice is quivering, but combative.

I realize I'm on shaky ground. "This man's killed by another man," I say. I'm supposed to talk about freedom, about self-determination, but with my vocabulary that's a task equal to digging a grave without a shovel. "People are killing people and all you worry about is your next bowl of rice."

"You don't need to eat?" she snaps. "Fine, don't eat. It costs money to put food on the table."

She keeps talking this way, but I tune her out, giving my all to Johnny. That guy from the San Diego Zoo's on, and with him is the fleshy pink offspring of an endangered species of wild boar. It knocks over Johnny's coffee, and Johnny jumps. The audience roars; I laugh too, but it's forced, a forgery; my mother's still sore and just sits there, holding herself in like a bronze Buddha.

While I am at work the next day, she calls me. She wants to know whether I've rented a car yet. My youngest brother owns a house on the Island, and we're invited out for the weekend. My mother and I have gone over our plans many times already, so when she starts in now I lose patience in a wink. But I catch myself—with my mother repetition is a necessity, as it is when teaching a child to speak. The rental car is my idea. She says we'll save money by taking the train. But she keeps forgetting there's three of us traveling—me, my mother, and my friend Deborah. Once we agree to go in a rental car, she then tells me I should get a small model in order, again, to save money. "I'll ask for one with three wheels," I say. And she says anything's fine, but cheaper is better.

Later the same day, my boss, Kyoto, comes to my office with a problem. Every time we meet he sizes me up, eyes crawling across my body, and lots of sidelong glances. *Who is this guy?* It's the same going-over I get when I enter a sushi joint, when the chefs with their long knives and blood-red headbands stop work and take my measure, colonizers amused by the native's hunger for their superior culture. Kyoto says a client in the personal-hygiene business wants a "new and improved" scent for its men's deodorant.

"They want to change Musk 838/Lot No. i9144375941-3e?"

He bows his head, chin to chest. "You take care for Kyoto, okay?" Kyoto says.

I nod, slow and low, as if in mourning. He nods his head. I nod again.

Musk 838/Lot No. i9144375941-3e. Palm trees and surf,

hibachied hotdogs topped with mustard, relish, and a tincture of Musk 838/Lot No. i9144375941-3e. Amanda Miller. Mandy Millstein. She was my love, and I followed her to Los Angeles. Within a year, about the time Sony purchased Columbia Pictures, she fell for someone named Ito, and broke off our engagement. When that happened, my siblings rushed in to fill the void Mandy's leaving left in my life, and decided I should be my newly widowed mother's apartment mate. My mother had grown accustomed to Mandy. She spoke Chinese, a stunning Mandarin that she learned at Vassar, and while that wasn't my mother's dialect Mandy picked up enough Cantonese to hold an adult conversation, and what she couldn't bridge verbally she wrote in notes. They conspired together to celebrate Chinese festivals and holidays, making coconut-filled sweet-potato dumplings, lotus-seed cookies, daikon and green onion soup, tiny bowls of monk's food for New Year's Day. Beyond all that, Mandy had a ladylike manner of dressing that appealed to my mother's own vanity, and to her notions of what an American ("If you're going to marry a non-Chinese, she might as well look the part") should be: skirt, nylons, high-heel shoes.

Kyoto's request saddens me. Musk 838/Lot No. i9144375941-3e, a synthetic hybrid of natural deer and mink musks, spiced with a twist of mint, was, and always will be, our special scent. Taken internally, it had an aphrodisiacal effect on Mandy. One night, as was my custom, I had brought samples of our latest flavors and fragrances home from the lab. As usual, Mandy eagerly sniffed the tiny corked vials; when she tried the musk, she said it smelled dirty. I told her that to fully appreciate its essence it needed to come in contact with the heat of one's skin. She, of course, refused to experiment with her own flesh, so I volunteered my hand; as she poured, I warned her that this was a concentrate, each drop equal in potency to the glandular secretions of a herd of buck deer. Clearly my warnings unsettled her, because the next thing I know Mandy had dumped the whole works onto my palm. Later that evening, as planned, I made pizza, working the dough with my well-scrubbed hands, but Ivory soap, as it turned out, was no match for the oily compounds in Musk 838/Lot No. i9144375941-3e. The baking pie filled the apartment with a scent reminiscent of horses. But the pizza itself was a sensation, every bite bearing a snootful of joy: tomato sauce that seemed to have fangs, cheese as virile as steak, onions so pungent they ripped our eyes from our heads. "It tastes alive," Mandy said.

"Wild," I said.

"It's the basil," she said.

Her eyes caught mine. I shook my head. "Not basil," I said, "not oregano."

She creased her second slice and dipped her fingertip in the reservoir of orange grease that pooled in the resulting valley. She touched her glistening orange finger to the gap between my eyebrows, then let it slide south down the bridge of my nose, stopping at the fleshy tip of my northernmost lip. At that moment I realized we'd been eating Musk 838/Lot No. i9144375941-3e. If it had any toxic properties, it hardly mattered then. Mandy started giggling, as if she were high on grass, and I laughed to keep her company. She drew circles on my cheeks with the orange musk-laced oils. A regular pizza face. She cackled in the manner of chimps, and when I returned the favor and greased her with gleaming polka dots, I got the joke: no doubt I looked as dopey as she did then.

After that we spiked our food and beverages with Musk 838/Lot No. i9144375941-3e whenever Mandy was feeling amorous but needed a jump start.

I wonder how she has managed since she left. When she

needs that little extra, does she do the same trick with Ito? Has he noticed that his California rolls smell funny—not fishy, but gamy like a herd of deer? If Mandy wants to recapture that old magic she had with me, she'll have to act quickly. Kyoto says it's time for a change. The manly scent of musk is no longer manly enough.

It's a sad day for love, Mandy, everywhere.

T his is a fancy car," my mother says in Chinese as we stop-and-go up Third Avenue. "It must've cost you a bundle. Tell me, *how mucha cents,*" she says conspiratorially. I look at her and say nothing.

"Isn't this nice of Bagel," my mother says a few minutes later. My youngest brother, the landowner in Bridge-hampton, has always been called "Bagel",in the family. His real name is Billy, and God help him who drops "Bagel" in front of Bagel's friends. My mother's the lone exception. When she says Bagel, he knows his friends simply think that's her immigrant tongue mangling "Billy." "Out of you four brothers and sisters," she adds, "only Bagel asks me to visit."

"What are you saying? How can I invite you over when I live with you?"

"That's right. You're a good son."

"I didn't say I was a good son, but didn't I bring you out to California?"

"*Ah-mahn-da* invited me."

"I told *Amanda* to invite you while she was talking to you on the phone."

"That's right, that's right. You're a good son," she says. "Good son who doesn't know how to talk to his own mother. His American girl speaks better Chinese."

"*Forget it,*" I say, waving her off.

"That's right. Always '*fo-gellit, fo-gellit.*' *Ah-mahn-da* never uses such words."

I swing across Twenty-third heading for Park. "Look at so many Puerto Ricans," she says. "Just like in California."

My brain stops, wrapped around a telephone pole that is my mother. I tell myself, *Try*. Explain the difference to your mother, who knows next to nothing: in Los Angeles what she thinks are Puerto Ricans are Mexicans and Chicanos. But I don't even know the words for Mexico, so how do I begin? In Chinese I'm as geography-poor as my mother, who knows only the streets and fields she's walked. Maybe I should use my hands. This is California, Amanda and I lived here, and over here—by my right hand—is another country Americans call Mexico. But that requires the patience of a special-ed teacher. In her mental maps, California is a few hours' drive from New York. That's what I'm up against.

Deborah is a bean pole. As a joke, my mother calls her "Mah-ti," water chestnut, the squat, bulbous tuber that tapers to a point like a mini dunce cap. She has hips that flare like the fins of an old Cadillac, but no rump to speak of. She wears glasses with a rhinestone frame—she's had the same ones since the eighth grade; this is not a stab at style here—and photosensitive lenses that have the annoying quality of never being dark enough or clear enough; she's always in a haze. On the rare occasions she's visited me at my mother's, she's come dressed in a most unladylike fashion: penny loafers or running shoes, chinos, and shirts bought in a boys' department. Today is no exception. I stop the rental car, a big Chevy four-door, at Park and Thirty-third. She grabs the front-passenger-side handle and stands there expecting my mother to climb into the backseat like a dog. I hit the power window switches. "You can sit in front when we stop to pee," I say.

Deborah slams the door behind her. She leans forward in her seat. "How are you, Mrs. Pang?" I've heard her speak more warmly to the bald mice she tends at Sloan-Kettering. That's where we met. At the lab we had had a small-scale scare, a baby version of the Red Dye No. 3 controversy a few years back, that forced Kyoto to send me, his right-hand slave, across town to have the stuff tested in Deborah's mice.

"*Goot,*" my mother says. "*How you?*"

Deborah doesn't answer. Won't waste her breath on someone who can't take the conversation the next step. Mrs. Pang, the linguistic dead-end street. Barbarian, I think. But a savage in bed she is, even without Musk 838/ Lot No. i9144375941-3e. Early on, my mother caught us in the sack—her sack, in fact—bony Deborah, with breasts like thimbles, on all fours. At that moment, as my mother's eyes burned holes through our nakedness, I meant to say, "What are you looking at?" full of indignation, but it came out a meek, "What do you see?" Fine, Deborah, I think, trash my mother; you're not a keeper anyway, as the fishermen say. She's the rebound among rebounds; only somehow she's stuck. If I had the words I'd straighten my mother out, allay her fears. What is she so fond of saying? "Are you planning to marry Mah-ti?" To which I tell her, emphatically, no. "So why," she says back, "you always hugging that scrawny thing?"

The trouble between Deborah and my mother runs deeper than the fact that my mother's seen the glare of Deborah's glassy bare rump. There are things I can do to soften their feelings toward each other. I might buy Deborah a pair of high-heel shoes, or register her at Hunter for Cantonese classes, or rent videos of the Frugal Gourmet cooking Chinese; I might ask my mother to stop calling Deborah Mah-ti and teach her, with patient repetition, the difficult syllables of Deborah's given name. But Deborah wants me to move out of my mother's place, says I'm a mama's boy, calls me that even as we make love; and my mother's still sad about the loss of Mandy, her surrogate Chinese daughter-in-law. My mother is subtle about this: "Mah-ti has no smell," she says, "like paper." That is to say, she misses Mandy, who made a point of showering herself with the perfumes I brought home from the lab whenever she visited my mother. There's no clean dealing with either of them.

When we pass the gas tanks along the Expressway, my mother tells me this is the very route Bagel always takes to his house. She says this with a measure of pride; I can tell what's going on in her head: I'm driving the same road my brother has driven, and to my mother's way of thinking that's not only a remarkable coincidence but a confirmation of the common thread between us, our genes, our good blood—ah, her boys, her talented womb! So why bother telling her the Expressway is the only reasonable route out to Bagel's?

Her last time out, she says, she drove with Bagel and his friend "*Ah-Jay-mee*" in the latter's two-seater, with Bagel folded into the rear storage area, best suited for umbrellas and tennis rackets. Then she wistfully adds that Bagel's former apartment mate Dennis had a car that had an entire backseat, but that luxury is "washed up" since he moved out.

After a while Deborah taps me on the shoulder. "What's she saying? She's talking about me, right? I heard her say my name."

"She said Dennis."

"*Dennis-ah cah bik*," my mother tells Deborah, spreading her hand to show size.

"Tell her this is a 'bik' pain in the you-know-what," Deborah says in a huff. "Tell her I'm tired of your secrecy, of being gossiped about in front of my face."

I say, "Slow down, okay? We're discussing my brother."

"What's Mah-ti saying?" my mother asks.

"She's saying her parents have a big car. She wants to take you on a drive someday."

My mother turns to Deborah and says, "*Goot!*"

There's not much traffic eastbound on a Saturday, not at this hour. Deborah's listening to her Walkman; I take the tinny *scrape scrape scrape* of the headphone's overflow as a token of peace. My mother stares out the windshield. Her eyes look glazed, uncomprehending. She seems out of place in a car, near machines, a woman from another culture, of another time, at ease with needle and thread, around pigs and horses. When I think of my mother's seventy-five-year-old body hurtling forward at eighty miles an hour, I think of our country's first astronaut, a monkey strapped into the Mercury capsule, all wires and restraints and electricity, shot screaming into outer space.

With Deborah occupied, I figure it's safe to talk. A chance to humanize the speed, the way pharmaceutical companies sweeten their chemicals with Cherry 12/Lot No. x362-4d so a new mother will eyedropper the stuff into her baby's mouth.

We speak at the same time.

"Ah-Vee-ah," she says my Chinese name in a whisper, "why is it that *Ba-ko* has no girlfriends? You have too many. You should marry. Look at Ah-yo. See how content he is?"

Poor Ray! If she only knew half of his troubles.

"Why is *Ba-ko* so stubborn?" she asks. "I tell you something, when I offer to take him to Hong Kong to find a bride, you know what he says? He says he's already married to his cat. Ah-Vee-ah," she says, touching my hand, "he upsets me so, I wouldn't even mind if he dated your Mah-ti."

I laugh a little; she shows her gold mischievously. "Tell me," she says (we're confidants now), "what do you make of your youngest brother?"

I shrug my shoulders. "*I don't know*," I say, turning palms up. "Ask him."

"I'm talking to you now."

"Talk to Bagel."

"*Fo-gellit!*" she says.

At some time or other, my mother's offered to take all the boys on bride safaris in Hong Kong. Ray's the only one to take her up on it, and came back to the States with a Nikon and telephoto lenses and horror stories about pigeon restaurants. He's married to a Catholic girl named Polly, who insisted, probably to get back at her parents for some past sins, on taking his name—Polly Pang. Even Ray tried to dissuade her. Following my example, Bagel has turned my mother down every time. Once after a family dinner, I overheard my mother working on Bagel. She said, "I want to see Hong Kong again before I die. I first went there in 1939 because of the Japanese. How proud I'd be returning to old friends with such a fine young son! 'An overseas bandit,' they call you. They line the prettiest girls up for you. Whatever you like. You pick. Take her out. If you don't like her, you try another. *Too muchee Chinee girl.*"

My brother said, "I'm too busy for a wife."

"She cook for you."

"I won't be able to talk to her."

"They're all very modern. They're learning English. If you take a young one, you can teach her yourself."

"I'm already married to my cat."

"Such crazy talk," she said. "What kind of life is that, hugging a cat all the time. She give you babies?"

"*Forget it*," he said. "Too much trouble."

"You're killing me," she said. "Soon I'll be lying next to your father. You crazy juk-sing, you do as I say. Before it's too late, marry a Chinese girl who will remember my grave and come with food and spirit money. Left up to you, I'll starve when I'm dead."

Bagel's house is white. Even the oak floors have been bleached white. A stranger in a white turtleneck and white pleated trousers opens the door. He's very blond, with dazzling teeth and a jawline that's an archeologist's dream. "Well, look who's here," he says, "the brother, et al." We shake hands, and he says his name's Nino. Nino leads us to the sun-washed living room and introduces us to Mack, who's sprawled over a couch with the *Times*. My mother whispers that she'd warned my brother against buying a white couch because it wouldn't "withstand the dirt," but she's surprised at how clean it looks. Mack's dressed like Deborah, and this depresses me. "Billy," Nino says in a loud singsong, "big bro and Mommy's here."

Jamie of the two-seater comes into the living room. He hugs my mother, shakes my hand, and nods at Deborah. He's in a white terry-cloth robe and Italian loafers, and offers us coffee. Down the hallway someone starts to run a shower.

While Jamie grinds coffee beans in the kitchen, Nino says, "I had the worst night's sleep." He's stretched out on the other couch, his hand cupped over his eyes. "What a shock to the system, it was so damn quiet. How do the chipmunks stand it?" Then my brother makes his entrance decked out in hound's-tooth slacks, tight turquoise tennis shirt, and black-and-white saddle shoes. "God, Billy," Nino says, "you always look so pulled together."

Hugs and kisses all the way around. Bagel's got bulk. He pumps iron. I feel as if I'm holding a steer.

"*Ah-Ba-ko*," my mother says, once we have resettled in our seats, "come and see." She leans forward in her easy chair, a white plastic shopping bag of goodies from Chinatown at her feet. "I told her not to," I say as she unloads bundles of raw greens and paper boats of dumplings onto the armrests. When she magically lifts the roast duck from the bag, soy sauce drips from the take-out container and lands on the chair, spotting the off-white fabric. Bagel has a fit: "I invite you to dinner and you bring dinner."

"So what else is new?" I hear Deborah say.

Within seconds, Nino, Mack, Jamie, and Bagel converge on the stains with sponges, Palmolive dishwashing detergent, paper towels, and a pot of water. An eight-armed upholstery patrol.

Soon after, we're having Jamie's coffee and nibbling on my mother's dumplings, which Bagel has arranged beautifully on a Chinese-looking platter, as much a conciliatory gesture as it is his way of doing things.

"Bette Davis was buried yesterday," Mack says, from behind the paper.

"Really?" says Nino. "God, now there's a lady. Hollywood heaven, open your gates. May she rest . . . in . . . peace."

"What eyes she had," says Jamie, "like two full moons."

"Old bug eyes," Deborah says.

Nino makes a hissing sound. We all look at Deborah. "Oh, hell," Nino finally says, "what does she know?"

"How old was she?" my brother asks before Deborah can answer Nino back.

"Who knows? I saw her on Johnny Carson and she looked like hell."

"*Johnny Cahson?* He said *Johnny Cahson*, right?" My mother giggles, thrilled she understood a bit of our conversation.

Bagel rolls his eyes at me like Johnny. I shrug my shoulders as if to say, I didn't invite her to the party.

"I wanted so badly for Bette to be beautiful, but she looked like leftovers that even the cat won't touch. I swear I cried, she was such a mess."

"He did," says Mack. "Poor Nino, it was tragic. He cried the biggest tears ever. But you have to admit, she still had those fabulous eyes."

"Sure, eyes. The rest of her had been run over by Hurricane Hugo."

"I saw that show," Jamie says. "Her mind was still there. She was very sharp."

"Oh sure," says Nino, "so's broken glass."

Deborah laughs; then my mother laughs. "What is she laughing about?" my mother asks through her own laughter. I shake my head to quiet her down.

Bagel holds up a gray-skinned dumpling to the ceiling. A toast: he says, "*What Ever Happened to Baby Jane?*"

"*Jezebel*," says Jamie.

"*All About Eve.*"

"*Kid Galahad*," I say.

"Oooo, that has Edward G. Robinson in it," Nino says.

Bagel's cat, Judy, and her husband, Vavoom, enter the living room, led by their noses. My mother surreptitiously plunks a shrimp dumpling on each armrest. She sees I see her doing this, and I scowl at her and she scowls back, then covers her gold mine with her hand as she breaks into a smile. She's surrounded by cats. "Look! What an adorable picture!" says Nino. "Judy, Vavoom, and Mrs. Pang, the goddess of treats." Then he adds, "Truthfully, I wouldn't give away any of these delicacies to cats; I wouldn't give any to Bette, even if she begged from her deathbed. Mrs. Pang, you've made lifelong friends." My mother, hearing her name, looks up from the cats, but the dim heat of her eyes tells everyone she's understood little else. "Silly me," Nino says, "did I say something?"

Bagel's a commercial artist, Nino's a jewelry designer, Mack's a book editor, Jamie's a city attorney. During a lull in the conversation, which we fill by watching the cats walk across my mother's lap from one armrest to the other, Jamie asks what's new at my job. I consider the Kyoto-Musk 838/Lot No. i9144375941-3e affair, but realize if I mention Mandy's name my mother will start in on me. So, instead, I improvise: "The rumor going around the lab," I begin, "says the chemists are developing a spray for the homeless, a time-release formula that'll simulate, in succession, the smell of a living room in a Scarsdale Tudor, a regular coffee (cream and one sugar), a roast-beef dinner, and fresh sheets washed in Tide."

"How ingenious!" Nino says. "The nose is such an amazing organ."

"When someone asks you for change," says Mack, "you give him a squirt of the comforts of home."

"Picture this, a panhandler in a subway car: 'Spare spray, spare spray?' "

"This is sick," says Deborah.

"I'm just giving you the latest gossip," I say. "The other rumor is that the city plans to distribute the stuff to the homeless."

"Cheaper than shelters, I suppose," Mack says.

"This is news to me," says Jamie, the city attorney. "But I wouldn't put it past the mayor's office. Remember those prints of potted flowers the city put in the windows of abandoned buildings up in Harlem?"

He pours himself a cup of coffee. "I'm working on a homeless case right now," he says. "This couple, the Montezumas, show up at Bellevue one day. They're carrying one of those Express Mail envelopes and inside there's a baby, hot and sticky from being born, the cord still on. She's purple, in real trouble. The doctors hook her up to machines, but in a few days she dies. Only she doesn't look dead. The machines pump air into her lungs, and somehow her heart keeps beating."

"Then she's alive," I say.

"No, she *looks* alive, but that's what Montezuma claims. Her chest goes up and down. But her brain doesn't register a single blip on the screen. Specialists are called in, and they tell Montezuma the same story. But Montezuma says God is testing us all, and he won't let the hospital pull the plug. Meanwhile the city is footing the bill. More specialists are consulted; Montezuma still refuses to sign the forms, so finally the city steps in and turns off the juice. The next thing you know, half the attorneys in town are fighting for the chance to sue the city, and I have lots of work."

Bagel, Jamie, and I spend the afternoon playing tennis while my mother watches us from the car. The others take a drive around the "countryside."

We eat dinner late. Jamie barbecues chicken. My mother chops her duck into rectangular chunks. We drink three bottles of chardonnay. Afterward, we're in the kitchen, slicing pies, making coffee, putting away leftovers, washing dishes.

I hear my mother calling for Bagel. We find each other in the busy kitchen, and he asks me to see what she wants.

She's in the master bedroom standing in front of the TV set. It's turned on; the screen's filled with pink and blue snow.

"What are you doing?" I say. "This is Saturday. There's no Johnny Carson."

"You think I don't know," she says. "Saturday night has to have wrestling."

I flip through the stations with the remote control. For as long as I can remember, my mother has been a wrestling fan. It's good pitted against evil; the clean-shaven, self-effacing, play-by-the-rules good guy versus the strutting, loudmouthed, eye-gouger. No language skills required here. A dialogue of dropkicks, forearm smashes, and body slams. It's a big fake but my mother believes. And for a long time, as a kid, our family gathered in front of the set Saturday nights, drinking sodas and cracking red pistachio nuts, true believers all.

In one of my strongest memories, a man from ringside wearing a pea coat and knit cap, with a duffel bag slung over his shoulder, leapt into the ring where the champ, a vicious long-haired blond, was taking a post-victory strut on his victim's chest. The fans in the arena, my mother beside me, were voicing their indignation when this mystery man, who looked as if he had walked in off the streets, caught the champ unawares, lifted him onto his shoulder, and applied a backbreaker, soon recognized as his signature hold. What joy, what gratitude, what relief we all felt! Justice restored! Later in the program, the ringside announcer interviewed our hero. He was an Italian sailor, he said, in heavily accented English, a recent immigrant to U.S. shores.

It was myth in action. The American Dream in all its muscle-bound splendor played out before our faithful eyes.

My mother and I sit at the edge of the king-size bed. On the screen, a match is about to begin between a doe-faced boy named Bubby Arnold and the Samurai Warrior. The All-American Boy meets the Yellow Peril. The outcome is obvious to everyone except my mother. She yells encouragement to Bubby, "Kill him, kill the little Jap boy!" as he bounds across the ring, all grit and determination, but promptly collapses to the mat when he runs into the Samurai Warrior's lethal, upraised foot. I shake my head. By then my thoughts are full of Kyoto and Mandy's Ito. My Musk 838/Lot No. i9144375941-3e, testament to our love, and my tenuous hold on Mandy are crumbling, going the way of Bubby Arnold under the Samurai Warrior's assault. I ache for Bubby, the poor schnook. I can't bear to watch. But my mother hasn't given up. She screams for her man to step on his opponent's bare toes, to yank on his goatee. But that isn't in the script. He isn't paid to be resourceful, no Yankee ingenuity here. No one, not my mother and her frantic heart, can change the illusion.

At the commercial break my mother says, "The Japanese are so cruel. He almost killed that poor boy." She goes on that way, recounting the mugging, and I tell her not to take it so seriously. "It's all a fake," I say. "He's not really hurt."

"I have eyes," she says. "I know what I just saw."

I'm surprised by the sudden heat in her voice, by the wound beneath the words. The fights matter: in them, she believes her heart's desire, her words of encouragement have currency. What *she* wants counts. But the truth is she doesn't believe what she has seen. The good guy should win. Somewhere in that mind of hers she carries hope for the impossible. Bubby Arnold triumphant, Mandy back in our lives again. I look at her, a woman against the odds. What a life of disappointment!

I won't let her down as Bubby Arnold has. She needs to hear the truth: there is no Santa; the Communists aren't leaving China. Her beloved Amanda is gone for good.

"I have to tell you somthing." I take a deep breath and say, "Amanda," and as anticipated, she's startled, expectant, hanging on my next word.

I regret I ever started. That hope is flickering in her irises, and it's poison to my enterprise. But I have no recourse but to get on with it; as my mother likes to say at such a juncture, "You wet your hair, you might as well cut it."

I know what I want to say in English. My mind's stuffed full with the words. I pull one sentence at a time from the elegant little speech I've devised over the months for just this occasion, and try to piece together a word-for-word translation into Chinese. Yielding nonsense. I abandon this approach and opt for the shorter path, the one of reduction, simplicity, lowest common denominator. "*Ah-mahn-da*, what? Talk if you have talk." There's music in her voice I haven't heard in years.

"I like *Amanda*," I say.

My mother nods. On the TV, wrestlers being interviewed snarl into the camera and holler threats that seem directed not so much at future opponents, but at the viewers themselves.

"She doesn't like me," I say.

"Crazy boy. Like? What is this "like"? I lived all those years with your father—who worried about who liked which one? Tomorrow, you call her back here."

Samurai Warrior's grinning face fills the screen. In the

background his manager carries on about the mysteries of the Orient, tea ceremonies, karate, brown rice, and his client's Banzai Death Grip.

"Look it, look it. He's so brutal, that one is," my mother says. She touches my cheek, her hand warm but leathery. I can't remember this happening before. "You say you like her, so call her back."

"What's wrong with your ears? I said she doesn't like me. She likes him." I point at the TV.

"Crazy boy. What are you saying?" She dismisses me, her fingers pushing off my cheek, as if they have springs.

"*Amanda* likes a Japanese."

"That one?" she says, meaning the wrestler.

I pound my fists against my thighs. "No, not him." I stand up and pace the carpet between my mother and the TV set. "*Amanda*," I begin, "*Amanda* . . ." And each time I say her name and hesitate, my mother sucks in breath and inflates with new hope. I stop pacing. She looks up at me from her seat at the edge of the bed. I touch her cheeks with both hands. I don't know where the gesture comes from, movies or TV, but it has nothing to do with what went on in our household. I am on strange ground. In my palms her face is a glass bowl, open and cool. "*Amanda* likes you. She doesn't like me. She likes a Japanese boy in *California*. I can call her, but she's not coming back."

My mother pulls away, not just from my hands, but receding, a filament inside her dimming. "*Ah-mahn-da* makes a delicious dumpling," she says in a small, distant voice. "She rolls the skins so delicately."

During the next match she is uncharacteristically subdued. The fight has left her. On the screen two masked wrestlers beat up Bubby Arnold clones. Nothing issues from her, no encouragement, no outrage, no hope. I've robbed my mother of her pleasure, of her flimsy faith in Americans, in America, and in me. And I don't have the words for *I am sorry*, or fine sentences that would resurrect her faith and put things back in order. I'm the pebble in her shoe, the stone in her kidney. Now I see that she's Montezuma from Jamie's story: she would hold on to the slimmest hope, while I, as I have just done, would rush in and pull the plug on her.

At the next commercial time-out she turns to me and says, "Ah-Vee-ah, all the men in this house have good jobs, they have money, why don't they have women? Why is your brother that way? What does he tell you? I don't understand." She speaks somberly, with difficulty, as she had when she described the raids.

Her eyes, I see, are filled with tears. I know that she cries easily and often since my father's death. I've heard her in her room late at night.

I put my hand on her back, as round as a turtle's, but hot and meaty. "I don't know," I tell her, and for the first time I am stunned by my deception of her. "I don't know why there's no women here."

Bagel comes to the bedroom announcing coffee and dessert. He turns off the set. I can read his mind. He doesn't want his friends to know he dropped from the womb of one who loves something as low as wrestling. "Come eat *pie*," he says.

"*Pie*. Who made them?" she asks.

"I did, who else? I stayed up last night baking pies for you. Come on."

"Yours I won't eat," she says. "I want to taste your girlfriend's baking."

"You crazy? I don't have a girlfriend," he says. "She's driving me crazy!" he exclaims, then leaves the bedroom, and we follow.

"*Ca-lay-zee*. Who's *ca-lay-zee*? You hammerhead. Hug

your dead cat the rest of your life. How fragrant is that?"

"*Forget it*, Ma," I say. I touch her shoulder, but she flicks me off.

"Ah-Ma," she says. "How can I be your mother if nobody listens to what I say?"

At the table we are confronted with big wedges of apple pie. My mother's still upset. She stares at the pie as if it were a form of torture.

"Where've you two been?" Deborah asks.

"In the bedroom, watching wrestling."

"God, how retro," she says. "What's happening to you?"

"Bagel," I say, stopping his hand as he's about to spoon sugar into my mother's coffee.

"Bagels?" Jamie says. "You're hungry for bagels? We're having bagels for breakfast."

I say nothing. I pull from my pocket gold-foil packets the size and shape of condoms. Inside each is a tablet developed at the lab. You dissolve it in your mouth, and it will disguise the sourness of whatever you drink or eat. I pass them to everyone at the table.

They won't know what has happened. They will laugh, delighted by the tricks of their tongues. But soon the old bitterness in our mouths will be forgotten, and from this moment on, our words will come out sweet.

Love
on the Rocks

I

W hat do I know about Buddy Lam? First, I can still see poor Enid, after an hour under the hottest shower a body could stand, sitting on the edge of our bed, towel over her shoulders, eyes staring like two miniature CRTs loaded with data: inscrutable and obvious at the same time. She said, "I can't wash the chill off," and then said it again a thousand more times that night. That's one memory: Buddy Lam condensed to a silicon chip. But don't be misled. I'll go on record as saying Buddy Lam was a friend of mine. He was loyal to his wife, his friends, his job. We both worked at FutureFun, where we were known as the Chinese Connection; Buddy and Bruce, the Chinese Connection. We had some big hits together—Kill the Cat, Laundry Shoot, Ax Man—just to name a few. I took care of the technical end of things and Buddy dreamed up the plots. A regular yin-and-yang team. He was famous in the Valley for those eccentric plots of his. Normal people just didn't think like that. We were a hot property until the bottom fell out of the home-video-game market. In an economy where PhDs were soldering circuit boards, I was demoted from design engineer to Guy

Friday. One Saturday morning they had me in front of a computer punching in the names of employees scheduled for termination. Up came LAM, BEIJING (BUDDY) on the list, and instead of ignoring it, I just punched him in with the rest, when with half the trouble I could've skipped him and kept Buddy on the payroll. He knew what I'd done, but on the day he received his form letter he bought me my lunch. I saw Buddy and Cookie a lot those first weeks after he lost his job. He couldn't find any work but that didn't seem to dim his outlook on things.

2

Miriam unloads the bags of groceries from the backseat of her Valiant. "Keep low, okay?" she says to Buddy. "Al drives around sometimes when he works." She smiles conspiratorially and blinks her translucent lids. "Restrain yourself," she adds, her voice reduced to a whisper, "this is an adult situation." Her skin glows; her eyes sparkle through the stalks of celery poking from the bag in her arms. There are times when Miriam seems more excited by the peripheral intrigue of their affair than by the affair itself. Two nights earlier they had slept together for the first time. Al was out of town, and after Buddy had promised to keep his fly zipped and his hands above her waist, she agreed to share her bed. All night long Buddy couldn't sleep, his love for Miriam working on him like pure caffeine, while she snoozed soundly, giggling at some jokester in her dreams. At 4 A.M. the alarm rang and she sent him dazed out the back door. He roamed the street for nearly an hour unable to relocate his car—parked, at her insistence, blocks from her house.

She goes to deliver the sacks of groceries to an elderly

couple in the apartment complex where they are parked. Buddy, who's short, folds neatly into his predicament. Knees to chest, head tucked, eyes level with the cavity in the passenger door where the lost window crank belongs, Buddy listens to the diminishing clicks of the smart red pumps he bought her earlier in the week and tries not to feel too glum. But why had she stopped the car just shy of the shade tree? What was she thinking? The sun beats down on him like a giant eye watching his every move. Under its glare he bakes in the woollen suit he wears expressly for Miriam. He knows if he tries to take off the jacket, the guilt-seeking eyes of Cookie's friends will instantly spot him, much the way cruise missiles zero in on their targets. A car honks in the near distance and he sinks deeper into his seat, snagging the jacket on a loose spring jutting from the vinyl seat. He reads all kinds of significance in the cotton batting spiraling from the shoulder pad. Were the forces in the universe that balance off one man's duplicity finally catching up to him? When might he rise from the treachery that forces him to sit among flattened Diet Pepsi cans, Baby Ruth wrappers, and bottles of sour baby formula? For weeks hundreds of disembodied eyes have followed him the way steel bars follow a prisoner around his cell.

When he hears her heels, Buddy reaches up and adjusts the rearview mirror just in time to see Miriam turn her face up to the sun, catching rays as a dish collects rain. Her skin is the same shade of walnut as her hair. She's wearing a man's undershirt and a baggy pair of camouflage pants rolled up at the ankles to show off her shoes.

She slides behind the wheel. "These people must think I'm with the United Way," she says in a huff. "They claimed one bag was half-empty and wanted to cheat me out of three bucks. Do I look like a charity? Just wait till next week. We'll see if I remember their prunes." Her rage delights Buddy. In the time he's known her, she's displayed a maddening equanimity toward her miserable life. Buddy is her way out; the shoes on her feet are material proof. He knows she wants more than her husband can ever offer. The afternoon they'd first met, at the Grand Union, he noticed her flipping through the fashion magazines, and it was apparent from her expressions that she envied not only the women who wore the fancy clothing but even those who could afford to buy the magazines.

The Valiant pulls away from the curb. "Forget about them," Buddy says. "You deserve better than this. I'll give you the money. The time you're supposed to be out shopping for your clients you'll spend with me."

"I like you, Mr. Lam, but I can't take your money."

They both look down at her red shoes.

"Don't call me that. You're trying to put distance between us again."

"Oh, I'm just afraid of what Molly might say when she learns how to talk. She saw you the other night." Miriam signals for a left-hand turn. "Maybe we should only meet at the Grand Union from now on. Look, Mr. Lam, you have a good life. You're established. You're an important executive. You wear nice clothes. I like you but you're different from me and Al. I mean, it's eighty-five degrees and you haven't even loosened your tie. My God, most people I know don't even own ties. The way I figure it, Al's twenty years from where you are, but someday he'll get even with you."

"How, by selling Bibles?"

She swings the car into the supermarket parking lot and pulls up alongside Buddy's Buick. She switches off the engine, plucks a half-eaten candy bar from the ashtray, takes a big bite, and then sighs. Her husband, Al, owns an inspirational bookstore and gift shop over on Mission. "Al says if the Lord wants him rich he'll be rich. If it means selling Bibles, then that's what it means. I have nothing to do with the store. I don't believe, not even on Sunday. All those little Jesuses hanging up on crosses give me the shakes. Last time I went in there, Al was talking to this crazy lady who believed Merv Griffin was the Devil. And there was my Al, nodding his big old head, saying, 'I know how you feel.' "

"You don't sound very convinced about his prospects." Miriam shrugs.

Buddy grabs her by the wrist. "Let's finally do it," he says. "Why don't we hop into my car and go to my place. I'll introduce you to Cookie and get things out in the open. Then we'll go talk to Al."

"Sorry, Mr. Lam," Miriam says. "I don't want to talk about that again." She shakes her head emphatically, no, no, no, no.

At that precise moment Buddy finally deciphers Miriam's peculiar smell: a mix of ripe peaches and French fried potatoes. He adores it.

3

I'm sure it's already written down somewhere but my guess is that he's about forty-two, which makes him twenty years older than Miriam. That's scary stuff. He could be her father only he's Chinese and she's not, but that never seemed to bother her, so I won't let it bother me. She said he wanted her to dump Al and go off to L.A. with him, even though he was married also. That means the two of them would have three marriages going on at once between them when some of us don't even have the prospect for one. At any rate, she couldn't drop Al, not with the kid around, but she sure liked having a big-time, sugar-daddy businessman hot for her. He'd buy her a bank, she said, if that's what she fancied. Well, I don't know about a bank but she sure adored those cute little shoes he got her. She must've told me a zillion times they're genuine cow leather and hand-sewn in Italy by genuine Italians, like she was afraid I might confuse them with the jellies I wear made of real Korean plastic. Ninety-five bucks those shoes cost him, she said; he didn't even blink when he paid up.

Miriam's nothing but a real nice girl, that's all. She works as a professional shopper buying groceries for old people and invalids at five bucks a bag. Forget shoes, you can't buy Italian bread on that kind of money. And that husband of hers isn't retiring too soon either. He runs a Christian bookstore. He's got books in there with names like *With Him at My Side* and *30 Prayers to Thinner Thighs*, and in the back he's got a room full of Jesus statues, veronica hankies, Holy Ghost mugs, and Shroud of Turin baby blankets. I told Miriam, "Face it, girl, so what if he's not the best-looking guy on the street. A quarter of the world looks like him and none of them's got his kind of dough."

Don't get me the wrong way. He was one strange customer. I used to work the express lane at the Grand Union when he came looking for Miriam. Same time each day for two weeks he'd show up, walk Miriam up and down the aisles while she shopped, and help her out to the parking lot. Afterward he'd come back and pick up the same things each time: a six-pack of Tab and six bags of party ice. I made small talk with the guy, partly because I was supposed to, and partly because I felt like I knew him through Miriam. I'd ask, "Having another party tonight?"

and he'd turn red behind his black-frame glasses. But he never lost his cool except once. It was before he and Miriam became an item. I'd just got done teasing him about the ice when I started putting it away in bags and he just flipped. "Don't touch!" he said. You'd think I was foaming at the mouth, the way he looked at me. Then he was embarrassed and apologized.

After that I played it cool. Didn't put my hands on nothing, but I couldn't help teasing him. "Having another party tonight?" I asked him that night.

"Betsy," he said, reading the name stitched on my uniform, "last night's party isn't over yet."

"You must be a popular guy," I said.

I asked Miriam about all that ice and Tab. She said she didn't know what I was talking about. I wondered if the stuff had anything to do with his Oriental love technique, and Miriam acted all insulted and said I had a dirty mind. But I asked her another time, "You sure he doesn't do something kinky with that ice?"

4

My daughter made those two. Cookie had the personality and the looks. She had the savvy to ask for directions when they were lost, and on her legs sweat socks looked as sleek as seamed stockings. When they walked down the street, Cookie towering over him, people rubbernecked as if they just saw Jackie O. pass with Arafat on her arm. The only thing they had in common was a certain roundness, only she curved and bulged in ways half the world envied and the other half adored. Why she married that barbarian will live as one of the great mysteries of the civilized world.

I put her through Vassar when it was still a respectable thing to do, before the freak show took over. She had great prospects back then. She could've married a congressman, a baseball player, or even a movie star.

Grant it, he loved her, doted on her. But any man would've done the same.

I'd like to call his mother and tell her what a monster she raised for a son, but she wouldn't understand a word I say. Cookie left me with in-laws who speak a lawless tongue. Look, at least if they were French I could use a dictionary.

I suppose I should mention that I knew about Cookie's affair. He sounded perfect: Yale grad, tall, bearded, feet planted firmly in the financial world. Call it adultery if you like, but I told her not to feel guilty. She was only trying to return to her roots. I said, "There's nothing wrong with what you're doing just as long as your husband doesn't find out."

5

Buddy announces his arrival but Cookie doesn't respond. For weeks, since she confessed her indiscretions, she's been touchingly contrite. She's devoted her energies to proving how loving, deferential, and faithful a mate she can be. But now it's just wasted effort. Buddy has decided her fate (oh, she did that herself when she chose to have that affair!) and is determined to bring Miriam home and make his intentions known.

He lugs the ice and Tab into their bedroom. Among the day's mail he finds a letter from a collection agency threatening to repossess his car. He totals up his debts on a pocket calculator and concludes he can't possibly afford to give

Miriam any money outright. Perhaps she can work for her pay, he thinks, do his shopping, buy the ice; that way he'll be assured of seeing her daily, and gain the added bonus of avoiding the obnoxious girl at the checkout lane. He's pleased with his new scheme until he realizes it still represents an outlay of funds he doesn't have.

He inspects the rip in his jacket. He needs to have it mended immediately, but he won't ask Cookie because she'll want to know where he tore it, and since he's a terrible liar he doesn't dare risk such an exchange. On the other hand there's Miriam, but she thinks he's rich, and rich people can afford tailors. He goes to the closet and finds his only other suit, the one he was married in, a powder-blue affair with satin trim at the cuffs and lapels. It will do as a temporary replacement while his business suit mends. Miriam will have to be patient. Besides, he thinks, what does she know about an executive wardrobe?

Buddy goes downstairs and puts Cookie's favorite record on the turntable, which he adjusts so the song will replay automatically. He increases the volume and returns upstairs.

Through the cheap speakers the singer sounds as soulful as a pup whining in a tin can. But Cookie likes it that way. Sometimes this music makes her weepy, and when she cries or just gets in the mood to, Buddy can have his way with her. Tomorrow, Cookie must face the consequences of her past intrigue. He will convince Miriam to come to the house and all the sneaking will end. Then, as planned, off to Los Angeles, where among the sprawl his creditors won't find him. But first, tonight, he wants to do what's fair and break the news to her gently.

He's in the half-bath off the bedroom swilling mouthwash and combing his hair. He builds a tall pompadour from which he plucks a few strands that then dangle loosely on his forehead. When he wears his hair this way, Cookie says he looks sexy. He rinses off his glasses. He slips on the wedding jacket. He takes up the Tab and sacks of ice.

Buddy tiptoes to the door at the end of the hall. He knocks gently. "Cookie, are you in there?" he says, turning the doorknob. He throws the light switch and the rows of bulbs that ring the mirror fire up like a movie marquee. Cookie is stretched languorously over the length of the tub. Her eyes wear the familiar expression of detached amazement that she greets his nightly return with. Her parted lips wish to utter the gratitude and relief she feels— out of the infinite goodness of his heart, he has forgiven her for yet another day. Already the music has touched her, for she is quiet and somber. Buddy sets the ice on the floor and stacks the Tab on top of the other six-packs piled on the edge of the tub. The rows of pink cans form a barrier between husband and wife. Buddy sits on the toilet seat and tells her about his long day of job hunting. He confesses his doubts of ever finding decent work again. Cookie's sympathetic silence moves him. Her undying support makes Buddy ashamed of the real news he has in tow. He looks at her lying there holding back her tears, her perfect body still and tensed as if she were steeling herself for more bad news.

He senses his resolve slipping. He needs a drink to fortify his nerves. "How about some wine?" he asks.

He goes downstairs and removes a bottle of chablis from the refrigerator. As he unscrews the cap, the telephone rings.

"What?" he barks impatiently. He stuffs two glasses into his pockets.

"Who are you 'what'ing? Let me say happy birthday to Cookie. I won't take up any more of your time."

Her mother. Perhaps this explains Cookie's tight-lip

act. Although she has little reason to expect a birthday celebration this year—not after what she's done—she's probably still disappointed that he hasn't at least acknowledged it.

"Cookie's in the tub."

"Don't disturb her then. Let her relax. I'll try again later. So what've you got planned for the birthday girl?"

"Just a quiet evening home—a little wine, the two of us."

"How exciting, Buddy. Sounds like you've put a great deal of thought into my daughter's birthday."

Here," he says, and wraps her unwilling hand around a glass. "Let's have a drink." He hopes the wine will warm her spirits. Otherwise, what kind of gentleman would he be if he drops bad news on her when she's already down? He fills their glasses and then nestles the bottle between her feet. As he sips, he peeks over the lip of his raised glass and sees she won't even taste hers. She's obviously crushed. It's the birthday. She loves celebrations, but what does she expect? Her disappointment weighs on her; he can see it in her droopy lids and the slackness in the muscles of her face. He pours himself another glass of wine, and when he returns the bottle to the tub he says, "Would you care for some ice?" He notices how confused she looks. "Not for the wine!" he says. Buddy stands and empties the sacks of ice into the tub, compacting the loose cubes over her languid body. "Relax," he tells her, "close your eyes. Listen to the music. It's your favorite record. Taste the wine." But she's too busy pouting. "Okay, you win. I'll be back in a little while."

He switches off the lights. When he returns, he'll enter with candles blazing and sing "Happy Birthday." Get her in a good mood. Then they can talk. He hurries to the Grand Union.

6

Mr. Lam must've asked me fifty times to go meet this Cookie lady. Now this might sound young and idealistic, but is that any way to carry on an affair? Not in books it isn't, or on TV, or in the movies. Secrecy is as good an emotion as love. I tell you, he was one of the sneakiest people around. That first time we met at the Grand Union, he followed me up and down the aisles for forty minutes, faking like he was shopping. I didn't know if he was there shoplifting or because he thought I was. We came dangerously close to a meeting at the meat counter. He was over by the chicken parts, I was next door at the chopped beef, but this old gal was standing between us, fingering two packages of wings. I still remember how I kept squeezing this pound of ground chuck, pretending it was his hand. Well, a few minutes later in the soft-drink aisle, while I was getting my Diet Pepsi, he came up from behind and said, "Why not Tab?" I mean, if you saw him, you'd never think he's capable of such a pickup line.

Pretty soon he's talking to me about this Cookie lady. He was in a funk over something she did. So I listened and nodded a lot. A week or so later, he started asking if I'd go home with him to meet this Cookie of his.

Listen, I was attracted to Mr. Lam. Any girl likes a man who talks. You know, really talks, from the heart. But what really turned me on was how nervous he was about being seen at the store with me. There were times we'd be chatting and suddenly he'd split like we're total strangers because he saw some friend of his. He said he hated sneaking around, but he was so damn good at it. I swear, it was like playing "Man from U.N.C.L.E." again. I loved how he slid down in the passenger seat of my car that time he came with me on my deliveries. At each stop I told him to scrunch up small, and he did, just like a cat asleep, and when I came back eight, ten minutes later, there he was still balled up, his head tucked way down low. That's dedication. Whatever I said went. I let Betsy talk me into giving him a little loving. She said I had to do something to keep up his interest. But I wasn't sure that was for me, so I said we couldn't take our clothes off, and he didn't put up a fuss at all.

After that night he wanted me to drop Al. I had this theory that he wanted to set Al up with that Cookie lady. Anyway, Betsy thought Mr. Lam's money and career were good enough reasons for me to leave Al, but neither of them understood Al. Al's the father of my baby girl. And Al's spiritual. He's not selling Jesus key rings to make his fortune. He got into the business because of the car wreck. The doctors said he was dead. That's right, he's one of those weirdos you see on TV all the time who die and come back to tell about it. While he was under, he said this pretty man with a beard and white robes told him, "Al, get your butt off this damn slab; your wife's pregnant with a baby girl." So that's what he did, and that bearded guy was right on the money, because I was with Molly then but Al had no way of knowing it at the time he died. The way I have it figured, Al is a ticket to someplace most of us know nothing about.

7

On his way to the supermarket, Buddy rehearses what he wants to tell Cookie. It boils down to a single key statement: "There is someone I want you to meet." But the words don't come out; in his mouth his tongue's a fish, thrashing at cross-purposes with his teeth and lips. How can he ever hope to match the eloquence of her confession? What a well-orchestrated seduction that was! She met him at the door wearing his favorite dress and the perfume he adored; her lips were polished to a high gloss; a leg of lamb was roasting in the oven; the Vivaldi he loved—and she despised—danced in the delicious air. He remembers how he ate it all up, smiling foolishly at his own executioner, kissing her greased mouth, her thick lips engulfing his own cannibalistically. And when she finally confessed she spoke with the ease of one reciting a familiar recipe.

Dazed by the memory of that night, Buddy steps through the automatic doors. He hopes to see Miriam there, buying a last-minute jar of mayonnaise or quart of milk. He listens for her heels, sniffs for her peculiar hybrid scent. He wanders the aisles before crisscrossing back to the baked goods where he selects a boxed cake with pink, blue, and yellow rosettes on white icing.

Buddy hurries to the checkout lane, anxious to get home before he loses his resolve. The cake will make his task easier, his answer to her leg of lamb.

As he turns the corner at a mammoth paper-towel display, he collides with a shopping cart steered by a nattily dressed woman done up in lavender. "Mister, if I were a truck, you'd be dead," she says as Buddy stumbles past. "Buddy Lam, is that you? Come back here."

"Lorraine Marcus," he says, walking toward Cookie's friend. "I didn't see you."

"Of course you didn't. You were speeding." She smiles, her teeth smeared with lipstick. She extends her hands out to Buddy. Her lavender fingernails are so long they curl. She draws him close so he can plant a dainty kiss alongside both her cheeks. "I see that wife of yours has you picking up your own dessert. Where's that woman been hiding? When I call, no one ever picks up." Lorraine Marcus takes the box from Buddy's hands. "Whose birthday is it?"

"Nobody's. We just like birthday cake."

"Oh, come now, Buddy, no one on earth likes store-bought birthday cake. It's Cookie's birthday, isn't it? I know she's a Taurus."

"You're too smart for me. Look, she's at home waiting for this. I have to hurry back."

"I trust you're not having a big shindig without inviting the Marcuses."

"That's unthinkable," Buddy says, taking possession of the cake again. "I'll tell you what, I can give you a chunk of this out in the parking lot. Cookie won't mind."

"Sure, let's have a tailgate party. We can share this rump roast." She pats Buddy's cheeks and rolls her eyes. "Buddy, you just tell that sweet thing that Lorraine says happy birthday and give her some spanks for me."

Buddy goes over to the only available checkout lane. "Oh boy," says the Betsy girl, "now a birthday party. But no candles? No ice?"

The birthday candles are on a rack behind him. Ice is a splendid idea. If he buys some now, he can avoid the annoying register girl tomorrow. He tells her to ring up six sacks of ice and heads for the freezer, pushing a cart.

After he returns to the register and pays for his purchases, Betsy says, "Can we talk?"

"I'm running late," Buddy says, easing the cart from the checkout lane. "The party's waiting for this cake."

"You know that girl who shops for the invalids? You know, Miriam?"

Buddy stops, his joints seem to lock. Could she really know his Miriam, even though she's so young and unpleasant?

"We talked before I came to work tonight," she says.

Lorraine Marcus swings her cart up to the register. She says to Buddy, "You say you're in a big hurry, but I see you can find time to flirt with the help instead of me."

"Come on, Lorraine."

"I have a tip for you, Mr. Lam," Betsy says. "Miriam's not shopping here anymore. It's the truth. I know a lot. We're best friends. It was my idea you spend the night at her place."

"Buddy Lam," Lorraine Marcus says, "what are my ears hearing?"

"I guarantee she won't be here tomorrow. And don't follow her to the A & P. Oops! That was supposed to be a secret. But I don't mind telling you because we're friends too, aren't we?"

Buddy walks away trembling. "Who's this Miriam person, Buddy?" Lorraine Marcus calls after him. "And is that party ice I see in your cart?"

Buddy steers the Buick in the direction of Miriam's house. They need to talk. She has to go home with him tonight before Lorraine Marcus blabs it to the world and Cookie hears the news secondhand.

8

Miriam was changing Molly on the kitchen table when he came to our door. The Good Lord sent that little Chinese man to us. I had been discussing with Miriam the possibility of expanding my operations. I couldn't decide what I should do. Earlier in the week, a video-game salesman planted the notion in my head of installing a video arcade in my store. At first, I called Mr. Ledbetter an agent of the Devil, and I would've tossed him out on his behind except the Lord stayed my hand. I granted Mr. Ledbetter an audience. He explained that an arcade would draw children into my store, where they can come under the direct influence of the Lord and His merchandise. He showed me these games and, indeed, they were truly Christian amusements. In the one called The Saint, Satan tempts you with every imaginable sin and you must resist or be damned. For a quarter, there's a genuine chance for redemption. On one screen there's a maze of harlots and adulterers, and you weave past their wanton grasp by wrapping your faith in Jesus around the joystick and letting Him guide your hand. Every temptation you pass scores you points. The more points you earn, the closer you move toward sainthood.

I was at a loss. Then Miriam said, "Maybe old Jesus will give you a sign." And moments later that Providential hand knocked at our humble front door. The little Chinese man said, "I know you, you're Al, the Bible salesman; I was certain when I first laid eyes on this house that within its walls charity had made its home."

He said he wanted to borrow the telephone. He had been in a minor auto accident and needed to contact the authorities. I welcomed him into our modest home. I told the story of my brush with death in a burning wreck, and how the Lord delivered me from limbo and sent me on my life's mission. To my surprise, the little man seemed familiar with my tale. He said, "You can spend all the money in the world on medical doctors and still not get the results a little faith can bring." When I heard these words, I had no doubts that he was the sign Miriam had asked for, the messenger of the Lord. I knew then I had to buy those video games. I was so happy and relieved and grateful Someone still was watching after me that I embraced the little man and then showed him off to Miriam. And if she didn't believe before, she was a believer then, for her face blanched white as the Spirit seemed to enter her the very instant she first set eyes on that Angel of Commerce.

I pointed out the direction to the telephone but he started toward Miriam instead. What a wondrous sight she was to behold! Trembling, wide-eyed, pale as a pine board, as the Spirit found a home inside her. The Angel said, "Miriam, come with me." She picked up our Molly and held her out in front of her, the way people in movies scare off vampires with crosses. For an instant I thought he might sprout wings and fly off with mother and child. And I wouldn't have lifted a finger to stop him.

"What are you doing here?" she said. I said, "That's no way to talk to our guest. He's come a long way to help us, and now, in our own humble way, we must help him however we can."

The little man took Miriam by the arm. "Will you please leave me alone?" she said.

I said, "I'll call the police."

"Don't," he said.

"But your car, what about your accident?" I asked. I

dialed the operator. Our visitor kept talking at Miriam and she kept shaking her head and saying, "I can't, I can't." So when I got off the telephone I asked her what it was she couldn't do for our honored guest.

She said it was none of my business. He said, "I want her to come see my wife." I said, "Mister, we are Christians under this roof. Is something the matter? Is your wife ill?"

When the police sirens came up the street, the little man ran out the back door. Miriam and I followed. I wanted to thank him for bringing His word. We saw him hop into his car and drive off. What better confirmation could there be? The Lord had come and fixed his car.

9

We hadn't heard from Buddy and Cookie in about two weeks. Enid Chin called and said it was Cookie's birthday. We figured with Buddy out of work and all, they probably weren't planning anything. So Scott and I and Enid and Bruce Chin decided to chip in and throw a surprise party. We got to their place at nine with a cake, a fifth of vodka, some chips and dips, and a bottle of Mateus. The house was dark when we arrived, so we figured Buddy had taken her out for dinner. We tried the door and it wasn't locked. We went in, and as soon as we heard their car pull up we lit the candles on the cake and hid in the kitchen. When the door creaked open, Bruce hit the lights and we all shouted, "SURPRISE!" but it was just Buddy, standing there in his wedding suit, his glasses crooked on his face like he'd been in a fight. He was carrying a boxed cake and all this ice.

"Where's the birthday girl?" I said. "Hey, Cookie."

"It looks like Buddy's planning his own party," Scott said.

"Ooo, ice," Enid said. "There isn't a cube in the house."

I took the cake from his hands. I said, "I hope we're not spoiling your plans."

Scott patted Buddy on the back and asked where Cookie was hiding. Buddy just shook his head and then he said to me, "Did you talk to Lorraine Marcus yet?"

"No," I said. "Is that who you've invited to your party?"

Scott, Enid, and Bruce were in the kitchen fixing drinks when the telephone rang. Bruce picked up. "Hey, Buddy," he said, "it's Cookie's mom." Buddy took the receiver and stretched cord out to the living room. I heard him say, "She's still in the tub. She won't talk to any of us."

Enid had to duck under the telephone cord as she left the kitchen with her glass of iced Mateus. When she righted herself, she caught Buddy's eye and mouthed, "I'm gonna use the john." Buddy shook his head but Enid was gone. Buddy said to his mother-in-law, "Enid's going up to get her now. Hold on. I'll be seeing you soon."

10

Enid screams, and the neighbor's stereo goes dead, and dogs up and down the street are crazy barking, and the front door flies open like the doors at the market, and Buddy is off. This is the night. Who would've suspected Enid capable of such a noise: turned the lights on in every house, sent that poor man running, like a starter's pistol was popping in his ears. He tore across the lawn, slipping free of his shoes, eyeglasses flying. He ran up the fender of a car, feet coming to rest on the cool hood. He staggered backward, losing balance, as if suddenly punched by the air. What did she say? He could stay "as long as you keep yourself zipped, Mr. Lam." Mr. Lam loosened his tie, opened his shirt, unbuckled his belt, and they all dropped away. Moon on shoulders, air between legs, he dove fences, trampled flower beds, ran over cars, disturbing dreams and the uneasy sleep of illicit lovers. Dogs tensed their chains. Cats looked on amazed.

Eyes in the windows, eyes in the streetlamps, eyes in the headlights, in the stars, in the satellites above. He had been so quiet until now, but that's over. Buddy, the mouse scratching at the floorboards, the stray rustle that shifts the rhythm of sleep, that quickens the breath, that stiffens spines in the dark; Buddy, the burglar in the basement, the murderer behind the door. So silent!

The night has been filled with so much noise. Her scream, the dogs, his friends, now sirens, now the many words shooting through his brain. The things he wants to say. He stops running, his legs leaving him and becoming one with the air. He leans against a lamppost, the cold metal dividing him in two. He starts to rehearse, but can't hear past the noise. The hum of tires, the swish of leaves, the stone beat of Cookie's heart. He'll hold on to his stories then. Things will have to quiet down. Then the words will come. There will be plenty of time later for their telling.

The Movers

A week earlier we had left our old jobs, friends, and habits, and had driven across the state so we could start over fresh. Now we were in the place we had just rented, waiting for the Salvation Army to deliver our furniture. I was sitting on the edge of the kitchen sink fidgeting with the twin spigots, both running cold, when Suzy came right out and said we were out of love. She had this way of talking when she was mad: her lips scarcely moved, and she would point her hip at you and pat it as if it were a dog about to pounce. "We've made a mistake," she said. "We don't love each other anymore."

What could I do in that situation? Tell her she's wrong? That she's loved? I told her her news was no news to me, that her very thoughts had been incubating in my head, but I managed to keep them to myself. I wanted to believe that as long as we kept our mouths shut and let the negative thoughts that popped into our brains die there, there was hope for us. I told her this. She slapped her hip black and blue. Then, in menacing detail, she catalogued all that was wrong with me. She surveyed our common history, touching on incidents I thought were at worst benign, some even happy, that she now cited as reasons for her discontent.

Minutes into her testimony—by then I had already heard enough—someone knocked at the front door, and I gladly left the kitchen, thinking it was the furniture, anxious to catch my breath. A small kid was standing there. "Collect," he said.

"What?"

"Collect."

"They moved," I said, finally catching on.

"Collect," repeated the boy. We went on this way for a few more rounds. The kid was a tangle of woollies. Snot was frozen on his face. "Can't you see," I said, "you've never seen me before?" I heard Suzy coming to the door. "Send it back. We won't be needing the furniture anymore," she was saying before she saw I was talking to a kid. "Collect," he said the moment he laid eyes on her. "You're making a mistake," I told him.

"Ha!" Suzy said, brushing the boy aside as if he were a swinging gate. "*You're* the mistake." She ran out to the car. When she slipped on a patch of ice and almost fell, my heart stopped. But she quickly regained her balance, and so did I, and while the kid held back the storm door, I peppered her with insults, mostly names of barnyard animals, each leaving my lips with the ease of habit. All my screaming did little to mitigate my rage, so I cocked my middle finger and waved goodbye as she drove off in our car.

The kid stuck his mittened hand in my gut. "Collect," he said one last time. I reached into my pocket and brought out a crumpled dollar bill. I promised him more if he'd go. Then I apologized for the scene he had witnessed. "She's not always so difficult," I said as he left me.

waited alone for the furniture. The manager at the store had promised delivery at three. By my watch it was already past four.

In the empty living room I sat on the floor near a window that faced the street. Cool air whistled through the cracked panes. Snow clouds darkened the sky. Beneath me the cold of the linoleum seeped through my pants; I felt as if I were sitting on a block of ice.

I got up and took down a set of bamboo blinds left by the previous tenants. As I unrolled the blinds, each slat clicked against the polished floor like beetles underfoot. I stretched out on this mat, hands dug deep in my pea jacket, and pretended I was dead, lying in a morgue in China. This succeeded where obscene gesture had failed. I felt transported, dead in a foreign land where the language of Suzy wasn't spoken. Who would understand our petty complaints there? Who could translate our squabbles and make them palatable to another tongue? No, I was a dead man, and all I had to do was shut my eyes and listen for the Salvation Army to come.

In time, I fell asleep and when I woke my legs were filled with sand. They were open in a V to the corner of the room reserved for Suzy's loom—there, she said, the northern exposure was perfect for selecting colors of thread. I scanned the adjacent wall where the fireplace stood. Above the mantelpiece there was a large opening of exposed lath, perhaps the work of a shotgun blast, over which Suzy's tapestry was to hang, hiding the blemishes of our domesticity.

Then I returned to the morgue. A heat vent nearby started to hiss, blowing damp, refrigerated air against my cheek. I needed to have the gas turned on, but I couldn't call because I didn't have a phone yet and I couldn't go because Suzy took the car. No phone, no heat, no car. No electricity at least for another day. I was out of love. And, even worse, I had no modern conveniences.

I had almost dozed off again when someone knocked at the front door. I got to my knees and peeked out the window but saw no truck on the street.

I heard the storm door pulled back, the lock turned in a single, sensuous click. Although a wall separated the vestibule from the living room, still I crawled quickly into Suzy's corner, where my hands came to rest on mounds of dirt that someone had swept up and left there.

"You're crazy, George," a girl whispered.

"Nobody's here," said her companion. "You heard me knock."

The door was shut and the lock secured.

She said, "I still think this is crazy."

My visitors ran upstairs, their footsteps echoing throughout the empty house. I remained frozen in place, afraid I might be discovered. Even though my pulse thumped loudly in my ears, I was still able to hear every word that passed between them.

"But where's the bed?" she asked.

"My parents just took everything out," said the boy. "Just be glad nobody's moved in yet."

She said, "We're trespassing, you know."

"Phyllis," he said, "I opened the door with my own key. How's that trespassing? Can't you be more spontaneous?"

I crept to the foot of the staircase.

"Here, smoke this gizmo," the boy said. "Who's going to hassle us? This is my house."

"But you don't live here anymore."

"Don't be so picky. Nobody lives here. This is open territory, like outer space. Now hold your breath."

The heavy scent of marijuana rolled down the stairs.

"Slow down, George. You're strangling me," she said. "Shut the door, at least."

I guessed by their voices they were in their teens. My watch said it was four-thirty, and according to the wall, where trees earlier had been shadowed, the sun had set. The furniture probably wasn't going to show.

Someone shut the door upstairs. I could no longer hear them. And so, I reasoned, they couldn't hear me. I climbed the stairs.

I peered through the old-fashioned keyhole in the door of the room Suzy and I had designated as our bedroom. Inside, the light was as gray as a low-contrast photo. Still I saw plenty through my sharpshooter's squint: with his jeans knotted at his knees, his jacket half off, his arms free of his sweater, which was still looped around his neck, the boy thrashed about between the girl's skinny, naked legs. Her arms were extended out to her sides, each hand clutching a piece of clothing. At once, my intruders looked like a spirited heap of laundry and an exotic form of torture. But when their taut young bodies touched who could mistake the sounds of the wondrous suction of love, like water slapping up the sides of a tub? My intruders improvised with a bamboo blind. I wondered, if she were here—I didn't think of Suzy by name; names are for parents to give and strangers to learn—would we also make a mattress of bamboo, or would we dutifully wait for our bed's arrival? And even then, would we spontaneously fall onto our new used mattress where countless others had slept and loved, or would we wait longer still for our sheets due COD from UPS?

"What's that noise?" The girl pushed up on her elbows.

I heard the noise too. Another set of knocks at the front door. Sharp and urgent, a bare fist, I thought. The boy sat back on his heels and threaded his arms through the sleeves of his sweater. He scanned the room and then finally said, "Relax. It's the dumb paperboy. He collects on Fridays." The boy pushed the girl down onto her back. Her white hands disappeared inside his sweater. She lifted her knees. He rooted for her lips. She shook her head.

My name is Grey," said the silhouette at the front door. His voice was full, confident, mature. He said, "I believe you know my daughter Phyllis. Our children are schoolmates."

With his back to the streetlight—or was it the moonlight?—my visitor didn't have a face. I couldn't see the scar that might've slashed his cheek in two or the desolate hole that once was home to a missing eye. All I was certain of was the silhouette's general shape—rounder and squatter than my own—and his voice, not just its sound, but the way it looked as it billowed in the chilled night air in fat, legible puffs like the speech of comic-strip characters.

"I didn't mean to barge in," he said, "but I tried calling, and the girl said your line had been temporarily disconnected." His presence sent the temperature of the house plunging. "Have you seen my daughter?" he asked.

I thought of my intruders up in the bedroom. Pictured the tiny figure of this man's daughter, her white knees, bare and strangely luminous, two moons in the gray light of the room, reaching for the ceiling—or, more ambitiously, straining for the heavens—as they cradled the boy.

"I can assure you," I began, "your daughter's safe with my boy." Those last two words, "my boy," thudded in my ears. I was astonished by my daring, and certain, despite my thirty years, that my voice lacked the easy authority of a parent. Without question, my "my boy" had just made its maiden voyage from my lips. So I took a precautionary step back into the dark house where age could best be discerned by a careful touch of my skin.

"Phyllis has to come home right away," the silhouette said. "My wife and I—it's our anniversary, and she has it in her head the kids should come to the restaurant with us." He sounded like a man who fretted over what his children dreamed at night. He said, "I asked her, 'Where were those kids when we got married?' But what's the use? When she gets something locked in her skull, you might as well be talking to a snail. You know how things go a little sour when kids come on the scene."

"Sure I do," I said. But what did I know? I took another step back from the door. I imagined having a man-to-man talk with the silhouette one night. And after a few beers he would say, "I'll get this eye fixed. Put in a fake one like that Sammy Davis, Jr. The ladies like that sort of thing. Makes a man mysterious, and gets the woman feeling sorry for you. I tell you, my wife can keep the kids. She can take them for burgers the rest of her days. You and me, we'll go out, we'll make a great team."

"That's right," I'd say. "Fathers have to stick together." And we'd shake hands like men.

He said, "Would you call Phyllis for me?"

"If she shows up," I said, "I'll send her straight home."

The silhouette's shoulders rose and fell. "She's not here? Look, I'm sorry I've troubled you. Please ask her to call home. But your phone, it's out of order."

I reassured him I'd send her right home.

"Thanks," he said, "thanks." The silhouette extended his hand toward the storm door, but when I didn't make a move to offer him mine he clumsily stuffed his back into his pocket. Then he switched subjects and advised me to work things out with the phone company. "Drive a person mad being cut off from the outside like that," he said.

"I'll have it fixed first thing in the morning."

"Good. Now how about your lights? No juice, is there?" He cleared his throat. "Through our children, you can say we're friends. Phyllis has told me about your money troubles. Let me know how I can help."

"That's kind of you," I said, "but I'm okay. I'm just trying to conserve energy." I started to laugh but he didn't follow my lead. "Forget about me and Phyllis. Go have a nice dinner, and wish Mrs. Grey a happy anniversary for me."

I watched the silhouette step into the night. I was almost rid of him when his body was suddenly cut in half by a set of oncoming headlights.

It was the Salvation Army truck. The driver honked at the silhouette, who stopped to talk to a man hanging out the open passenger window of the truck's cab. The silhouette then turned and came halfway up the front walk toward the house. He stopped and called, "Are you expecting some used furniture?"

"Me?" I said indignantly. "What does a man like me need from the Salvation Army?"

"That's what I thought," said the silhouette. "But something's odd. They have the correct address on their invoice but the name's all wrong. I'll just send them on their way."

"Wait. Let me." I almost stepped out of the house, but thought better of it. "You've done enough already. Mrs. Grey's probably wondering where you are."

He stood there as still as a tree stump and stared in my direction.

"Mrs. Grey," I said, and finally he left, shrugging his shoulders at the truck as he passed.

You got a Suzy Tree here?" the guy in the passenger window asked. Half a fat, unlighted cigar tugged at the corner of his mouth. He had on an old felt baseball cap, its bill tipped so low on his brow that his face seemed to start at his nose.

"That's us," I said.

The cap leaped from the cab. "Who's your boyfriend?" he asked as he pumped past me on his stumpy legs. "He almost chased us away."

"I should've let him," I said, watching the cap unlock and then disappear into the truck's dark trailer. "You're over two hours late."

"The snow," the cap said. "It's the damn snow."

"What snow? It's not snowing."

"Of course no snow," he said. "I'm talking about the idea of snow. People do things different when they're living with the idea of snow."

I didn't try to answer him. All I knew was if Suzy were here, this guy would be apologizing for their tardiness; he'd be almost too polite. I said, "Let's say I don't want this stuff anymore."

"Can't do," said a deep voice behind me. I turned and saw the driver, a man a head taller than the cap. He was wearing gloves with the tips cut away, exposing sausage-thick fingers that scissored what must've been the other half of his partner's cigar. "We only unload," he said. "If you don't want the merchandise, call the office and they'll send the pickup crew over."

I didn't care for these two men, but they certainly could work. At first, I thought it was an illusion of their cigars and stubble and utilitarian jumpsuits that gave me this impression. But in no time they had the vestibule filled with a gigantic tangle of wood, steel, Formica, and foam.

"It's a wrap," the driver announced as he carried in an armchair and lowered it on top of the heap.

"What do you mean?" I said. "Where's the bed?"

"What does that mean, where's the bed?"

Now that we were in the house, I could no longer see their faces. My guests had turned into shadows in the vestibule where there were no clean edges, no distinct boundaries.

"You say you got a bed coming?"

"No, I just said that so you'd stay a little longer."

"Hey, he's a pretty funny fellow," said the cap. "I better get me a chair so I don't fall over from laughing."

"Drop it," the driver said. "Let's get moving before I starve to death. You see anything left in the truck?"

"Nothing I'd put my back on," said the cap.

His partner chuckled.

"There was something rolled up and standing in a corner."

"Sounds like one of our mattresses all right." The driver clapped his big hands. "Let's get it and get going." They moved for the door.

"Hold it," I said. "I'll carry it in." This was one of Suzy's ideas. She wanted us to bring the bed into our new home, a variant of the bride-over-the-threshold ritual. I had opposed such a scheme from the start. And this she interpreted as proof that I didn't want to live with her. So she pointed her hip at me. Then the paperboy came.

"Can't do. Totally against regulations," the driver said.

"This is no time for amateurs," said the cap.

I clenched my fists. I could feel the muscles in my neck coiling into snakes. A sudden rush of heat thawed the tip of my nose. My breath turned quick and shallow.

But who was I mad at—the movers? Suzy?

I said in the voice of reasonable men, "Let me do the mattress. I'll make it worth your while."

The mattress was damp and musty. In all likelihood it had labored in a dank basement for years under piles of *National Geographics* and cracked clay flowerpots. I dragged it out into the night air. It seemed to sigh as it folded in half across my shoulder.

By the time I reached the house, I was in a sweat from the struggle the mattress had put up. I propped it against the wall but it slowly slithered to the floor as if it were filled with heavy syrup. "This isn't the one we bought," I said.

"We only unload," the driver said. "You don't want, call the office."

"Look, feel this. This is Jell-O. Would you want to sleep on this?"

"Sorry, bub," said the driver, chomping moistly on his cigar, "you're not my type."

The cap danced in carrying the box springs. He was whistling an inane tune. "You have to admire the work of a professional," he said as he let the load slide off his back. "Hey, what's the matter here?"

"He doesn't want the mattress."

"What's the matter? It's too firm for you?"

They chuckled.

"Forget it," I said. "Just leave me alone."

"Love to. But first we need Miss Tree to sign this invoice." The driver's heavy fingers tapped a clipboard he had magically produced out of the night air.

"I'll sign," I said, reaching for his pen.

"Can't do. We need the lady's signature. Company policy, see: 'Accept only the signature of the party named on the invoice.' "

The cap struck a match against a table leg and held the flame over the clipboard so I could see their silly rule. On the same match they lighted the cigars. With each puff I saw their faces, like gruesome orange masks. I could tell the driver from the cap by the relative height of the burning nib at the tip of his cigar.

"If I sign, you can go."

"I see we're dealing with a devious individual," the taller nib said. "You want us to break Army policy. Joey, should we give him an opportunity to deceive us?"

The shorter nib bobbed up and down.

"Okay then, what's your relationship to Miss Tree? You Mr. Tree?"

I told them no.

"Her brother?"

"No."

"I know you're not her father."

"How can you be so sure I'm not?"

"You don't sound like anyone's father," said the shorter nib, and instantly I touched my throat and thought back to the silhouette.

"Face it," the taller nib said, "no self-respecting father would let his kid near this kind of crap."

"For your information," I said, "I have a sixteen-year-old son."

"Sure you do. And my father's Smokey the Bear."

"That's not so hard to believe."

The shorter nib came at me, puffing wildly, but then suddenly stopped.

"Leave him," said his partner. "Tell me," he continued, "are you Miss Tree's sweetheart?"

I had to chew that one over. "You could've asked her yourself if you showed up when you were supposed to."

"S-s-shit," the taller nib hissed. "We're wasting our time. Let's move this stuff out of here."

"I thought you only unloaded," I said.

"We load, bub, when it's our mistake."

"So you admit you're wrong."

"Sure we're wrong. We'll take the rap for everything wrong in this town, in this state, on this planet. So what?"

The orange nibs floated through the vestibule burning smoky orange loops onto the black canvas while the hands and boots of the movers untangled the furniture pile.

"I paid for this junk," I said. "It's legally mine."

"Not till Miss Tree signs."

"Gentlemen," I said, wondering where that word had come from, "if you don't stop I'll be forced to call the police."

The shorter nib said, "Hey, you suppose we get overtime for this?"

I backed away to make good on my threat. I heard the tear and creak of furniture in distress. I heard the movers' steamy breaths, the *clomp clomp clomp* of their boots. Then I turned my back to the vestibule, and immediately, involuntarily, I threw my arms out in front of me. I saw nothing. My eyes were useless. In the dark the hands are what count. My fingers combed the air for the phone's smooth shell, solid and sleek, but I soon realized my movements lacked purpose. I was, of course, phoneless. But I continued on, simultaneously hoping for and dreading collisions.

There are no directions in the dark. All one has is memory and I had no memories of that house. I took recklessly long strides away from the vestibule, as if I were trying to outstep the darkness, as one steps over puddles. I waved my arms like a drowning man, groping for anything solid. I heard the nibs curse and grunt. They could've been singing "Whistle While You Work" and I wouldn't have been surprised. But what spooked me was the peculiar way their voices seemed to come at me from every angle, even though I hadn't veered from my original course.

A brief eternity later, finally, a collision. Two walls, one on either side of me—a narrow hallway. Here I moved with confidence. Each hand pressed flush against the walls, my fingertips tracing the cracks they found there as a palm reader follows a lifeline to its end. I stepped easily now, content inside that enclosed space, when without warning the walls gave way to air, and my arms spread open like the bellows of an accordion. My hands once again swatted at nothing. My legs turned wooden, my body froze, but my mind traveled on, back to Suzy and dark rooms where we once lay, where I extended my arms and at the ends of my fingertips I'd find her. It took a few moments, but soon I realized my flailing hands were moving in a distinct pattern. She was within reach. My hands had molded her from air.

Then I heard fresh footsteps. Not the dull thuds of the movers' boots, not my own because I still hadn't budged, but bright steps—a child's, perhaps, tentative in their approach.

"I'll sign," said a female voice.

I turned in time to see a match struck. Through the sulfurous smoke I saw illuminated by the fragile flame a most implausible trio—the bovine faces of the movers sandwiching Suzy's likeness.

"Where you been hiding?" asked the cap.

She answered by blowing out the flame. "Where do I sign?"

"Smart. She blows out the light and then wants to know where to sign. Sign in the dark, lady." The cap struck another match. The trio reappeared. The lambent flame washed over her close-set eyes, her fringed forehead, her brown lips, giving substance to the voice that said, "Where?"

"Right there, Miss Tree," the driver said. She signed and then blew out the flame.

The nibs bobbed toward the door. "Enjoy the bed," the shorter nib said, and they were gone.

"Thank you," I said to the darkened room. "You've been a great help." I moved in the direction where I believed I saw her last.

Those tentative footsteps suddenly took life. Quick, whispery steps, louder and then fading, the way an echo loses energy. They were somewhere behind me, and when I turned, they were behind me again. I spun around once more and saw the door opening.

"Go home," I said. "Your father wants you."

She was momentarily silhouetted in the doorway. She briefly looked in my general direction.

"Tell him I sent you home," I said as she left me, with a slam of the door.

I realized my hands were clutching the front of my shirt. Beneath it my ribs felt loose; my heart needed massage; in my stomach a little man was trying to punch his way out.

Before I knew which foot to move first, I heard a voice from above: "Hey, mister, I want you to have this key."

"Who's that?"

"You don't need my name. I used to live here."

"It's you," I said. "You're the one." I could tell he was on the stairs. "Please, strike a match." All I wanted was to see his face, to see myself there as I had seen Suzy in the girl's face.

"I don't have a match," he said. "I don't smoke. But, mister, here's the key."

I heard the metal clatter on the floor. Did he expect me to catch it? "Why didn't you leave with the girl?" I said.

"We meant no harm," he said. "Just taking a look around the old place." The stairs creaked under his weight as he started his descent. "You get the key?"

"Why did she leave you?"

"I'm coming down now," he said. "I don't want any trouble."

"You should go after her. Tell her you're sorry you did what you did. Tell her you love her, if that's what it takes."

"She's at dinner with her folks. You met her dad."

"He's not a very happy man," I said. "You give him so much to worry about."

"*Me*? You lied to him. Man, that was great. I swear, you really messed with his head." The boy stepped onto the floor.

"That was my mistake. I shouldn't have done such a thing. And don't get carried away. I didn't do it to impress you."

"Okay, mister, don't get hot." He pushed aside some furniture, clearing a path to the door. "Stay back now," he warned. "I'm leaving now."

"Wait. Give me a hand upstairs with the bed." I felt his body close to mine. I could reach out and turn his hand away from the door. But how long could I keep him? What did I have to say to a boy his age? I'd tell him about Suzy, then what? We could count snowflakes, if it snowed, and in the first light of the new day, I might see all we had in common. Surely there would be something—the slant of our eyes, the breadth of our noses, the cut of our hair, and, should Suzy appear, our mutual love for the same woman.

"Pick up the key," I said. "I want you to have it. Come back with the girl anytime."

"I'm gone, mister."

"No, not yet."

"I'm late." He turned the doorknob. I cupped my hand over his. How warm it felt.

"Where are you going? Maybe I'll come along."

He opened the door. An icy wind struck our faces. "I have to go eat dinner. That's all." He stepped outside. I didn't try to stop him. I asked if he had gloves, a hat, a scarf. I told him zip up tight. "Don't run if it starts to snow," I said.

"I'm okay, mister." With his back to me he looked up at the low sky. He took a step and made a half-turn toward the house. "Thanks for the visit," he said. "I think you'll like it here."

One Man's Hysteria
—Real and Imagined—
in the Twentieth
Century

When the first bombs fall, I will be ready. Not with fishing nets or Geiger counters or fallout shelters, but with poetry—memorized, metabolized, and ready to recite. Only poetry can save us now. Civil Defense will blow its sirens and jam the airwaves with survival tips, but after the bombs fall these will be nothing but desultory noise in a world of sound and light.

They call them missiles now. Not simply missiles, but missiles with multiple nuclear warheads with enigmatic names: MX, MIRV, ICBM. But I prefer to call them bombs. "Bombs" sounds homier, cozier. The world frightens me, but I haven't lost my good senses. I don't suspect the Communists of suicidal leanings. In theory the Soviet Union is a fine idea; I believe the Chinese are among the most humane people on earth. But the experts at the Pentagon don't agree. They are suspicious and eager to defend. This I find more troublesome than a source of comfort. I'm not paranoid but neither is my skin lined with lead. So, owing to the recent preponderance of doomsday forecasts, I've taken up the reading of poetry. One can never be too cautious in these subatomic times.

t was Sunday morning and, as had been my habit each weekend for the past few months, I read poems to Laura from the anthology I kept in a strongbox beneath our bed. "Shut up, sweet," Laura mumbled to the wall, "let me sleep a while longer." Since we were back-to-back and I couldn't see her speak, I pretended I couldn't hear her either. Propped on my elbow, I leafed through the tome. I said, "Sleep at that reading, later. I always do." I glanced at the head of each ragged column, page after page, waiting for a familiar title or name to catch my eye. "Okay," I said, "who wrote this?" It was still early, so I started her with something easy:

> *"Awake sad heart, whom sorrow ever drowns;*
> *Take up thine eyes, which feed on earth . . ."*

But Laura feigned sleep throughout my reading of Herbert, filling the silence I had come to expect her snap response in with thick, labored breaths, until the baby cried, and then she grudgingly slowly opened her eyes.

Of course, she is not our child. With the world the way it is, babies, in good conscience, aren't a reasonable option for the thinking couple. We live on Dill Street above the Wicks, an unexceptional family of three, soon to be four. In these dangerous times, they have managed to achieve an alarming degree of complacency. They are indifferent to current events; when they hear "Star Wars," they think only of the movie. Some might say they are fearless and full of hope but I say they're fools.

" 'Wick,' " my wife says, peering over my shoulder. "You can't use their real names in a story." She pauses a moment, hands on hips. "Stephen, listen to me, it's not ethical."

Leave me alone, I think, writing's hard enough without you standing over me. Actually, I would've preferred saying these things out loud, but my wife wouldn't take kindly to them. Besides, I'm too busy to listen to her accuse me of being testy, melodramatic, and paranoid. Then I'll feel obliged to answer her back, and I'm not up to the task. Still, it's tempting. Who can resist getting in the last word, even if it does mean a fight? But then, as if to save me from my moral weakness, the omnipresent screams of baby Melissa rush up the heat register and into my study.

"But, you know," my wife says, rolling her eyes in the direction of the baby noise, "Wick is perfect. Baby wickedness terrorizes the neighbors again!" She says this as if she were reading a headline off the front page of the paper.

Downstairs, in reality, they possess modest hopes, hopes so bland they would humble a saint. The Wicks don't realize that the mechanical tapping this typewriter rains down on their heads is their only true hope. Though my typing might seem no more significant than Melissa's screams, or the Air Force jets that boom overhead, or the tornado siren that sounds the first of every month, I am, in fact, imbuing their lives with substance, giving them the permanence of print, offering salvation from their naïve optimism of a future time.

Upstairs we are a ménage of writers. My wife—actually she isn't my wife, but for my purposes here I'll dispense with the truth and designate Laura as wife. What more convenient and evocative way is there to refer to the person one lives with? My cohabitant? My lover? My apartment mate? Too ugly, too changeable, too vague. I'll happily sacrifice accuracy for expediency. My wife writes stories and poems, while I, far less versatile but nonetheless supportive of her dual talents, dabble exclusively in prose— short stories, mostly—but I do aspire toward a novel, a great Faulknerian saga that will blanch the critics' ink. But I wonder, given the pace I work, will there be time enough for its writing? Will there be trees for its printing? If I finish, who will have eyes to read?

Together our aspirations tend toward the mundane. Our public goal, what we say in passing to friends, is to own a food processor with a French sobriquet. Privately, I'm relieved we lack the financial means to justify such a purchase. As a man of the twentieth century warily eyeing the twenty-first, I'm well aware of the social implications of achieving such a goal. In the etiquette of the nuclear age I know the presence of such a contraption in our household (the modern-day equivalent of the exchange of wedding bands) would consummate our recent domesticity. The first tomatoes it purées will be remembered like our first kiss; as it kneads the tan dough of a Swedish rye, we'll be tempted to equate this with an aspect of our initial love-making. And naturally, in keeping with the ways of modern couples, a microwave oven can't be far behind.

During the past election, my wife and I voted for a full slate of eventual losers. Although this has been a source of considerable self-righteous chest-beating among our friends, we've approached these defeats with an air of composure, a spirit of conciliation, and limited displays of public indignation. It's never been our belief that either major political party can save us.

"Who wrote this?" I asked, reading from the anthology.

"The population of the world consists of three principal types of people—the creators, the consumers (those who make the creators necessary), and the retainers (those who digest and hold on to what they consume)—here, specifically, I refer to those people with the talent to memorize and recite poetry. Of this trio the retainers are best suited for the post-apocalyptic world. Who else among the survivors—those who manage to be liquid in fire, steel to flying glass, granite against shock, alchemists all; those who miss the express (vaporization) but catch the local (irradiation)—who will have coherent speech except the retainers? Who else will possess things to say? Bombs will scramble thought. And while non-retainers might speak, they will do so in Melissa-like utterances. In such a world the retainers will emerge and recite in sibylic rote—deaf to the ironically playful rhymes and joyous metrical schemes—the poems they had committed to memory, the world's last true words. These are the only viable progeny our civilization can leave to this genetically poor future landscape. These are our bravest children, our strongest.

"Laura, are you listening?" I said, nudging her gently. I chose a poem I thought would tease her from her alleged sleep:

> *"I saw Eternity the other night*
> *Like a great ring of pure and endless light."*

"Vaughan," she said. "Henry. Underrated. Seventeenth century. Now, please, let me sleep some more."

"First give me the next line."

"Stephen, it's too early for this asinine game."

Laura fails to understand. She takes me for a morbid fool. She must remember that I tease her memory not to test her knowledge—she has her degrees—but out of a sense of duty. I see the danger and have taken appropriate action. In this case poetry is the only practical approach to life.

" 'I caught this morning morning's minion,' " I read, trying to create some momentum for my endeavor.

"Hopkins, Hopkins, Hopkins!" she exclaimed and slapped her fleshy palm with its long sinuous lifeline to her forehead. Ah, there she goes! She possesses a good heart really, and I love her, even though she deliberately fails to look beyond the apparent. How many times have I told her that when the atom was split, "atom" became, semantically speaking, a centuries-old lie. So I kept reading, hoping that one day she'll see through to my motives and readily join forces with me.

I continued with Hopkins, one of Laura's favorites. At first she was snoring, taking the long, even breaths of sleep; but halfway through the poem her legs rustled the sheets, producing the sound of large fish thrashing in shallow water. She was warming to the task, and soon, draping her long legs over my waist, she picked up where I had left off and recited:

"Brute beauty and valour and act, oh, air, pride, plume, here
    Buckle! ['Yes, yes, yes!' I said. 'Go on, go on!']
      And the fire that breaks from thee, then ['Say it!']
      a billion
  Times told lovelier ['How lovely!'], *more dangerous . . ."*

"Oh, Laura!"
" 'O my chevalier!' "
She nestled her nose between my shoulder blades. Her secret signal. She wanted more. I happily acquiesced and quickened the pace.
" 'I must complain, yet do enjoy my love,' " I read.
"Campion."
"How's that?"
"You heard right. Thomas Campion—no *h*."
She was, as usual, right again. She was in top form. I quickly found another poem, assuming the role of quizmaster with great relish, confident my work with this contestant would in the end benefit mankind.

" 'These lines that now thou scorn'st, which should delight thee . . .' "

"Stop!" said Laura, massaging her eyelids, lost in
thought, leafing through the tomes in her head. "You
bastard," she said, "that's not the beginning."

"Did I say it was?" Much to my own distress, I feared
I had finally stumped her.

"Quiet," she said. Her face twisted as if she were in
pain. "He's a—sonneteer. Drayton. Major poet among the
minor poets. First name—Michael." Then she recited the
poem while I followed along in the book. She was flawless,
iamb perfect, pausing only at grammatical breaks.

"There's no threat," my wife says as she returns several
pages of my story back to the tray beside my typewriter.
"You're letting all that rhetoric coming out of Washington
get to you. I can assure you, Stephen, no one in North
America, Europe, or Russia is going to die from a nuclear
device."

"Quit dreaming. You're too idealistic."

"Just remember Hiroshima."

"Yes, Hiroshima. Uranium-235 bomb, the equivalent
of twelve-point-five kilotons of TNT, killed over seventy
thousand civilians."

"Don't forget Nagasaki."

"What are you trying to say?" I pick up the anthology
on my desk and open to a poem I had planned to use later
in the story. "Listen to this," I say. "Shelley had it right
back in the eighteenth century."

"Nineteenth."

"Okay, nineteenth. You think you're so smart. Listen
to Shelley:

> *"The awful shadow of some unseen Power*
> *Floats though unseen among us . . ."*

I slam shut the book. "You see, it's all there in verse. It's been anticipated for ages. We live in an ugly world. We have to face up to it."

"Stephen, I agree," my wife says, "even if you have taken Shelley out of context. But my instincts tell me nothing's going to happen too close to where you're sitting now. Radioactivity might be color-blind, but those who control the bombs aren't." My wife is pacing back and forth behind my chair. She says, "I find it more than a little curious that they never dropped any atomic bombs on Germany, after all the trouble it caused, and then went ahead and unloaded on Japan." She claps her hands together, twice, directly over my head. "*Boom!*" she says. "Not once. They went back three days later for an encore. Those yellow-skinned barbarians are slow learners, I guess. If any place is destined for the Stone Age, it's China, Vietnam, or a crazy country like Libya. We're safe in Ossining. I mean, Cheever lived here, and *Reader's Digest* is close by."

"What about the South Bronx or Chinatown? Or Detroit?"

"I'm sure Washington lets Moscow take aim at any area where the natives don't, as a rule, wear Lacoste shirts and Topsiders, as special non-military targets. Missiles are capable of pinpoint accuracy, you know. They can hit Harlem and leave Bloomingdale's open for business."

"Well, even with Cheever's ghost and Bloomingdale's on our side, once the ozone layer is wrecked, we'll all go blind or else shrivel up from deep tanning."

"Oh, Stephen, you have such a downside."

In the middle of a protracted silence, like the eerie calm that follows the fireball's flash and precedes the deafening explosion, my wife wraps her arms around my neck and leans her soft bosom flush against my back, a sudden,

welcomed peace initiative. "Hi-ro-shi-ma," she whispers
as Emmanuelle Riva, the actress who played the forlorn
actress in Resnais's film, had done. "Hi-ro-shi-ma," she
whispers again, reaching her hand down the opening in
my shirt.

"Na-ga-sa-ki?" I ask as our cheeks touch. I take her hand
and position it at the top of my pants. "Na-ga-sa-ki?"

Although I lack the mental apparatus of a retainer,
I have tried to memorize what I can. One never
knows when one might be called upon to speak.
" 'No more, my dear, no more these counsels try,' "
Laura recited. She was on a roll, she was on fire. Her
tongue and memory clicked like a teletype machine. Un-
prompted, she was belting out some of her favorites. " 'O
give my passions leave to run their race.' "

"Sidney—right?" I said.

Laura suddenly stopped. She hated when I interrupted.
She hated when, in my small way, I paraded the bits of
poetic knowledge I had gathered from our years together.
Memorization of verse was her domain, her special talent.
I pleaded with her to finish, but she turned to the wall and
was silent.

We had met along a river under an ancient tree surrounded by ducks. We were both new in town. I had come
in from the east and she from the west. I was navigating
my bicycle with its twin flat tires to the garage when I
passed Laura and recognized the book, with its enormous
girth and gold printing across its spine, splayed open, face-
down, on her lap. With her eyes shut, she moved her lips
as if she were saying the rosary or kissing an imaginary
lover. As I approached, I heard Keats whispered from those
lips. I snuck up behind her and chipped in the last line as

a way of introduction. But she turned on me, a total stranger, and scowled, just as she was doing now. The ducks scattered as Laura, refusing to speak, climbed the riverbank with the tome pressed to her breast.

I leafed through the anthology for someone else's words to shake Laura from her dark mood. Too many critical minutes slipped past before I found the perfect lines. " 'The grave's a fine and private place, but none, I think, do there embrace.' "

"How trite," she said.

"What? This is a classic."

"You don't have to tell me. 'I think the dead are tender,' " she said, quickly and without enthusiasm. " 'Shall we kiss?' "

"Yes, let's," I said. I moved closer to her but she pulled away.

"That was Roethke's invitation, not mine. I said it only to preserve the integrity of the line. If you want to kiss, kiss him, kiss Roethke." Laura turned again, preferring the wall to me.

If I didn't act fast, I would lose her to the bathroom and her morning routine. That would put an end to the game, even though she needed the training. For such emergency situations I have learned to hold in reserve a secret weapon—J. Alfred Prufrock. Laura was a sucker for Eliot. Quickly I located the poem and began to read. At first she played dead, aware of the blatant manipulation, but I was confident I would weaken her resistance. When we first made love, a Book-of-the-Month Club record of Eliot reading played in the room. It was a multi-orgasmic night for her. She said she had never had such satisfaction before she had me. Or, as it turned out, heard the record. Soon Laura was reciting purlingly as I read aloud. Her words, Eliot's words, fell hot and sticky against the nape of my neck.

"Stephen," my wife says, "this is a lie, a myth, pure silliness. I don't even like Eliot." Now she is poking a rigid finger into my back. "And I won't have you soiling my good name in this smut; multiple orgasms—what a dream!"

"What's the matter with you?" I say. "And what's so suddenly wrong with multiple orgasms?"

"Nothing. I know nothing about them from firsthand experience. I haven't been privileged to such delirium. But my memory is good. I remember our first time. Your pal down there between your legs took the night off."

"Ah, the wonderful, lurking past, forever poised to rush up from behind with ice pick in hand," I say.

"And it wasn't Eliot on the turntable, it was Dylan."

"Dylan Thomas."

"Bob Dylan."

"Stop. You're ruining the poetry motif I've built into this story. Now look, if you insist my Eliot's a fake, then you'll have to agree this is just good, honest fiction. So don't be so touchy."

"Call it what you like," she says, "but don't call me your wife when I'm not, get rid of your damn orgasms, and for God's sake disguise those poor, innocent Wicks. I mean it, or else Laura comes out of the story."

Now why is she so upset? Laura isn't even her name.

Laura and I kissed. I thought I felt Eliot percolating beneath her scalp. I rolled her over on top. Her body was pliant but her kisses were cold. I was perspiring, ripe for the smooth friction of love. But despite my finest efforts, she would not make a commitment to me. She was distracted, busy with some other pursuit.

I asked what was the matter, and when she muttered that mermaids were singing, I no longer minded her indifference. It was Eliot and poetry that denied me satisfaction. And for them, for the great cause, I would gladly sacrifice countless days of pleasure.

"Tell me about the mermaids," I said.

" 'I have heard the mermaids singing, each to each,' " she said. " 'I do not think that they will sing to me.' "

And soon, after a dozen lines or so, she was mine, seduced by the poetry in her head. We kissed, or I kissed her, as Laura's lips shaped around Eliot's words. I shut my eyes and imagined the ocean at night or a bay beneath a giant bridge. We kissed and I squeezed my eyelids tighter, sealing in the dark of the ocean floor. We kissed, our tongues struggling like mating eels, while fish of many colors swam in my head. Often, I made love to Laura this way.

But do I dare make love? Despite my obvious sophistication, my liberal thinking, and a solid foundation in ancient and contemporary love techniques, I want sex only during periods of heightened world tension. I have no more control over my urges than an animal has over its estrus cycle. Ever since I saw an Air Force film of a nuclear warhead being loaded into a missile silo, military hardware and human sexual apparatus have merged in my libido, and lovemaking as a result has seemed dangerous and vain. Mushroom clouds burgeon in my skull whenever the caressing begins. How can a man be sufficiently aroused under a blanket of Mutually Assured Destruction? In today's political atmosphere, intercourse yields no real hope, and as for pleasure—well, the pleasure is undeniable but slightly perverse. But when a new trouble spot flares up in the world I'm more than eager for loving. I was ripe during the incursions into Angola and Afghanistan; I wearied my wife during the Salvadoran revolution; I could've serviced all the concubines in ancient China (and Mao's five wives too) during the four hundred and forty-four days of the hostage crisis. When Washington threatens Managua or Moscow shoots down an airliner or truck bombs go off in Beirut, I'm lustful, eager. I attain critical mass.

My condition might seem strange but it's nothing more or less than instinct at work. While the world teeters ever closer to Armageddon, my most urgent need is to propagate my species. I want a child to bear my name into the future, its bleakness notwithstanding. But I know a child will be ineffectual against the fallout, the light, the infection. How could such a child grow? What sad gnarled shapes and combinations will its genes assume? There is but one sane alternative. Now, when we love, I try to propose that my wife write and commit to memory an antebellum elegy, a poem in which my name appears at least once in the text, not necessarily spelled out but hidden perhaps in the manner Shakespeare is buried, as it is rumored, in the Forty-sixth Psalm.

"Stephen," says my wife, "get me out of this story." She drops the manuscript pages she has just read onto my desk. "You have me in bed on the brink of some lascivious feat, and here you make this absurd confession of your own perverted sexuality. My God, Stephen, if you're not embarrassed by all this, think of me. I have to live with you even if it isn't true. You know, someone might actually publish this."

"But it's all true," I say, looking at the typewriter. "It's the sorry truth."

"What is?"

"The risk of bringing a child into this world."

"Stephen, you're just afraid."

"Of course. We live in a dangerous world."

"No, I mean you're afraid of children."

"Me? Uh-uh. I'm afraid *for* them." I turn around in my seat and take my wife by her broad baby-bearing hips. "Why don't you write me that poem?"

"What's wrong with you? We're safe here." She has more to say but stops and exhales a long breath, as if her lungs had contained all the frustrations of the world. "I want out of this story," she says. "Go back and cross me out. People will think it's autobiography."

"I'm not an autobiographical writer."

"There's no talking to you. Please, leave me off those pages." She exits and crosses the hall to her study and slams the door behind her.

I have great faith in my wife. Her recalcitrance and contentiousness will enable her to persevere through the coming madness and eternity of radioactivity. If she were a mother, she would hide the face of our child in her lap until the firestorms abated. If she were a doctor, she would tear her skirt into strips and dip them in the last cool waters and soothe my wounded eyes. But she is a poet, and I want to ask her—when the screaming subsides (or when we hear no more), when those of us huddled together in disbelief can no longer sleep, cry, or speak—to recite the poem, my poem, all poems. For as light will darken our eyes, so our thoughts will turn to shadow.

My wife's temper reminds me of steel—in my hands, both are unbendable. I knock on her door, armed with a surprise, but she continues to type away at her little portable, which makes a sound like cats lapping milk from an aluminum pan.

I let myself in. She is staring straight down at the sheet of paper curled in the roller. I rest my hands on her shoulders. This is accomplished without incident. She turns the platen backward until what she has typed disappears into the machine.

"Why so tense?"

"You know I hate when you read over my shoulder."

"Honey," I say, stroking her fine hair, "I've made you a mother." I guess I must have accidentally given her hair a tug at that moment because she lurched forward and groaned.

"I made you a mother," I repeat, saying it as if for the first time.

"I don't want to be your wife if we're not married, and I don't want to be a mother, real or imagined, under those conditions either."

"I thought you'd be pleased with this development."

"Leave me alone, Stephen. I want to finish typing this poem before we go."

"Go where?"

"To see Carla read."

"We saw her yesterday. What, is she doing the whole thing herself?"

Carla is Nancy's friend, who is participating in a marathon presentation of *Finnegans Wake* at the bookstore downtown.

She read the opening yesterday, and she is scheduled to read the last few pages today.

"How very circular," I say.

There is no point to our discussion. Our attendance at the reading is inevitable. So I return to the subject of our child. "His name is Todd," I tell her.

"Who?"

"Your son."

My wife, with her love for the dramatic, snatches the paper from the typewriter and knocks over her chair as she stands and marches into the bathroom.

"Don't you like the name Todd?" I say, following at her heels. "The two *d*'s, I think, give him character."

"Retodd," she says as she draws her eyes with pencil. "That's what you are, retodded."

"Don't be so cruel to your own son."

"He's yours. He's your baby."

"I thought you wanted a kid."

"Christ, Stephen." She pulls her lips tight and applies a colorless gloss.

Two months ago we had visited a pet shop. Since our lease stipulates that we may not keep a dog or cat in our apartment, we went out in search of a cold-blooded companion.

"Sperm," my wife said, pointing to the tiny fry darting among the translucent plants in an aquarium. We watched as a male tried to couple with an already pregnant female swollen to nearly twice his size.

"Want some?" she asked.

"What? Sperm or guppies?"

"Babies."

"Let's see how we do with fish first."

We linked arms, found the proprietor, and chose a pair of guppies. On the drive home one of us had inadvertently set the plastic bag of fish on the narrow shelf space between the windshield and the dash. The defroster was blowing the entire trip home. When we arrived, the fish were floating belly-up in tepid water.

N*ote: Revise from beginning. The two characters in bed do not make love, not even off the page. They kiss, Nancy stretched out beneath the narrator. He believes she is singing Dylan instead of reciting Eliot as he tries to interest her in sex. Ultimately they have no time for love. Now they have a child to tend.*

We walked the eight blocks or so to the bookstore. It was just minutes after noon. Todd held our hands, doubling his steps to keep pace with us. We were on our way to see Nancy's girlfriend Carla, an English teacher at the high school, read the opening pages of *Finnegans Wake*.

"I'm glad Carla got involved in this reading," Nancy said.

"It's better than some of those jerks she gets involved with," I said as we passed a lawn sale.

Todd tugged at Nancy's arm. "Carla's the crying lady," he said.

At a second lawn sale, we stopped to browse. Books and records and kitchen appliances weighed down several tables. Boxes with men's shirts and shoes and ties littered the yard. A food processor, almost new, with a French sobriquet, gleamed in the sun.

I asked the woman in charge what she wanted for the machine. The price she quoted Nancy was quite reasonable, but I could hardly say the same for her manner. Not only did she refuse to speak directly to me, she wouldn't even look at me. She was young, plain-looking, and naked beneath her gingham shirt. This last detail was not so extraordinary and neither were my powers of observation. I offer it for the sake of accuracy in reporting.

The food processor was a wedding gift, she told Nancy. "Why else would I own one?" she said, tugging at the red bandanna wrapped around her frizzy blond hair. "I only used it when his parents came to visit. Everything had to be a purée. Meat had to look gray before his father could eat it. What a horror. But I don't have to do that anymore. We're separated. I don't have any use for it." Her voice became progressively dimmer, hoarser, as if with each phrase she spoke she were swallowing a handful of sand.

"I'll take Todd for a walk," I said, feeling that I was the cause of her discomfort.

We found a cooler around the side of the house. After considerable rumination Todd selected a grape soda and I handed him a quarter to drop into the jar.

"I've asked you not to feed him junk," Nancy called from where she stood with the woman.

"We're fueling up for *Finnegans Wake*."

Passing the bottle between us, Todd and I browsed through the books.

"That lady is a Carla too," he said.

I looked over and the woman was crying. Nancy loosened the red bandanna and held it to the woman's nose. The woman, her eyes focused on the ground, was talking and shaking her head, and Nancy kept nodding hers sympathetically.

"So many books," Todd said as he ran his little fingers across the row of spent spines.

"I'd say there are over a hundred million words on this table," I said. I picked up a book titled *Ahead of Their Time: Selections from Berryman to Sexton*. "What would you do with a hundred million words?"

"I'd throw a hundred million *thousand* words," said Todd. "I'd throw, throw, throw, throw, throw!" He acted this out, drawing his tiny arm behind his head, then thrusting his fist forward. It was a strange and unsettling outburst, as if he had stepped away from the reach of his brain, the way we are in a moment of fear.

"Stop it," I said. "No. That's enough." I reached out to arrest his little fists, and our hands collided, his stubby fingers bending back against the heel of my palm. I was startled by the force of the blow. We had never touched this way before.

Todd and I went to the rear of the house, where we discovered a screened-in porch with its door wide open. There was a glass table inside surrounded by wicker chairs. On the table was a fishbowl with a single goldfish in residence. Todd knelt and watched the fish while I sat in one of the chairs and leafed through the book of poetry I had found. I read two lines out loud and asked Todd to repeat them. I read the same lines again and asked him to memorize them. After a third reading he said them back to me perfectly. A natural retainer! I felt hopeful and proud. As Todd watched the goldfish, I focused down on his shiny black hair, trying to peer through that blackness to the tight convolutions underneath and the budding confession there: Stephen, this world scares me. But why put such a thought in his head? One crazy in the family was enough. Still, I saw no reason why he shouldn't grow up loving poetry.

I was flipping through the book again when Todd called out, "Look at the fish!"

The fishbowl was a transparent purple globe. The goldfish, barely visible in the slightly effervescent solution, hovered near the surface of the water, swimming uncertainly.

"Can you fix him?" Todd said.

I dipped my hand in and scooped out the fish. "Make a bowl with your hands," I said. "Here, hold him. He's okay, his gills are still going. See that?" Todd accepted the fish in his stiff little palms and brought it up to his nose. I dumped the purple liquid outside and refilled the bowl from a spigot near the door. "There," I said, "put him back into his house. Gently, now."

As we made our way to the bookstore, Todd clutched Nancy's skirt and told her about the goldfish. Nancy was quiet. Some of the lawn-sale woman's strangeness had apparently rubbed off on her. Nancy was also peeved about the food processor. All I said was that I didn't want to lug it to the reading, but I had also been quick to add we could take a second look at it on our way home. This wasn't good enough. She took my pragmatism as a rejection of our domesticity. When I hooked my arm around her waist as an act of appeasement, Nancy bolted, agitating the hem of her skirt into a flurry of wavelets that seemed to carry her away from Todd and me. Nancy, I thought, can be a bit of a Carla too sometimes.

At the bookstore we found Carla leaning against the biography shelf, conversing with Ian K., a clerk at the shop, novelist, and the organizer of the reading. He was stuffing his pipe, paying more attention to the tobacco than to Carla's presence. She was as lovely as I had ever seen her, even if her elegance was misplaced in the sunny bookstore. She wore a sliplike black dress with spaghetti straps, and light blue ceramic beads circled her neck. As we entered, Nancy commented that K.'s beard was an affectation. She had little patience for his type. She feared for Carla, who routinely fell in love with unhappy men, whose lives improved as hers became more miserable.

I tend to be at my worst at readings. I simply do not care for them. Todd and I wandered off to the back of the store and sat in an isolated nook we found in the fiction section instead of using the seats Carla had reserved for us in the front row. I rested my head in the angle where two shelves met—Robbe-Grillet in one ear, Sand in the other. I pulled my knees to my chest and closed my eyes. Todd did the same. When I opened them, Todd was squatting several feet away with an oversize bottom-shelf art book on his lap. He turned the big pages, rubbing his sticky hands greedily over the colorplates while Carla read in the near distance. I struggled with my indolent eyes and tried to maintain a focused picture of my son. Falling in and out of sleep, the best I could manage was a series of flickering images. And if my imagination had been operating then as it is now, I would say I saw him growing bigger and stouter with each blink of my eyes.

"Come look," Todd said, nudging me with the corner of the big book. "Look at all the blood."

It was a reproduction of Gauguin's "Jacob Wrestling with the Angel" that he had shoved under my nose.

"That's the angel," I said, pointing to the blond alated figure. "Angels don't bleed. They have holy water in their veins, which keeps them light."

"Oh," he said. He sat on his heels and asked, "Where does all the blood come from?" Todd brushed his hand over the broad areas of red that covered three-quarters of the page.

"Red isn't always blood," I said, "just as black isn't always hair." I stared at Todd, fingers in his mouth, his head bowed to the page. I looked at the painting. The grass was red, so was the sky. It can, indeed, be construed as a bloody scene. Gauguin took liberties. He dared to presume. And in the same spirit I wonder now what color Todd's blood is. Does it even have color? Is there blood between us, me and this creation of mine?

"Your hair is black too," he said.

And as red is blood, I thought, then black must be death, isn't it, Todd? Isn't it?

After the reading, I directed our small party straight to the lawn sale. As we stood at the table with the food processor, Todd, right on cue (when I tapped the plastic mixing bowl), recited the lines I had taught him: " 'There are no stars tonight/But those of memory.' "

Nancy knelt on her skirt and gathered the boy in her

arms. She asked him to repeat the lines. He did, again and again. "Hart Crane," she said. Todd shrugged his shoulders and held his palms up to the sky. "Hart Crane," he said.

"You're teaching him about war, aren't you?" Nancy said in an accusatory tone of voice. "Don't you see how irresponsible that is? Well, you're staying up with him if he has nightmares."

"Come on, Nance, you heard him. That was poetry."

The woman came out of her house. She was in tears, the red bandanna held to her nose. "It's dead," she said. Nancy took her into her arms.

Todd and I exchanged glances. The lesson I should have taught him at that moment was not apparent. Was I supposed to admonish Todd for something he didn't know? He had been giving the fish a drink. We worked hard to teach him to share. So now who should assume the responsibility? When the bombs fall, who takes the blame?

"Stephen, I'll be out in a minute," Nancy said as she led the woman into the house. "Make up your mind about the Cuisinart while I'm gone."

Stephen," my wife says, "let's get going. We have to be at the bookstore in half an hour." She enters the study and reads what I have written up to this point. "Well, do they buy the Cuisinart?"

"You know we didn't."

"But do they?"

"I'm not sure. Why don't we go look at it again today?" I get up from my chair. "What've you been working on?" I ask, to change the topic.

"I typed Prufrock out. After seeing those lines you used in the story, I decided to take a look at it again. It's not a bad poem." She puts her arms around my waist. She kisses me and it's a total surprise. "Thanks," she says. "Eliot has risen from the dead." She massages my shoulders. "Let's go," she says, "we have less than half an hour."

Half an hour, thirty minutes. That's how long it takes Soviet missiles to reach our shores. Thirty minutes to recap the highlights of civilization, to wave flags, to sing hymns and anthems—then chaos, then an eternity of sickening calm. In half an hour you can write a will (if you are hopeful), or say dozens of prayers, or rape and steal and know you'll never be caught. You might open that Scotch you saved for special occasions. You can hoard canned beans and jugs of water, gather guns and ammunition to defend your supplies. *Carpe diem* is yours, in ways the Metaphysicals never imagined. You can write a poem or reread an old favorite, if your nerves are good. Or you can defy all logic—thirty minutes is ample time to make a baby.

"Todd sounds like a nice boy," my wife says, then kisses my cheek. "Good work, Dad." She goes to our bedroom and returns with my sports coat.

"I guess there's no escaping Joyce," I say. On a scrap of paper I start to write myself a note so I'll know where to pick up with the story when we return.

"I'll meet you downstairs," she says.

"Okay, just give me a minute."

I take my time to scribble:

> *You are Stephen*
> *Nancy is Laura*
> *You are Laura too*
>
> *Take out Wicks?*
> *Work in Luddites?*
> *Don't forget Todd, he changes the world*

Warming Trends

Hank got laid off before the recession made the cover of *Time*, but everyone, especially his own family, lumped him in with the trendy new wave of unemployed. "I lost my job," he'd say with a measure of pride, "before Reagan was ever invented." Since the day the funeral parlor shut its doors for the final time, Hank's life had increasingly come to resemble one current-event item after another. Through no fault of his own, he was simultaneously sucked into an embarrassing number of popular social movements. At any moment he expected Connie Chung and camera crew on his front stoop, waiting to solicit from him, the personification of the eighteen-percent jobless rate, his feelings about inflation, the deficit, or some other fad.

"I love it," Hank said aloud as he played the scene in his head outside the corner market where he'd purchased the morning *Post*. "I love the new higher prices." He chuckled and his athletic gray sweatshirt rode up his belly, which shaded the once baggy khaki slacks now snug at the seat as if two plump koalas lived there. Only his maroon jogging shoes with the silver chevrons fit, but he hated them just the same. They were so damn fashionable, every pseudo-jock in the neighborhood owned a pair.

Hank squatted beside a parking meter, sinking his amplitude down on his haunches. He scraped a limp cigarette from beneath one sweat sock and a soggy book of matches from the other. His fat fingers seemed particularly cumbersome that morning as match after match mushed to pink paste against the bald flint strip. Successful finally, Hank puffed mightily, drawing smoke through damp tobacco, his brow studded with sweat from his effort and nerves. Using the meter for leverage, he hauled himself up, the modest change in altitude momentarily dizzying the big man.

He quickened his pace homeward, taking the murderously long strides his doctor prescribed for his high blood pressure and excess poundage, which had conspired to put him on a low-cholesterol diet as well as the exercise regimen. Being healthy was so chic he almost preferred the idea of death. Sunrise jogs, liquid meals. If not for his family, he'd be eating egg foo yung three times a day and napping after each dessert.

The ponderous steps kept his bulk heated; the smoke made his breath as short as the winded gasps of marathoners; and reading the sports page gave him the illusion of athletic accomplishment. For finishers, Hank stopped at his neighbor's garden hose, gargled, and doused his head for a ragged, sweaty look.

He hulked into the kitchen where his wife, Elizabeth, and child, Natalia, were sitting at the table, Elizabeth stabbing the innards of her new shoes with a wrench and Natalia hunched over a bowl of cereal.

"Have a good run?" asked Elizabeth without looking up from her shoe.

"Ran all the way to the market and back. Almost didn't stop to pay for the paper." Hank smooched his wife and slid into the chair beside her.

"You smell like smoke," she said. "You sneaking again?"

"Wo-ho! not me. That bastard Berkowitz was burning his leaves and I got too close." Hank had been advised by his physician that his lungs were in as sorry a state as his waistline and that he needed to quit smoking, which he did for two weeks, until Elizabeth started selling cosmetics door to door.

"They won't stretch," Elizabeth said, working the wrench into the shoe in a most provocative manner. "I should've bought the lower heels, but these were so pretty on in the store. I can wear them to the opera."

"Opera, sure," Natalia sneered. "Right after Hank treats you to Burger King."

"You can't work in those shoes," said Hank, thumbing through the paper. He mumbled into the newsprint, "I think you should quit and stay home."

"Wear the ballet shoes you had on yesterday. They're pretty cool," Natalia said, looking into her bowl of Cocoa Puffs. She was trying to keep the little orbs submerged beneath the milk's silver-blue surface with a spoon.

"I must wear black or navy pumps," Elizabeth said, as if she were a telephone operator reading the Bill of Rights. "If my Lady Eve field rep catches me without my regulation pumps on again, she says she'll fire me right out of my pantyhose! What a laugh!" Natalia giggled.

"That wouldn't be so bad," said Hank. "I don't like you tramping through strange streets, ringing unknown doorbells you don't even know who's touched, and showing weirdos the proper use of cuticle clippers. It's perverse and unsanitary." As he spoke, Hank was flipping through the newspaper.

"I think it's degrading, if you want my opinion," said Natalia.

"Eat your food," snapped Elizabeth.

"I'm chewing, see?" The girl opened her mouth for inspection. "I masticate thirty-six times before I swallow.

Don't care if it's steak or cottage cheese. With my mother out begging door to door and my father idle as a dog at the pound, it's my daughterly duty to maximize the nutritive value of each food dollar."

"You hear that?" Hank said to Elizabeth. "Where did she learn to talk like that?"

"Health class," Natalia said. "But I can stop going if you'll write Miss Leach a note."

"You stay put and get healthy like your father."

"You call reproduction healthy? That's next week's topic, you know."

"Elizabeth, you hear that? She serious?"

"Forget it, Hank," his wife said. "Did you have your smoothie yet?"

"What diet you on now?" Natalia asked. "Scarsdale, Cambridge, Beverly Hills?"

"It's all b.s.," he said. "You want to lose weight, go on the Angola diet. Eat dirt and bugs. Wash it down with hyena's milk."

"Excuse me while I puke!" Natalia said, making obscene noises in her throat.

"Natalia!" Elizabeth said as she measured brewer's yeast into the blender for Hank's shake.

"Wo-ho! Now check this," said Hank, reading from the newspaper: 'JERSEY MOM ROMANCES BOSS FOR O.T. PAY. Too many mouths to feed, says Mrs. X.' Now, that's sick."

"Oh, Hank."

"Oh nothing."

"Oh, who cares?" Natalia said. "This Lady Eve stuff is plain beggary. I'd be mortified if my friends ever found out what Mother does."

"Honey, you can't wear those shoes. Call in sick. I'll make some waffles and we'll talk."

Elizabeth glared at him as she set down his smoothie.

"For your information, I am the office, and I'm the sales-man, the accountant, the secretary. Which should I call to tell me I'm sick?"

"Just making a suggestion." He sniffed the pink smoothie.

"We need the money."

Hank watched as Natalia poured more cereal into her bowl. Slowly, one spoonful at a time, she sprinkled the frosted puffs with milk. He was horrified when after what seemed an eternity the level of the cereal hadn't risen. The process reminded him of the way time crept while Eliza-beth was out wandering the dangerous streets and he waited at home.

"Just pour the milk," he barked, "or you'll be late for school."

"What school? Today's Saturday."

Without the mortuary's schedule of wakes and embalm-ing deadlines to organize his time, the days had melted into one giant weekend. Hank said to his wife, "If it's Saturday, where're you off to in that fancy getup?"

"The Lady Eve manual says that business booms on Saturdays." Elizabeth held a shoe over a pot of steamy water. "The people not home during the week are home today."

"I wouldn't be home during the week either if old man Muncie didn't die on me," Hank said, turning the *Post* over to Natalia. "He told me I'd be the director of the funeral parlor someday—"

"But Muncie died and those damn out-of-town relations came in," Natalia said, finishing the often heard lament, "and closed down the business before Hank could make his million."

Filicide was on his mind, then suicide, then a smoke from the package of Tareytons hidden behind the crisper in the refrigerator. His nerves were jangled, and a man his size had big nerves to soothe. He threw a ferric glance in his daughter's direction. She was holding a tube of lipstick between her lips like a sucker.

"That's made from whale blubber and Arab oil," said Hank.

"Yuck!" she cried, tossing the gold-colored cylinder into the cereal bowl. "That's discusting!" Her mouth was smeared with vertical red streaks.

"Are you two going to get along without me here to referee?" asked Elizabeth, shoving her fist into the steamed shoes. "When was the last time you guys spent a whole day together?"

With nicotine now on his brain, Hank said to Elizabeth, "You better get moving." Once she was out of the house, he could rehabilitate his nerves. "And you don't even have your face on yet. You better have me do your makeup. I've won awards."

"For dead people, dear," Elizabeth said. "You're great with embalmed surfaces. I'll never forget the beautiful job you did on Aunt Margie. She looked so natural."

Hank's shoulders fell, his eyes shrank, his double chin dropped to his chest and quadrupled. Elizabeth ran upstairs for her Lady Eve sales valise. When she returned, she said, "Okay, do your worst."

Tears almost welled in his eyes. It was the first work he'd had in three weeks. Others might've been rusty, but not an experienced dermasurgeon like Hank. Everything went without a hitch until it was time for the mascara. "Hold still," he demanded. "No one's ever twitched so much while I worked."

"I'm also the first who's talked back to you." She jumped out of the chair and nervously looked into a hand mirror she had pulled from the valise. A bit heavy on the rouge and liner, she thought; lips like a bloody wound. But who's to say she looked any worse than the models in the Lady Eve brochures?

"You're a sight, Elizabeth. If we could figure out a way to pay Hank for doing your face, you wouldn't have to work."

"We've raised a genius," Hank said.

Natalia held the newspaper up in front of her so that only her fingertips were visible. "Say, Hank, you see this article about the Yankees?"

"No, what article?"

"An unidentified player claimed that another unidentified player is having an affair with an unidentified batboy."

"You're kidding me. That's *too* corrupt."

"Read it yourself." She slid the tabloid across the table. He flipped through the sports pages again, and found nothing.

"Whale blubber," she said, giggling through her slender fingers, "like in my lipstick." She pushed away from the table and tossed her head as she stood, her pigtails whipping around menacingly like live wires. Hank trained his eyes on her as she stalked from the kitchen, her nose tracing the ceiling. His gaze rode across her taut throat to the bewildering little shapes alive beneath the thin fabric of her T-shirt.

Elizabeth looked from Natalia to Hank. His ruddy face was now ashen. His smooth, fleshy skin had fractured into hard, perpendicular lines. He looked as though he had just glimpsed his daughter's daydreams.

Natalia went up to her room.

"She'll be sixteen in a month," Elizabeth said in a consoling tone of voice. She inspected the contents of her valise, reciting the names of the merchandise to herself. "Your daughter has tits."

Hank clutched the front of his sweatshirt with his thick hands. "That's lovely. Are you trying to give me a heart attack? I know you think it's fashionable to use degenerate language, but how can you say that about your own daughter?" He hid his face in his hands. "How can she be so grown-up when she's not?" He spread his fingers and stared at his wife.

Elizabeth laughed. "Oh, come now. Don't act surprised. She's not so young anymore. You've heard her talk."

"My God, yes. Why don't they teach her something useful in that school? She never says a word about fractions, parameciums, or Magellan."

"Don't get hysterical, Hank. I have to get going. It'll be good for you two to see more of each other."

"I don't think I can stand to see much more. Aren't you worried about her?" he asked. "Where was she last night?"

"You know. Out baby-sitting with Holly."

"That's exactly my point. Two growing girls alone in a house stripped of parental supervision. Who can say what went on? Boys could've easily stopped by. You know, with their dirty hands and even filthier minds. Black-nailed carriers of disease. Don't laugh, I wasn't an adult all my life." In his upset state, Hank suddenly looked almost skinny. "Boys have gutterbrains."

"It sounds like you must've been a lot of fun as a kid. Sleazy little Hank."

"From you I guess that's a compliment. Listen, boys today are worse. They drag in beer and drugs. Their vocabulary begins and ends with four-letter words. But you probably like that."

"I have to go." At long last, she wedged her feet into the shoes. She didn't say they hurt her, but it was obvious from her expression. "Tell Natalia your theory about boys.

She'll get a kick out of it." She picked up her valise and stepped gingerly toward the door.

"You don't have to do this," Hank said, grabbing hold of her wrists.

"Cocoa Puffs cost money."

"We can stop feeding her. She's big enough as it is."

Elizabeth laughed and kissed the air alongside her husband's cheek, careful not to disturb her makeup.

She was gone for no more than a minute when Hank went to fix his nerves. He rescued a Tareyton from the refrigerator and smoked it hungrily in the garage.

After he saw that the Game of the Week was going to be between the Yankees and the Indians, Hank convinced himself he couldn't let health stand in the way of his watching the National Pastime in the manner it was meant to be enjoyed. Besides, Natalia had gone out for the afternoon.

With his feet lagging behind his intentions, Hank hastened to the corner market and charged a six-pack of Lone Star and a bag of pretzels to his account.

By the third inning, almost halfway through his beers, he was thoroughly irritated by the work of the two men broadcasting the game. The way they tossed clichés around and upended the rules of grammar made him wonder why the world rewarded such incompetents while first-rate performers like himself sat idly on the bench. He munched a handful of pretzels and felt his stomach become comfortably bloated. This unaccustomed fullness triggered fresh and daring ideas: he could kidnap the bald play-by-play announcer and ransom him for enough cash to cover the cost of reopening the funeral parlor, with Hank, decked out in a somber black suit, as its new director. He was certain there were families in town who still required his services.

Between innings Hank sneaked a Tareyton in the kitchen, blowing the smoke into the switched-on range hood. Then he grabbed another beer and returned to the living room, where his beloved Yanks were threatening to pad their 8–0 advantage. He slouched into his favorite easy chair, the beer balanced on the dome of his belly, each finger of his right hand ringed with a pretzel. He chewed and sipped and belched and excavated bits of dough from between his teeth. His Yanks had quickly demonstrated to the national TV audience that their combination of power and grace far outstripped the minimal talents of their opponents. The faint of heart or the casual observer, unaccustomed to the twin spectacle of brute force and pitching wizardry, had probably gone back to mowing the lawn or washing the dog. The game was a mismatch from the start. A rookie pitching sensation—the reason the network broadcast the Indians—was humiliated for six runs before he recorded a single out. Hank knew the Indians were a sorry bunch, but this afternoon they exceeded all expectations. They struck out and hit into double plays as if on command.

Hank belched and the Yanks scored two more runs. It wasn't a pretty sight.

They got great baseball tradition here in Cleveland; don't let one game fool ya; in '54 they brought home the pennant.

Hank chuckled so much the beer fizzed in his nose.

That was three decades ago almost, Joe; the only tradition here is losing.

Hank picked up the empty cans at his feet and launched them at the TV set. "You cluckers!" he shouted at the announcers.

"You call?" It was Natalia from the kitchen. He didn't

know the monster had come home. He could hear the hum of the refrigerator motor change pitch because its door had been open for too long. "Get your nose out of there before it freezes," he said, afraid her snooping might lead her to his tobacco.

She strolled into the living room with a peanut-butter sandwich dangling from her mouth. Hank scrutinized his daughter's act. "Why you eyeballing me?" the monster-child said. "I never guessed you were a pervert too."

"Don't mind me, sister. You watch out for the real perverts." Hank grunted conclusively. "And watch what you say. I am your father." He looked at the TV. "Where've you been hiding?" Hank asked, calmer now.

"I was out at the record store with Holly and Bilbo."

"Who's Bilbo? Holly's dog?"

"That dog happens to be William Rex Daily, known to his friends as Bilbo."

"Hey, what do you think you're doing?"

Natalia had swiped the beer off his belly and brought it up to her mouth. "No big deal. I only tasted it. There's more in the fridge. Besides, since when were you such a puritan? You know, Hankie," she said, sitting down, "it stinks of smoke in the kitchen."

"You're imagining things. Things like you're old enough to drink. Things like it's okay to call me Hankie."

At the end of six New York leads, 10–0.

"It's a slaughter. What's the point of watching?"

"Because slaughters give me pleasure. I like to see the Yanks punish the other team."

"Well, you don't look too happy to me," she said, reaching again for the beer. "You look like the team plane just crashed into Lake Erie and Elizabeth was found on board." She watched for Hank's reaction.

His soft flesh seemed to calcify. "What inspires you?" he asked, already fearing her response.

7

"I just wanted to impress on you how sad you look," she said. "You should get out more. Don't you envy all the fresh air and exercise Elizabeth is getting? You used to complain you never saw the sun when you were working at Muncie's. But here you are, cooped up with a TV set."

He sank deeper into his seat. The unctuous smell of peanut butter weighed on the air. He could feel the calories accumulate in his nostrils. On the screen the first Yankee up in the seventh swung at ball four, as if he were trying to make an out, and tapped a bouncer to short where it was mishandled and kicked into left field. The batter slid safely into second. *Gee, Tony, I don't know; if I was management, I'd think about giving these fans a refund.*

"This is too painful to watch," Natalia said, getting up to leave.

"You finished with that sandwich?"

"Say, what happened to your diet? I might have to report this to Elizabeth. You better go walk off some of those pretzels." She stuffed the sandwich into her mouth.

"I've had it up to here with you today." He indicated the level of his eyes. "Mind your own business. You're giving me heartburn."

Her pigtails flew wildly. "What did I do? Am I so awful? I know some fathers who would gladly trade their brats for me." She turned and ran upstairs.

You'd think we're in Yankee Stadium. The staticky buzz of TV crowd noise suddenly intensified. On the screen the Indians' mascot in the center-field bleachers was thumping his tom-tom, inciting the hometown fans to root against their team. *Can you blame these fans?—thirty years of mediocrity.* Hank switched off the sound. He stared at the set as if it were civilization's first campfire and he was its inventor.

He dragged his body to the kitchen for a cigarette. Head under the range hood he smoked, the sound of the exhaust fan whirring in his ears. He puffed furiously to compensate for all the cigarettes he hadn't smoked because he wasn't supposed to be smoking. His knees quivered; toothpicks pricked his lungs.

"Hank, don't do it! Get away from the gas! Things aren't that bad!"

"You sneak." He bumped his head against the range hood and singed his fingers as he extinguished the cigarette. "Looks pretty bad, huh?"

A coy expression crossed Natalia's face. "We all have our secrets. I won't tell Elizabeth." She had changed her clothes. She was now wearing one of Hank's undershirts from his lean period, its neck-opening stretched out of shape to expose a bony shoulder.

He said, "That is the first cigarette I've had since—"

The doorbell rang. Natalia jumped. "Sure, Hank," she said as she raked her fingers nervously through her hair. "That's my secret."

"What?" Hank lumbered into the living room.

"Bilbo."

She opened the door. Bilbo was a few inches shorter than his host. He had a Mohawk-style hairdo that tapered down the back of his neck to a phlegmy green rattail. His clothes were black and otherwise unremarkable except for the ammo belt and hobnail boots. "Come meet my father," she said.

He grunted, shook his head, crucifix earrings striking his cheeks.

"Hank, this is William Rex Daily."

"Well, hello," Hank said. "Are you supposed to be a barbarian?" He glared at the slave of fashion. "What's that?" he asked, pointing to a series of brown dots in a geometric pattern on the boy's arm. "Tattoo?"

Bilbo grunted something.

"Cigarette burns," Natalia said. "I put those two there myself," she added, pointing at Bilbo's arm.

Hank felt queasy. He trudged back to his chair and flopped down. "No more cigarettes," he muttered to himself.

The two youths stood in the middle of the living room. Natalia asked Hank if Bilbo could smoke a cigarette, and Hank told her he didn't care so long as the boy refrained from putting it out on his arm. Bilbo grunted, lit a Marlboro, smothered the match in his hand, and shoved the red-and-white box of cigarettes into his ammo belt. They stood there talking quietly.

"We're heading out, Hank," Natalia said.

"Oh, are we going hunting? Hey, come here. Sit down and watch the game with your father."

Bilbo grunted and turned in the direction of the front door.

"Does he talk?" Hank asked Natalia.

"Of course he talks," she said, "but he doesn't watch baseball. It's too calm for him." Bilbo's accessories jangled as he squirmed under Hank's critical eyes. "We have to go now."

"Sit down," Hank growled, rising from his chair. "Be good Americans and come watch my Yanks beat up on the Indians."

"You can't do this to us," said Natalia, folding her arms across her chest.

"Young lady, bring us men some beer. You can have some too. We must rid the house of the evidence. And pretzels—here, Bilbo, eat my pretzels." Natalia went to the kitchen. "Bring me my Tareytons," he called after her. "They're behind the crisper." He told Bilbo to sit. Hank went up to the boy and examined his hairdo. It reminded him of a freshly trimmed hedge. At least it was neat. "Who do you like, Indians or Yankees?"

Natalia returned with the contraband. "Don't answer me yet," Hank said to the boy. "Here, drink beer." He flipped the top off. "Ha-ha. Baseball, beer, and Bilbo. Sit back, enjoy. Open up your brew, Natalia. Bilbo, smoke my smokes."

"You're holding us hostage," she said. "You're no better than those terrorists on TV. Wait till Mike Wallace gets wind of this. I can see it now. 'Stay tuned for *60 Minutes*. Tonight: Father takes teens hostage.' "

Hank ignored her remarks. "Bilbo," he said, "Yanks or Injuns?"

To the surprise of all, Bilbo answered: "I favor Third World nations. I am in sympathy with Third World peoples. I'll take the side of the poor, oppressed, underdeveloped team."

As Bilbo spoke, Hank's heart fluttered. Seldom had he been so moved by another's words. He could feel his allegiance shifting away from the brutish Bronx Bombers and moving toward the pitiful Tribe, a team at that instant without a city to call home. This upheaval had its physical as well as its mental aspect. As the shift in sympathies occurred, he felt as if he had swallowed a marble that was now squeezing its way through his small intestines. He realized his prospects for the future were no brighter than those of the Indians that afternoon. They were natural allies. It was so obvious. When you're poor, why love IBM? So Hank, for no palpable reason, adopted the classic mind-set of the chronically unemployed: he started to hope. He decided that if some great cosmic force granted the Indians a miracle, and they should win, his own luck, too, would change.

Hank's conversion was complete the moment he first hollered encouragement to his newly adopted team, and the Indians miraculously responded with four quick runs. *Stay tuned, we may have a ball game yet.* "Fucking apologists!" he yelled at the screen.

"Hank! Such language."

"Fucking apologists," Bilbo echoed the big man. He stood and shook his fists.

"Hey, Bilbo, let's split," Natalia said.

The boy looked over at Hank, who said, "You can go, but she stays."

"Go? Not till I see those Yankees on their knees."

"Ha-ha-ha. That's the American spirit. No matter how you cut your hair, we're a nation of sportsmen."

"Coward!" Natalia shouted at her friend. "Capitulator!" She fell back into her chair, hair flying.

Even though the boy was one of the most unsightly abominations he had ever come across, Hank forgave the errors of youth. For all their differences, he recognized that they shared the common bond of desperation. In Bilbo, Hank saw the skinny skeleton that lay miles beneath his flesh.

Together they watched the game to its conclusion, cheering, moaning, groaning, sighing, belching, drinking, and smoking in unison. Did it matter the Indians lost in the twelfth inning? Or the fact they staged their uprising against the Yankees' second-stringers? The comeback itself, the sheer nerve of the Clevelanders, was evidence enough a change in fortunes was in store for him.

He was preparing dinner and whistling the theme to "Bonanza." He trussed a chicken and set it down in a roasting pan. When he reached his hand into the fowl's body cavity, an overwhelming nostalgia took hold of him.

He waddled to the garage and retrieved a box of supplies

and equipment left over from better days. The sight of the box made him giggle. Hank was back on the job.

With a scalpel he lopped off the bird's appendages and zipped right through the neck stump. The blade was still good. He trimmed the skin around the neck, thigh, wing, and rear vents before suturing them shut and sealing each seam with generous applications of Leak Pruf. Now the chicken, the approximate shape of a football, was watertight.

Pleasant memories filled his mind as he worked. He recalled the time he had repaired a client's face by slicing off chunks of his buttock that Hank's divine hands had then used to reconstruct a nose. Aware that he was breaking new ground in the field, he had taken copious notes and Polaroid snapshots of each critical stage in the procedure. Later he had published the documentation in *Morticians' Quarterly*, raising his stock immeasurably with old man Muncie, who shortly thereafter dropped dead.

Hank shut the kitchen windows and opened the refrigerator and freezer doors. He switched on the air conditioner and dimmed the lights. Within minutes he had simulated the clammy basement environment at Muncie's, a dermasurgeon's paradise, and the chill on his skin made his creative juices flow.

He severed the chicken's tail, that most delectable triangular morsel of fat the uninitiated erroneously associate with excretory functions. After he carved and notched and folded this piece, Hank centered the greasy pyramid on the bird's breast. "Wo-ho!" he said, pleased with his handiwork.

All the brilliance and expertise wasted during the weeks of idleness now drove his beefy but still nimble artist's hands. He cut and sewed and powdered and waxed and puttied. For the sake of old times, he filled a syringe with

Ever Lyfe Lyk and injected it into the flesh. Always the perfectionist, Hank then shot silicone under the skin wherever minor ruts spoiled the geometry of his creation. Others wouldn't have bothered with such fine details, but most men weren't born, as the dean of the mortician college had described Hank, with embalming fluid in their veins.

Soon Hank could see his breath in the air. His hands were as dank as death. He stood back and admired his work. His body tingled, even in places he didn't think housed nerves anymore. But as he gloated a wave of uneasiness crept up his esophagus, undermining his triumph. The more he thought of the absolute authenticity of his creation, the more nauseated he felt.

But he pressed on with the finishing touches. From a trunk in the attic he fished out a pair of sunglasses and a wig from Elizabeth's '60s phase. Back in the kitchen he popped the dark lenses from the frames. While he trimmed Elizabeth's wig, he remembered she was still on the streets, roaming unsavory neighborhoods. He looked at the clock. It was half past six. And Natalia, brimming with those hormones that made her grow so, was soloing with Bilbo. Who could say where that hairdo might lead them? "There are a million loonies outside our door," Elizabeth had said at dinner the night before. "You know what I mean, Hank. You worked with the public."

"Sure, John Q. Corpse and Jane E. Dead. But they never whistled at me when I walked past. I kept polite company."

Elizabeth then followed with a story about a kook on Union Street who invited her into his house, a beautiful Victorian filled with precious glass objects and Boston ferns. She was seated on a velvet divan waiting for his wife to appear but, of course, she didn't. Elizabeth thought little of this because the *Lady Eve Fact Book* told her that many sales were made to men buying gifts. The kook, a blue-knuckled man in his fifties, asked to sample the perfumes. He sniffed her wrists, her forearms, shoulders, kneecaps. He wanted to sample more fragrances but she had run out of test spots. Finally, he placed an order for a hundred and fifty dollars' worth of perfume. As she filled out the requisition form, he leaned boldly forward and sniffed her shoulder again. The hard tip of his nose pressed against her like the barrel of a gun, but she didn't dare budge, the commission too dazzling to risk losing.

Even after she finished writing up the order, the kook selected nail polishes, lipsticks, and eye makeup. Her mind was preoccupied calculating her earnings. He asked which color she was wearing on her lips, and when she turned to flash him the smile the Lady Eve manual said would reassure her customers of the intelligence of their inquiries, she found herself staring into his depthless pores. He said, "How about some Moody Mauve on my lips?"

"Wow, sexual harassment! My own mother, a victim!" Natalia had said.

"You're quitting that job."

"Wait. I'm not through yet." Elizabeth said she told the kook to shut his eyes. He puckered his lips in anticipation of a kiss. When he opened his eyes to see what was holding up the kiss, Elizabeth said, "I zapped him with Femme Fresh."

"You douched him!" Natalia said.

"Lilac-vinegar formula, also available in orange blossom."

"God, that's too cool. I mean, he could've raped you!" Natalia squealed.

"Where'd you learn such language?"

"What's wrong with 'rape'? It's in the dictionary."

"Of all things," said Hank, "why teach them to spell?" He stared down at his creation. It was technically perfect but the queasiness in his gut prevented him from fully enjoying the sight of the carcass. Perhaps its nakedness bothered him. He was starting for the attic again when the front door opened. "I demand an apology, you hostage-taker!" Natalia shouted. Hank listened to her stomp into the kitchen. "*Mr. Muncie!*" she screamed. "You killed Mr. Muncie!"

When he returned to the kitchen, Natalia ran into the corner furthest from her father. He held an old-fashioned shirt collar and one of his ties up to the tapered end of the carcass. "That's really sick," Natalia squealed. "How long has Mr. Muncie's head been in the freezer?"

"What kind of craziness are you talking now?" He looked at the open freezer door and then down at the countertop. Indeed, there was old man Muncie looking smugly up at him. Muncie had a wicked expression on his face, and everything in Hank's stomach started to bubble. Why had his hands brought Muncie back? Muncie wasn't supposed to die. Others were supposed to die, and now that he was dead, he wouldn't stay dead. What good was he to Hank? Muncie didn't even protect him from the vultures who swept into town and sold the mortuary, ruining Hank's career. Hank despised the face. "Get out of my life, Muncie," he said, taking hold of the nose.

"Mr. Muncie!" Natalia shrieked from the corner.

"No, this is a chicken," Hank said. He hurried to Natalia with the lump of chicken fat riding on the palm of his hand.

"Stay back. Keep that nose away from me." She held up her hand to block Hank's advance.

"It's just the chicken's butt." He furiously rubbed the powder and putty off the lump of fat down the front of his shirt. "You see," he said, holding it out to her, "this is the piece I like to eat."

Somewhat mollified, she said, "What have you done to Elizabeth?"

"Oh, stop it. You know she's still out." He peered out the window. "It's pretty dark out there."

"Does she know you kept Mr. Muncie's head after you killed him?"

"What's it going to take? You want me to boil this up and eat it here in front of you?"

"Don't gross me out, now," she said, regaining her lost composure. She paused, then said, "You know, Hank, I think she's been kidnapped. We should call the cops."

"Don't say such things. They're not funny."

Natalia's imagination grew more extravagant. "What if she's been hit by a car? Or maybe a dog bit her. Hank," she said, her voice rising with her increased excitement, "what if that kook's grabbed her? Nah," she waved the theory off, "that's too logical. I've got it now—terrorists!" She clapped her hands. "We should call the cops." As she reached for the telephone, it suddenly rang. "I bet it's the hospital calling with bad news. Or maybe it's the kidnappers demanding ransom. Hank, we've got nothing to pay them with. Who in the world will give you a loan?"

Hank picked up the receiver. "Natty? That you, Bilbo?" Natalia took the telephone from her father.

"I can't talk now," she said. "We're expecting the cops to call any minute. My mother's a missing person. Yeah, no kidding. Jealous? Of course you're jealous." Hank tried to snatch the telephone from her grasp. "I have to get off. We're tying up the lines of communication." She abruptly hung up.

"Call him back," Hank said. "You can't tell people your mother's missing. You'll worry them for no reason."

"But she *is* missing."

"I hope you hope you're wrong."

8

She dialed Bilbo's number and then held the receiver out in Hank's direction so he could hear the busy signal.

"His parents are calling the FBI this very minute," Hank said. "I know it. Now see what you've done?"

"They're not home."

"What? You mean you were at that barbarian's house alone all afternoon?"

"Hank, it's cold in here." Natalia squeezed past Hank's stomach and went to switch off the air conditioner, shutting the refrigerator doors on her way. She lit the oven and the burners on the stove top. As Hank adjusted the thermostat, Natalia came up behind him and stretched her arms as far as they'd go around him.

"Were you like this when your mother wasn't working?"

"I was younger then."

"*Then*, kiddo, was just a few days ago."

"It seems a lot longer."

Hank turned to face her. Natalia's head was bowed; her stringy hair covered her eyes. "I'm scared about Mom," she said, pressing her forehead against his soft chest. He could feel her body tense, trembling slightly.

"You want to stand near the oven?"

Natalia said, "I'm already there."

Hank turned and lifted his heavy arms from his sides and wrapped them around his daughter. In profile her slight frame molded to the curve of his belly, like the moon emerging from an eclipse. Patiently, Hank let her go.

Disturbing
the Universe

The journey to the horizon is long. But trav-
ellers to the horizon persevere for they believe
such a place exists. Not just in illusion, but
in the realm of hands.
    —LEI ZU WEI, the poet-historian, on the
    construction of the Great Wall of China

I

t was a desperate hour. The sun sat in high sky. Water, as always, was scarce. The soldiers had cut our food with lime to deaden our appetites. Still we suffered hunger pains. The earth was dry. It was a fine dust that lined our lungs. Three from our crew were found dead that morning. The field report filed by the Colonel with the authorities in the capital alleged those men had died of mishaps, or had succumbed to the difficult climate of the Northern Frontier. We knew, despite the rumors circulated throughout the Empire, all three had perished from broken hearts. After all, ours was never a transient race; we grow thick, deep roots. Who could forget the approaching soldiers and their steeds when they came to raid our villages?

Who could claim to be free of the menacing shadows left upon our skin, those lingering impressions where our wives last held us as the soldiers swept us away? Hundreds have died at the Wall. These three men were merely its latest victims. As the Emperor's conscripts, we endured many hardships. But on the day in question other matters stole our attention. Early that morning we had witnessed a sea gull soaring overhead. Why had she flown so far from shore? We had witnessed a hare chasing a fox, trees bending against the wind. The signs were strong, calling for resolute minds and sharp instincts, but we were just interlopers in that mysterious region, bald-headed sojourners through a lifetime of rain.

II

No one slept well. No one ever did. Nights were cold, windy, and full of the shrieks and creeping of creatures unknown to civilized men. We watched the brilliant silver-yellow disc climb the indigo sky. For such an early hour, the sun was precariously hot. We feared the number of brokenhearted would swell before day's end.

The gray pap we consumed for breakfast was still warm in our tortoiseshell bowls when the Imperial Commission arrived in our camp. The Colonel slipped between the flaps of his tent and greeted the six commissioners with deep bows and courteous words. He nodded in the direction of their white steeds, bearing gifts and correspondence from his native province. This was nothing new. It was only right the Colonel should enjoy the comforts of home. He was our leader. What surprised us, though, was the sight of the silks on the steeds, embroidered with the colors and designs of our villages in the South.

By the glare of the sun's stark rays, falling in distinct shafts that seemed to isolate one body from the next, the curved spines of the visitors disappeared into their host's tent. Inside, it was said, they sipped fragrant teas and ate delicate rice cakes; they gossiped about politics and scandal in the capital as we started our daily drudgery at the Wall.

The Imperial Commission remained shaded in the Colonel's tent while the sun scaled the sky. The construction of the Wall seemed to be of little consequence to the commissioners. On previous visits here, they had inspected our work, unrolling the scrolls that contained the plans, and compared the abstract with the thing itself. Such was not the reason for this trip. When the flaps of the tent were finally drawn back, five commissioners mounted stallions, white as the fabled Indian snow. Where was the sixth? We all agreed that as sure as the barbarian drank the milk of cows and ingested the whey of goats and spread upon their tables the blue meat of monkeys, six men on six steeds had come to our camp, but now only five journeyed, their backs to the sun, leading away the sixth horse, loaded with provisions. It needed to be coaxed along, unable to step a straight path, rearing its head, haunted by the human absence.

After the ceremonious leave-taking, the Colonel returned to his tent. This incident, or the very lack of incident, was an invitation to us to work in peace. But even tranquillity seemed burdensome at the Wall. Any other day, as predictable as the winds at dusk, the Colonel would march to the Wall and inspire our labor. Attendant soldiers beat us; on the Colonel's orders, they would tear down a newly erected section, excoriating us for shoddy workmanship, extending our exile here in the North. Now his absence worried us. We were uneasy without the scolding, the blows, the humiliation. What greater confirmation could there be! We were truly slaves.

III

There were three classes of laborer in our camp: peasant, criminal, and scholar. The peasants were assigned the most benign tasks, such as earth-pounding and frame construction. The criminals—common thieves, killers, wayward eunuchs, and pretenders to the imperial throne—broke rocks and moved boulders. The scholars, said by some to be society's most useless men, suffered the worst fate. They were plagued with trench-digging, as decreed by the Emperor himself. With only sharpened rocks to cut the earthen canals, they were often wounded, and many perished, buried alive in the grave they had dug themselves. Still, despite the evidence, the sight of their red blood or their muffled shouts as we—for such were our orders—showered the fallen with loess, we knew their mortal deaths were secondary, an after-thought to the brokenhearted deaths they had already endured when first they laid eyes on the Northern Frontier.

With this history in mind, we gasped at the sight of the young scholar who went and spoke to the earth-pounders. It pained us to see his empty hands in open defiance of the ban against any work stoppage without official sanction.

"How does one work," the scholar said, "when one's strength is gone?" The earth-pounders kept on with their labor, tamping the orange dirt and rocks that comprised the Wall's viscera.

"I take my strength from the Colonel and his dogs. Yes, I admit I am guilty of hate and fear. But these ills of the blood are all the muscle I have with which to dig," said the scholar. "Tell me, how am I to slave without the nourishment of their abuse? Observe how they have domesticated us. Are we not peers of the dull zebu who wear the yoke and toil without sense or design? Let us suppose the farmer has lost his cane or has taken ill, do you think those zebu would take up their yokes and plow the field without the crisp crack of the whip alongside their ears?"

The earth-pounders were silent. They stood on top of the Wall, at a height of five men above the ground, and worked to make the filler solid, flattening the surface smooth so a layer of brick might someday be laid on top. It was rumored the Wall would serve as a land bridge, wide enough to accommodate five horses traveling abreast, linking the eastern shore to the mountainous region to the west.

"You see the entire world from up there," the scholar said. "Yet you remain on the Wall." He climbed from the deep trench and started for the makeshift ladder, a geometry of bamboo knotted together with hemp, and the only means of gaining a foothold on the Wall.

It saddened us that the eldest earth-pounder was forced, at great risk, to leave his station to block the troublesome scholar's ascent. "This is not your place," he said. His fellow earth-pounders flinched at each syllable he uttered, fearing for their friend's life.

Why bother with the treacherous scholar? Away from here other sons of Confucius had little to say to peasants. With far less risk, scholars never sought an audience with us, as this one did now. But here the gentleman must learn—that should not be a problem for a man of erudition—to crane his neck and gaze toward heaven for a glimpse of a peasant. "Go back to your work," said the earth-pounder. "We are equals at the Wall, and nothing before the Emperor."

The scholar anchored his sandaled feet on the ladder's first rung. "Let us abandon this perversion of nature," he said. "The way of the world is not linear, but circular. This wall is an insult to the kingdoms of the past. Nowhere in all the annals of those ancient times is a single word written of this monstrosity."

A youthful earth-pounder grabbed the ladder and tried to shake the rebel loose. But the scholar would not budge, clinging to the ladder like a splinter lodged deep in the skin. The old earth-pounder calmed the youth with an avuncular pat on his arm and instructed him to resume his chores.

"What is on the other side?" asked the scholar, climbing slowly. "Have you seen the legendary barbarians this mammoth lie allegedly saves us from?" He jumped onto the Wall. The earth-pounders stepped back from the rebel. "Don't be alarmed," he said. "I am a mortal, like you, like the Colonel, except he possesses us, and is himself possessed by demons. Perhaps that is where he is today. Lost in the Great Void, in counsel with his masters."

"Young sir," the earth-pounder said, "you have read the Classics. You have studied all that is worth knowing about the universe. But you lack wisdom." He paused and surveyed the land. "The Colonel soon will be upon us. Of this you can be certain. We are not forgotten. Miracles are rare anywhere but especially in the Northern Frontier. No one ever escapes, not even the dead. Each time I strike this dirt I hear them moan, those buried deep in these trenches." The earth-pounder studied the scholar. The scholar's eyes were clouds, his brittle skin a leathery brown. "Be not mistaken," the earth-pounder said, "they have harsh laws. As we talk, we sentence ourselves. Go back and dig. No one's life is tolerable here, but you still must care for it, as I do my own. Not another word."

The scholar's face tightened. "What would the Sages say

of this? Had the Emperor not burned my books, I would show you the passages that condemn such waste and extravagance."

"Is it not written we must obey our leaders as we do our fathers?"

The scholar ignored the earth-pounder. "We must save ourselves," he said, flapping his arms to indicate flight. "Look at the other side. It is no different from ours. In fact, it is better; it has no Colonel. We must seize the opportunity and leave."

The scholar peered over the edge. "Our only risk is the leap down from here," he said. "This is exceptional irony. We will make an ally of our hated wall; it will shield us from enemy eyes as we escape." He looked over the edge again.

Before the earth-pounder could say a word, the scholar had leapt off the Wall, landing in a motionless heap. The earth-pounders stared in amazement as the scholar slowly stood, brushing the dust from his robes. He started to run, limping slightly, gravitating close to the Wall, going easterly.

Such foolishness. It was a simple matter to leap from such heights but to vault them was impossible. In all the wilderness there was not a pair of hands that could fashion another ladder. Now the Middle Kingdom was lost to him. In his madness he had forgotten that the Wall not only kept out the foreigner but also prevented any rebel from coming back in.

The earth-pounders peered over the edge and watched the scholar, the only moving thing in the vastness of the wrong side.

"Soon," the old earth-pounder said, "he will learn."

IV

The Colonel and his mysterious guest, the missing sixth commissioner, suddenly emerged from the tent. Likewise, the soldiers materialized, appearing in two columns, each led by an official. They marched to the Wall's completed eastern segment. The sixth commissioner held a black book pressed to his chest. On the left hand of each soldier was what appeared to be the dried and stretched bladder of a pig. Several men also carried wooden clubs on their shoulders. We stopped to observe the procession, the soldiers perfectly erect, their eyes riveted to the head directly in front. We were puzzled by this latest intrigue. But our collective idleness went unacknowledged by the authorities.

At the tail of the column headed by the Colonel, a soldier had cradled in his arms four golden pillows. Beside him, in the bowl formed by his palms, another soldier held a peculiar orb, on which the character *people*, 人 , was stitched with lucky red thread in a pattern of parallel curves that wrapped around its entire surface. It could be said that these *people* held the orb together; hundreds of *people* in a continuous band of linked arms, without distinction between leader or follower, without beginning or end.

When the soldiers were ordered to stop, the sixth commissioner began to read. With the black tome balanced on one hand, he waved his free hand for emphasis. In turn, the Colonel translated what the sixth commissioner read into commands.

On the Colonel's orders, a pillow was placed at the sixth commissioner's feet. From this starting point a soldier, again on orders, paced off a prescribed number of steps, and there positioned a second pillow. Taking a quarter turn, the soldier measured the same distance and laid down a third. Another quarter turn, and he repeated the procedure, setting down the final one. Later, we learned the sixth commissioner had special names for each pillow. They were, in the order of their placement: Earth, Air, Fire, and Water.

After a lengthy conference and numerous consultations with the black book, the sixth commissioner and the Colonel divided the soldiers into two squads. The Colonel led his troops to the vast area behind Earth, where they huddled, and then turned to watch the sixth commissioner, who, with his nose buried in his book, assigned his men, one by one, to designated stations: the first was positioned beside Air; the second at an equidistance between Air and Fire, while a third was similarly placed between Fire and Water; the fourth manned Water; the fifth squatted directly behind Earth, facing the other four soldiers. The sixth commissioner then read an elaborate series of instructions to these men, again waving his tireless arm to emphasize key points.

All through these strange happenings, we watched idly.

At times, the sixth commissioner demonstrated for the soldiers the roles they were to perform at their stations. He did so with pantomime: first he appeared to be a monkey, then a swan, a frog, a shooting star; then a lake, a delightful spring breeze, and on and on. Finished, the sixth commissioner summoned three more of his soldiers and spread them beyond the arc formed by the four who guarded the pillows, from Air to Fire.

At the center of the pillows, with the peculiar orb cupped in his hand, the sixth commissioner summoned a ninth soldier. He showed the new recruit the most complex and beautiful task in the unfolding mystery. With the orb nestled in the pig bladder worn over his left hand and the fingers of his right hand hooked around the orb, he raised both arms directly over his head, and for one brief moment gave the impression of a human pagoda. Then he lifted his front—or left—leg, crooked at the knee, until the foot was raised to the height of his standing knee, like a blue heron stepping from an inhospitable pond. Leg up, hands high. Then, suddenly, all his movements tumbled forward: he dropped his arms, tearing the orb free of the pig bladder; the falling arms stopped, shoulder height, both parallel to the ground and to his now straightened leg suspended in midair, the pig-bladdered hand in front of his face, the orb slung behind his back; he lowered his leg, and when his foot touched ground, a full stride ahead of where he began, he slung his arm forward and launched the orb in the direction of the soldier stationed behind Earth. The orb popped in, then out of, the soldier's waiting pig bladder. The poor man, whose hand was barely protected by the dried pouch, cried out in pain. The other soldiers laughed and clapped their hands. On the Wall we did the same. This was our most brazen act to date. But then, we had just witnessed a miracle.

V

It was a glorious afternoon. The sun was very hot, but it did not matter. The soldiers performed their duty with vigor and showed no signs of fatigue. Not since the initial period of ineptitude—but so were we clumsy and tentative in our role as spectators—had the pace of the contest flagged. It was sublime entertainment. Any amusement, of course, would have been welcomed, but this stirred our passion, colored our memories, and transported us from our despair. We did not work: we merely observed the proceedings. This seemed agreeable to the authorities. We had taken the ladders from the earth-pounders and climbed onto the east wall, which served as the outermost perimeter of the sixth commissioner's spectacle. From here we had the best possible view. We sat or stood, crammed closely together, ten rows deep, filling the Wall's entire breadth. One soldier, whom we affectionately called Reji, Hot Chicken, after the way he kicked the dirt before he stepped up to Earth, was the most adept at making the club collide with the orb. Not only that, he displayed a propensity for propelling the orb over great distances. Each time he visited Earth, we rose to our feet and cheered, anticipating another swat that would send the orb soaring beyond the retrievers' outstretched pig bladders and ricocheting off the base of the Wall. After such a collision, Reji galloped from Earth to Air, to Fire, to Water, then back to Earth. We shouted our encouragement, forgetting that with the same strong arms the soldier had swung a bamboo rod against us. "Reji! Reji!" we screamed. It was treason.

In the near distance, criminals were engaged in their own version of the sixth commissioner's contest. A club was fashioned from wood borrowed from the frame-builders, an orb was chipped from stone. We played or watched as others played; we were enchanted; even at home we never had such an afternoon. The diversion was an opiate that reduced our suffering to a trifle; it seduced us like stories of the Empress's magnificent bound feet, lulled us like the hundred hands that wait on the Duke of Zhou's every need, mesmerized us by its calm and dignity. Our miserable lives were subsumed by the life of this exercise. Who could dispute its representation of the harmony between man and the ways of nature, otherwise absent here in the Northern Frontier? Mark the fact that the speed of a tossed or clubbed orb always exceeds that of a pair of running legs; mark the stubborn insistence of gravity on the flight of the orb and its uncanny, mathematically precise confinement within the limits of the Wall; mark how no one was tempted to escape, though we had the opportunity. Even the earth-pounders, with the exception of their leader, had abandoned their posts.

Our people possess strong instincts for conformity. The individual is most comfortable when merged with the great masses. The earth-pounder resisted this natural force and toiled alone, performing the work of a dozen men. He was thin but strong. A little brown man in rags, caked with dust and sweat—how it angered us to see him work! At that happy hour we did not wish to be reminded of our lives.

He thudded the earth flat, tamping the loose loam and rubble with a smooth-faced stone. He carried baskets of dirt from the loess bluffs and dumped them between the brick and mortar façades. He gathered boulders and broke them into fist-sized pieces. He joined frames and dug trenches and pounded the earth under the white sun.

From what we overheard the Colonel say, the military demonstration was approaching its finale. We had devised a system of tallying points for each squad. The totals were even; the exact count was of no consequence. What happened with the next release of the orb was all that mattered, for we had made wagers on the outcome. We are, undeniably, a nation of gamblers.

The earth-pounder worked feverishly. And so it happened that, under these rare and particular circumstances, he was positioned and possessed of the presence of mind to answer when the Wall decided to speak. "What have you mortals done to upset the sun?" said the Wall in a peculiar northern dialect. "I woke with the earth buckling beneath me. I felt your friends moving in my bowels all morning long."

"I am not surprised," the earth-pounder said. "They have upset me, too."

"Not a single tear has touched my granite bed," the Wall complained. "Have you stopped suffering all of a sudden?" The Wall sighed, sending a mild tremor along its spine. The old earth-pounder momentarily lost his balance. In its gravelly voice the Wall lamented: "There are many *li* of my belly that need digging, many *li* of flanks to erect, many *li* of my back to flatten."

"I am doing the best I can," the earth-pounder said.

"Am I not the headstone of your civilization, the only man-made object visible from the moon?"

The earth-pounder reassured the Wall of his dedication to its completion. The Wall sighed and its companion rose and fell, as if buoyed by the sea.

"I am the yoke that tames the wilderness, the nexus of the heavens, the elements, and human hands."

"Stop! I am on your side."

"Now you mortals have gone too far. You have disturbed the way of the universe. The sun and moon are the only spheres for man to adore. But look how you worship that ridiculous sphere that strikes my flanks and threatens my completion. The sun is jealous. Just wait until the moon appears."

"The others are lost," said the earth-pounder, kneeling to pat the Wall with his coarse hands.

"You are not a common laborer," the Wall said brightly. "You are an artisan of the first rank." It paused. "You possess the gentlest touch, you wield the softest rock. Besides, you are a worthy diplomat. I heard you with that scholar. Surely you can convince the others to return to work."

The earth-pounder caressed handfuls of the Wall's dry dirt. "The Emperor himself could not move them now. They are drunk with fun, neither concerned with monumental art nor matters of national security."

The earth-pounder pressed his ear to the Wall. Our shouts had increased as Reji stepped up to Earth once more. "You are human," said the Wall, "surely you know the ways of deception."

W e were packed tighter than the jewels in a pomegranate. We emptied our lungs and waved our fists. Scuffles erupted among our ranks. With Reji towering over Earth, those who had wagered against his squad begged to be relieved of their obligations. The worthy was savior and villain. He controlled our destinies. As he gripped the club high over his head, we abruptly, reverently, nervously fell silent, holding our breath as if we were awaiting a glimpse of eternity. From beyond the Wall a gigantic cloud floated over us, swallowing the ferocious sun. In the next instant the cloud dispersed, forming two distinct clusters that drifted apart in opposite directions, leaving in their wake a great expanse of blue, in which sat a somewhat muted sun and, to our utter amazement, the moon. The celestial spheres, twin silvery discs, seemed to shine with equal intensity. We could have been mistaken—we were truly dazzled by the lunar presence—but the moon appeared to be creeping toward the sun.

will sculpt you," the earth-pounder said excitedly, his face a fist's length shy of the tamped soil. "You will never suffer their insensitive hands again." The Wall shifted its immense mass menacingly beneath him. The earth-pounder assumed the shape of a snail, hugging the dirt so as not to be tossed off.

"You cannot complete me alone," the Wall said. "It is not possible. I see even the best mortals fall to madness."

"In the annals of mankind, you will be revered as its greatest achievement, and I its greatest sculptor—"

"Mortal," the Wall interrupted, "you forget, you are only mortal. How do you propose to do the work of a thousand men?"

"Have faith, my friend." He patted the Wall. "If you have faith, a thousand hands will sprout from these two."

Once again the Wall rumbled. The earth-pounder nestled his face against the hot orange soil.

The initial toss to Reji wafted up and down, veered left, and swooped right, as if the orb had encountered invisible barriers along its flight path. The orb crossed Earth and landed in the receiving soldier's pig bladder. The sixth commissioner, acting as judge, threw up his right hand and barked, "KAI!" We applauded and jeered his decision. On the subsequent toss, the orb collided with the club, making such a loud thud that our hearts momentarily stopped. The orb soared into the sky. When finally it crashed to earth, it took a mighty bounce onto the section of the Wall where the earth-pounder was toiling. Reji was speeding around the pillows when, halfway to the third, the sixth commissioner declared the orb had

landed in the forbidden zone where even the most pro-
digious collisions were magically voided, as if nothing had
happened. A buzz rose from us. We suspected foul play.
The exercises for the moment stalled. They did not have
another orb to replace the one Reji had struck.

The orb rolled to a stop near the earth-pounder. A soldier
from the retrieving squad ordered him to return the orb.
The Wall urged him to do otherwise, thus forcing us back
to work.

The earth-pounder said, "I don't need any assistance."

"I am not offering any," said the soldier. "Give me the
Colonel's orb." When the earth-pounder refused, the soldier scanned the length of the Wall for a ladder, but they
had all been destroyed under our weight. As we cheered,
other retriever soldiers came to their comrade's aid.

Above, the sun and moon touched. Gusts of wind
whipped in from the north and swirled the parched soil
into ghosts. The sky darkened. The world turned gray.
We cursed the earth-pounder for his intransigence, his
petty rebellion. He picked up the orb. Bits of his wretched
clothing were ripped and whisked away by the violent
winds. He looked in our direction and then at the other
side of the Wall. We saw nothing there. The sun melted
into the moon; day turned to dusk. A giant whirlwind tore
the remaining rags from the earth-pounder's sad frame.
The scraps of material tumbled over the forbidden soil of
the other side, until finally they came to rest, tangled in a
barren bush.

Meanwhile, like acrobats, the soldiers had formed a human ladder and scaled the Wall. The earth-pounder gazed
at the barbarians' wasteland. He dropped to his knees as
if to consult with the Wall. His naked body trembled. We
cheered the daring of two soldiers who had surmounted
the Wall and were now closing in on the traitor.

The earth-pounder was shaking his head in an apparent disagreement with the Wall over how to proceed when the two soldiers tackled him and wrestled away the orb. We cheered their heroism. The earth-pounder lay in judgment before our imperial laws. A whip cracked and bloodied his ear. A sentence was passed: "By order of the Emperor's faithful servant, our Colonel," said the soldier holding the orb, "you are condemned to death for the high crime of working during the imperial game." And so he was killed and rolled into the Wall for burial. In the sky the sun and moon were one.

VI

The activities resumed. On the very first toss to our hero, Reji clubbed the orb high into the heavens, through the darkness, to the divine landscape beyond, an offering to the gods. It was our guess that this was the reason for the spectacle. And the gods were pleased with us that moment, for they snatched away the orb.

Now the sun gradually separated from the moon, and night turned to dawn.

Then it happened, the most horrifying of sights: the orb descended, rejected by the gods, like a meteor hurled at the earth. We were frightened: it might as well have been the sun and the moon themselves dropping out of the sky.

But Reji hastened from pillow to pillow. He completed an entire circuit, and immediately the sixth commissioner proclaimed the end of the exercises. We cheered and hooted and cried; we fought and hugged, and, when finally sober, we wondered what dubious fate awaited us next.

The sun was an orange crescent. The moon the black green of a thousand-year-old egg. The din we raised subsided and we were as still as stones when the orb finally landed with a sickening thud on the other side of the Wall.

In the imprecise light, we saw movement, not the usual sway of plants or figments of swirling dust, but animal movement. Crawling as close to the ground as their reptilian kin, the fabled barbarians, the demons of the North, the obscene bandits were dragging their cheese-filled bellies toward the orb. They were terrible to behold, long and dark, covered in the skins of wild beasts, their faces matted with fur, with noses reminiscent of wolves. The barbarians, drunk on ass's milk, breathing in the manner of thirsty dogs, surrounded the orb in concentric circles and crept toward it in unison on their elbows and knees.

When those at the center of the concentric circles picked up the orb, the barbarian herd roared, and we jumped from the Wall, spilling over its edge like floodwaters, those leaping first providing a cushion for those who followed. Ours was never a courageous race. Otherwise, why would we hide behind walls?

VII

At nightfall the moon held its rightful place as proprietor of the sky. The barbarians camped around the orb. Their chieftain questioned the captured young scholar about the significance of the thing. He could not answer.

The barbarians were dining on roasted lamb. The scholar, exhausted and confused and hungry, opened his mouth to beg for some morsels. When he parted his lips, it was not his pleas we heard. Instead, he sang in a high, sweet voice:

"White birds over the grey river.
Scarlet flowers on the green hills.
I watch the spring go by and wonder
If I shall ever return home."

Later that night we lay under the stars. The appetizing scent of roasted lamb lingered in the air around us. Our mouths watered, our stomachs growled. Some conspired to kill and roast the Colonel's horse. Some dreamed of being a barbarian. Some wrestled with their esteem for the soldier Reji. Some wondered what tomorrow might bring. But most of us listened to the earth, with our ears pressed against its skin, while the Wall snored.

Inheritance

remember once, as a girl, when my parents were late
returning from Chinatown, how I tossed in bed, unable
to shake free of the vision I had of them side by side,
like loaves of bread wrapped in gauze, laid out in a shallow
grave. Then I realized they weren't old enough to die: at
that time I believed everyone lived a hundred years. I did
some quick arithmetic, and soon, comforted by the sanity
of numbers, I fell asleep. But my theory was tested a short
time later. On TV one night, I saw the actor Richard Long,
a regular in the show, slip from a rope that dangled from
an airplane door. With a full head of hair and wrinkle-free
face, he fell to his death on the screen. I was stunned—he
was too young. But a few weeks later, there he was again,
as handsome as ever, not even a scratch from the fall,
reincarnated as a cowboy in another show. I grabbed pencil
and paper: I had ninety-two years to go.

Of course, I wasn't so smart. Shortly after I turned ten,
my theory was dealt a severe blow. Edsel, my father, took
me and my sister Ellen to the cemetery that sprawled beneath the bridge on the way to Chinatown. I used to think
people were somehow crammed inside those tombstones.
Whenever we drove past I held my breath; I didn't want
to breathe the same air breathed by the dead ones in the

tombstones. Edsel guided the car through the cemetery's narrow lanes. Soon we came to a stop, and Ellen started to cry. She left the car and unloaded a pair of grease-soaked bags filled with food from the trunk. A picnic? I wondered. We scaled a rocky, yellow-dirt hill and stopped at a grave marker covered with pretty Chinese characters and a single word: ERNEST. Ellen arranged the food on platters and set them on the ground. She and Edsel lit incense and burned colored paper.

Meanwhile, at home, my mother had transformed the eating table into an altar; joss sticks, roast meats, dumplings, and oranges spread before framed photographs of a strange boy. In this way Edsel introduced me to my brother Ernest.

I wish Edsel hadn't done that because what happened next could make marble cry. Not long after he told me about my brother, Ellen, her husband, and their two kids were killed in a crash on Francis Lewis Boulevard. Then, nine months later, my mother died while ironing. People said that my mother had just given up, and when I didn't cry they said I'd run out of tears. You might blame Edsel because he told the secret. It was the power of suggestion, multiplied by bad luck, raised to the nth degree. On a smaller scale the same thing happens all the time—you say you haven't been sick in months, and within twenty-four hours you're in bed, your chest rubbed raw with Vicks.

After that, Edsel kept a close eye on me. Sometimes I'd catch him staring intently, as if I were creation's last sip of water set out under a blazing sun. He started to talk to me a lot—something Chinese fathers aren't predisposed to do—thinking perhaps that by talking, I'd have to stick around and listen. He pronounced us friends and demanded that I call him Edsel, straying again from Chinese-father orthodoxy. All this surprised me and took getting used to. He was very old-world Chinese even though in his public life he was, to anyone who asked, an American. He had served in the Army just after the First World War, was a member of the American Legion, and every four years voted for President, according to the ease with which he could say the candidate's name. In the '50s he finally acquired his Anglo-sounding name, given to him by the Mott Street apothecary from whom we bought our herbs. The apothecary knew more English than most; lots of families asked that he name their kids. He was proud of this service and had devised a system for the task, assigning each family a letter of the alphabet. We were the E's: Ernest, Ellen, Edna, and Edsel. Imagine the clans of X, Y, and Z.

A few months ago, I was on television. We were living in Buffalo, and the night before the women's health collective downtown had been bombed. The next morning, a group of us went to the scene to protest the bombing. All the local media were present; people with vid-cams scoured the ruins for shattered jars of fetuses. A reporter from KBUF ("No fluff on Kay-Buff!") interviewed me on camera. The network picked up the story and that evening I was on Dan Rather's show.

I did a respectable job. I said the bombing was an act of terrorism, encouraged by the President, condoned by the Attorney General.

Before the news ended, friends started phoning to congratulate me for my political courage and moral rectitude. Then anonymous callers said they'd pray for my soul, burn down my home, and/or cut out my womb. Miss Ott, my eighth-grade social-studies teacher, called from Queens and said, "You certainly did not get those ideas from my class."

Around midnight Edsel phoned. "I would have called

sooner," he said, "but I have been suffering little strokes ever since I saw you on the TV."

I rolled my eyes at my husband, Li, who was in bed watching a basketball game on cable.

"Your name was right there on the screen," Edsel said. "Everyone saw you. You know how it is when a Chinese comes on the TV—this one calls that one, they wake the little ones, and soon they are all watching. They know," he said. "They think I am your father."

I reminded him that most of his friends couldn't read my name off the screen or understand a word I said.

"When a Chinese is not cooking on the TV," he said, "we know it is trouble. I hope they have no news where they are now."

By "they" he meant our family: my mother, who refused the apothecary's name; earthbound Ernest, good with cars, in harmony with iron, steel, oil, and grease; Ellen, a born breeder, who married a Hong Kong jewelry clerk out of high school, and could mow the lawn in white linen high heels and not get a grass stain. I was the last of my parents' procreative work, the new and improved model, far outstripping my predecessors for durability and strength, who restored the order to the rise and fall of generations—at least I could say I outlived my mother.

Putting the outrage of my mother and siblings aside, what upset Edsel about my appearance on TV was my politics. He wouldn't say so directly, but he was shaken by the fact that his lone surviving child was, in his eyes, opposed to babies.

Politics had always been a problem for us. During the war in Vietnam, we had many battles over U.S. policy. It wasn't so much that Edsel favored the war as it was that he hated the Chinese Communists. We seemed to be fighting all the time, but all he wanted was for me to be more like Ellen, with her young brood, her pillbox hats, her heels and hose. But I wore blue work shirts and steel-toed boots, I listened to loud music, I went to peace vigils and moratoriums—though I was never one to shout slogans, no matter how well they rhymed; I loved the sight of hundreds of candles burning in the dark; I was a passive-activist, a handclapper, the rank and file of a popular move-ment. I didn't understand Edsel then. He should've known better than anyone what was going on in Vietnam: so much sudden death. But when I went to college (I was the first in the family to get so far, the Army and babies having detoured my brother and sister, respectively), Edsel's po-litical position changed. Even without the impetus of a draft-age son, he voted for McGovern, and against the war, even though he had difficulty with the Senator's name.

It was the morning after I became a TV star, and Li was getting ready for his softball game. He played first base on a team sponsored by an anti-nuke group, Dads for Peace, made up of new fathers and fathers-to-be. They called themselves the Peace Bombers. On his uniform shirt there was a baby's face. In arching letters above its head were the words GROW! NOT GLOW! Li's no father; he played because he was big and athletic (he was a starter for the Chinese national basketball team) and supposedly told the coach "Soon, soon" when asked about his status as a dad. So they made an exception in his case. The po-litical symbolism of a Communist in double knits playing for peace was too rich; besides, Li hit line drives. I found Li's enthusiasm for the dads goading. Clearly his was a political gesture directed at me. He wanted children. Hav-ing escaped China's 1.2-baby-per-couple pragmatism, he had looked forward to American bounty, capitalist excess: on foreign soil he'd revive China's traditional big-family system and father his own team.

As far as I could tell, Li was as crazy as those dads he played ball with. The world was a risky place, and they knew that, and they wanted to fix things. But they hadn't yet, and still they made babies before the world was fit. Now that the babies were here, how do they protect them? "Look, kids," they'd say, "a day will come when missiles drop from clouds, there will be beautiful light, and we will fall forward and not feel a thing, okay?" I wasn't alone in this clearheadedness. Lots of friends were equally concerned, although their political resolve was slowly eroding. More and more I was receiving birth announcements in the mail from them. All that dilating and pushing, all that energy, if focused, could fix the world.

Li left the apartment, but was back in two seconds. He shut the door, then opened it a crack. "What's going on?" I said. Without turning, he motioned for me to join him.

Downstairs the front door was open and beneath its lintel I could see the bottom half of a police car parked on the street in front of the house.

The police were in Mrs. Woo's apartment. She was eighty-two years old. She was legally blind, her vision evaporating in the short time we lived there. When we moved in, she stood at her door, as we were positioned now, watching us haul our lives up the stairs. Her nose was a moon in that shadowy opening, and when I looked her way, she didn't blink, like a knot in wood. She befriended Li; they spoke Chinese; she cooked medicinal soups of bark and berries, which she served in plastic containers saved from wonton shops, and gave Li the soup when he returned from work, waiting for him in that crack in the door. Once, she invited us for supper;

this was after her eyes were clouds. She refused our help. She fumbled in drawers, measured liquids with her knuckles, negotiated the kitchen by memory in a quick, uniform gait that resembled my mother's, a proper lady who could walk on the backs of snails. (How I distressed her with my sneakers and my springy step!) Mrs. Woo scared me with her work at the stove. The gas, the matches, her slow fingers. I thought she'd blow us up. When we sat down to eat, I lost my appetite at the sight of her: steam rose from her big bowl of soup noodles, curling past her creamy eyes, a shifting veil around her white hairs. Later that evening, I lay on my side of the bed and cried. Li heard me, said nothing, and lay as still as a body could, drawing the faintest of breaths. Our minds were fixed on great distances. He could ride a jet or hop a boat to China, fast or slow, and feel again his mother's hand in his hair—a trifling eight thousand miles, a dozen time zones away. I hated him for this privilege, this simple fact of geography. I burned colored paper to reach my mother; if I go to her, it must be on the gentle edge of a curl of smoke.

Mrs. Woo rarely spoke directly to me, which was a relief because my Chinese was no better than a six-year-old's. Once my sister started school and infected our home with English, I stopped learning Chinese, and after that my mother—who let Edsel negotiate this American life for her and who masterfully avoided linguistic accommodation of any form—spoke to me as to a little child. When Mrs. Woo had a question for me, she asked it through Li. Still I understood most of what passed between them—they weren't discussing, after all, the origins of the universe. I was nothing to her but an American. My blood was good, she'd say, I'd make good Chinese-looking babies for Li, but, she'd say, why didn't I dress fancy like real American

girls, why no lipstick? Translation: she's not quite the real
thing, neither Chinese nor American, and wouldn't Li be
happier with a culturally pure spouse?

As much as her ideas upset me, I couldn't let on that I
knew what she was saying or else she'd stop saying those
things in front of me. I didn't have the vocabulary to
answer her anyway, and if I said what was on my mind
in the language I thought it in, that would simply confirm
what she thought.

She left with the police and a young woman who had
the wide-face look of a Korean. Mrs. Woo cursed her for
a Japanese. I called after her, and the Korean said, as the
police led the old woman to their car, that she was a social
worker, that Mrs. Woo, at her children's request, would
live in a retirement home.

Li went to play his softball game. He walked to the car
with his bat on his broad shoulders. He was upset.
But this, as usual, wasn't easily detected. My husband's bigness exaggerated any display of emotion: angered, he seemed vindictive; frightened, he seemed meek.
When he saw Mrs. Woo with the police, Li's hand, resting
heavily on my bony nape, burned and gained sudden light-
ness, like the flash of heat that accompanies the spirit's
flight at the moment of death.

I wanted Li to say something about what we'd seen. A
snappy couplet, a specialty of my mother's, that would
reduce experience to bad poetry. Or experience distilled
to ideology: Mrs. Woo's arrest was emblematic of capitalist
consumer culture—use a person, throw her away. But Li
wasn't one to discuss matters of a personal nature. He
tended to categorize human experience into the three basic
themes of high-school English class:

MAN versus MAN
MAN versus NATURE
MAN versus SOCIETY

I met Li in college. He was an exchange student. My political-science professor thought Li and I should meet since we were both Chinese. We'd have lots to talk about, he said. I blushed, acquiesced, and went home to my room and was sick for a week.

Edsel liked Li from the start. He was serious, smart, and Chinese. Edsel wanted to give us a big wedding in my mother's memory. Her dying wish for her most durable child. One day we took Edsel out for lunch, and on the way to the restaurant we detoured to the courthouse, and we were married by a judge. Edsel was happy with the match, but fretted over what my mother would think. In the weeks that followed, he burned incense and colored paper to appease my mother's spirit. He even urged us to marry again, threatening to join her in heaven and soothe her hurt feelings in person if we refused.

We moved to Buffalo for Li's graduate school. For a period Edsel didn't talk to us. Then he showed up at our door one day, a new man. He brought a bottle of cognac for Li, and for me he had a pair of yellow baby booties he said he'd found among my mother's things. This was a lie. The booties were knit with acrylic, and chemists didn't start spinning yarn from test tubes until after my mother was gone. Big wedding or not, implicit in marriage was a promise of babies, fat bundles of Edselesque matter.

Babies. Li and the softball dads. What were their conversations like? Did they discuss the effect of strontium 90 on the food chain or calculate the half-life of U 235? More likely, they debated the relative merits of disposable diapers over cloth diapers, breast feeding over bottles; they fretted about baby's colic, stools, and vaccinations.

I put on jeans and a man's white dress shirt, the sleeves rolled to my elbows, and a pair of turquoise high heels that I bought on a whim; I had once owned similar shoes, hand-me-downs from Ellen, which in my youth I had junked as evidence of my sister's oppression. I thought I'd stretch the leather at the toes while I studied. I could barely walk in them. Why I bought such shoes, I didn't know. Lately I found this was a satisfactory answer for lots of questions. I hid the shoes from Li. Why? I didn't know.

I went downstairs and sat on the porch on Mrs. Woo's green bench, my feet propped up on the railing, my Education textbook open on my lap. I was taking classes toward a teaching certificate then, and I had to prepare a lesson for the first-graders I was student-teaching on Monday. I tried to picture their happy five- and six-year-old faces as they stared expectantly at Miss Edna, waiting to be initiated into the wonders of the alphabet: A is for Atom, B is for Bomb, C is for Chain reaction, and so on.

The sun was bright, hot for the first time that season. It bleached the words from the page. The birds were back and noisy, the maples feathered with tender green leaves. Our street was lined with rows of Depression-era houses, connected by clotheslines and separated by impoverished lawns and old cars in driveways, many of which never moved. For hours on end Mrs. Woo used to study this scene.

Across the street, two houses down from ours, boys were playing with guns. One boy held a pistol to the temple of another; bullets rang from his mouth and the victim collapsed to the sidewalk.

These weren't the kids in our textbooks. I tried to study but it was useless. I could never teach boys like that. Give these young murderers math and science, and they'll devise more sophisticated ways of death. No new lessons: they needed to unlearn the language of gunfire that shoots from their mouths so eloquently.

I shut my eyes and immediately my thoughts found Mrs. Woo. I hardly knew her. She had two children. Her daughter lived in Boston, her son in San Francisco. She said he had a head like a sledgehammer; his wife was recently in the hospital; after three quick miscarriages, she bled. Doctors had advised against any more babies after the tenth, but Mrs. Woo's son wanted a boy child, and they'd had three more daughters before her womb staged her happy rebellion. She scolded him, Mrs. Woo said; leave your wife alone, wear those things the doctors gave you, let her eat the pills. During the warm months, she kept busy on the green bench sending cards and five-dollar checks to commemorate every birthday, graduation, holiday. She amused herself by reciting the names of her grandchildren and great-grandchildren, trying to match each kid with his or her parent.

What I didn't know about Mrs. Woo's personal history I invented. For years she resisted marriage and motherhood, frightened by the thought of seeing her wasp waist thicken; she wanted to stay young, forever stepping into expensive shoes, plucking Chesterfields from a gold-mesh sack, sipping tea from white porcelain cups.

My textbook slipped off my lap. I opened my eyes. Everything was purple and yellow. When the world came into focus, my little terrorists lowered their weapons and ran.

The professor who supervised my student-teaching called. He began by saying he was sorry, then got to the point. The teacher whose class I was to teach had seen me on TV and now refused to work with me.

The School Board would discuss my case at their next meeting, but until then I wasn't allowed to teach in the district. My mind recalled my terrorists. Could I do any worse than what their teachers had already done?

The telephone rang again. This time my father was on the line. He was upset because two schoolgirls had asked to take his picture while he was standing outside his favorite cigar store. "I have turned into one of those eccentrics that people photograph for no reason," he complained.

I felt bad for him. Each day, he'd go for a cigar and smoke it just outside the cigar store. He'd stand there, puffing and gnawing at the end, with his Yankees cap on his milk-carton head and his hair sticking out conspicuously, like fungus on a tree. He loved that routine, especially after he quit working. When my mother died, she left a great deal of money that no one knew she had. Once Edsel recovered from the shock of finding the boxes of cash, he sold his laundry and bought shares in two parking lots in Manhattan. It turned out to be a great investment. He was proud of those fenced-in squares of asphalt. After Li and I were married, Edsel and Li sat down for a serious heart-to-heart. "I raised Edna on the fruits of my toil," he said. "And it wasn't cheap. She's used to brand names, Crest, Kraft, Green Giant. Learn English. Stop bouncing that basketball. You can't eat basketballs, and she has no hidden money. Do you understand, I am offering you lots?"

Li couldn't understand parking lots. From a country of a billion people, land devoted to idle cars seemed ludicrous to Li. Homes for people, not cars, he told Edsel.

"No," said Edsel. "It's money in your pocket. Del Monte on your table. There's no overhead, no inventory, and labor's cheap. I pay my Puerto Ricans the minimum wage; I can get away with less. All they want is to sit in Cadillacs and play the radio."

Li said, "You're a landlord. Land belongs to the people."

"That's an improvement," Edsel said. "Your wife says give the land back to the Indians. Look, you don't believe it, but I'm people too. Asphalt and fences aren't free; even Puerto Rican boys cost something. I'm not so bad. When your Communist friends take over, they'll let me pass. I'm no big shot. I read Chinese newspapers, not the *Wall Street Journal*. You don't like what I do, but you like my daughter. My daughter is one-hundred-percent parking lot."

Edsel poured a shot of whiskey. "Here's an ancient Chinese tale," Edsel said, "that I made up a long time ago. Two beggars are sitting on the ground. Number One draws a circle in the dirt. He calls this the earth. 'The earth is barren,' he says. 'Everywhere people go hungry.' Number Two nods. 'It's not good,' he says. Number One digs deep into his pocket and removes a handful of seeds and sprinkles them on the circle. His companion cannot believe his eyes. He says, 'You're throwing away our last meal.' By now, Number One has covered the seeds with a layer of dirt. 'Soon,' he says, 'the world will abound with food.' He upends a gourd of water over the earth. Number Two is horrified. The water washes away the circle. Number Two says, 'You've flooded the earth.' The hungry beggars go to sleep. They sleep for days. For weeks. For months. When they wake, there are beautiful, delectable plants before their eyes. They can't believe what they see and assume they are dreaming. They go back to sleep and never wake."

Edsel came to visit that Monday. Since I wasn't allowed to teach, I was able to meet him at the bus terminal. He looked the same as when I saw him last. As always, I first noticed his big gleaming head and his shiny face. For all his years and all his worries, he had hardly a wrinkle. Like me, he was wearing a white shirt and black slacks. He had on brown corduroy shoes, and I was in my heels. This last detail he noticed immediately: "You're finally growing up."

Edsel at first refused to ride in our new Toyota. He said Japanese cars were made of death. The seat covers, he said, were the skins of Chinese. "This is vinyl," I said. "Do you mean our ancestors came in oil drums?"

He cursed Emperor Hirohito, looked searchingly at the heavens, and got into the car. On the drive home, he told me about Judy Spiegel's daughter's wedding. Judy Spiegel had been Ellen's best friend when they were growing up in Queens. They did everything together. Judy Spiegel married a boy from the neighborhood, Ellen imported one from Hong Kong, and both girls never gave a thought to leaving. After Ellen died, Judy Spiegel and her kids often visited us. She'd kiss me and press my nose against her hard, milk-heavy breasts. "She looks just like Ellen," she'd say, tears wrecking her mascara, and then dash into the bathroom, followed by her kids. For weeks after such encounters, I'd study my face in the mirror and wonder what a life Ellen must've had with a face that made her friends cry.

"Maxine Spiegel married a flier," Edsel said. "U.S. Air Force. Red, white, and wild blue yonder."

He looked at me for a reaction. I kept my eyes on the road. "You would prefer I say he's a Russian spy," Edsel said. "He is everything you hate. A patriot and one day an airline pilot. Career and country. Two things you two know nothing about."

"What's his payload?" I said.

"Pay?" Edsel said. "I'm surprised. Such a sensible question from Edna."   •

"No. What weapons does he fly?"

"Now that is my girl," Edsel said. "Bombs, always bombs on her brain."

I shut up. He returned to the wedding. "They did it in the yard. Yards are for dogs, not nuptials. All day the ladies' shoes sink into the ground. I would rent a ballroom in a big hotel. No sod for our guests."

What he said next I knew by heart: my mother's plans for her famous daughter's wedding, with a guest list of show-biz types, royalty, and politicians; an evening of satin and silk brocade, exquisite jewels and filed teeth.

"You forget," I said, "we've been married for eight years."

He said, "Not in your mother's eyes."

The way his mind worked worried me. Sometimes it seemed my dead mother rode on his shoulders like a monkey, and all the difficult years had weighed on his brain like an iron, smoothing away the convolutions of good sense. I remember when I was away at college Edsel went to work at one of his lots. Back in China the Cultural Revolution, that plague of ideology, was lustily destroying lives, intellectuals banished to the countryside to unlearn learning among the masses. Edsel decided also to return to the land, showing up at a parking lot one day for work. His employees didn't know the old Chinaman was Edsel, their boss, so they put him to work filling potholes, sweeping gravel, and walking litter patrol, while they lounged in luxury sedans and smoked cigarettes and played the stereos. Edsel didn't complain. He actually gave some of his men raises for the supervisory skills they had shown.

"Edna, we will show Judy Spiegel how to do a wedding," he said, like a coach exhorting his charges.

"Stop, please," I said.

"Stop? Not now. I started this a long time ago. I started when your mother said yes. Then the three of you. How do I stop, I'm your father?"

Then he was silent. Suddenly, I felt as uncomfortable as

an urbanite honed on sirens and horns stranded in the country.

"You are right," he said solemnly. "I am a stupid man."

"I never said that."

"I am old, then. It shows in my brain—like a bladder."

"You're not old."

"I'm seventy-eight. Little girls want to take my picture for a school project."

We arrived at the house, but sat in the car a while longer. Again I assured him he wasn't old.

"Then you are old," he said. "And so is the singer your mother likes." She wanted Tom Jones to perform at the reception. "I am giving up on you," he said. "You are old and stubborn like me. So I give the wedding to your daughter."

"I don't have a daughter."

"Do you need me to tell you what to do?"

I opened the passenger door for Edsel.

"Very old," he said, getting out. "Compared to your brother and sister, you're ancient—a relic."

I slammed shut the door and leaned back against the seat, closing my eyes, running my hands over my cheeks. Baby talk again. Like a car salesman who gets your number and calls and calls. Only the sales pitch was slightly different this time. Edsel wasn't worried he'd die before seeing another grandchild; he wasn't worried about the biological clock that scared my over-thirty friends into bookstores for the vicarious comfort of child-care manuals. He was worried about my precarious stay on the planet. To his way of thinking, I was a car on the street with hundreds of parking tickets, and at any moment I might be towed away.

Was there something wrong with me? My fallen comrades now swear that wiping a baby's rump isn't only a joy but a political act as well—worrying about bombs is limiting; they kill, and that's it. But with a baby you have the big picture: all of human history asleep in your arms, ready to be remolded. I'd come to think of babies as ferns—both grow, both are messy.

We had tea and ate dumplings he brought from Chinatown. Then after I settled Edsel down for his nap, I went out to the porch.

On the green bench I felt drowsy, exhausted by Edsel's noise. But I was glad he had come and was comforted knowing he was just upstairs. An overall sense of well-being, a childlike intuition of life's wholeness, held me. I was reminded of the peace I felt that night twenty-four years ago when I calculated the years he had left with me.

I rubbed my stomach, full from dumplings, and thought of Old Ming, a family friend and a well-respected cook in Bayside, who, according to Edsel, dug a fallout shelter, fearing Mao's bandits were after him; when he failed to herd his family into the hole, he took up residence there by himself for two years before his death from "general conditions incompatible with life." So here was this celebrated cook, eating canned Army-surplus beans, waiting out the Big One, while his wife and kids ran off with a Filipino to the sunny, airy, citrusy West Coast.

A KBUF van pulled up in front of the house. The driver came out the back doors and piled video equipment and cables on the sidewalk. He monkeyed with the technology. Opening the passenger door, the reporter on the eleven-o'clock news, who covered stories like lions at the zoo with toothaches, mineral shows at the Armory, and trends in infant sleepwear, slipped from the van. She marched toward the house, taking quick, buglike steps in pink shoes with pink rosettes at the toe. The cameraman followed close at her heels.

"It's me," she said, tapping her lacy bodice with her microphone, "Christie Lovecraft, KBUF Action News." She was standing at the foot of the steps. I stared at her perfect teeth. On the street the neighborhood terrorists were caucusing by the rear of the van. "I speak for women all over the greater Buffalo metropolitan area," she said. "I want to help you. I can put you on TV." She wiggled her long white fingers at the cameraman. "Shoot her," she said.

Why couldn't they let me die a neat video death, like Richard Long falling to earth from a plane? I waved my extended arms in front of my face.

"The School Board has ruined you," Lovecraft said. "Think of the children who'll never benefit from your knowledge."

I couldn't risk another appearance on TV. I ran for the shelter of the house. That was my intent—action in the abstract. For a quick escape I needed mugger's shoes, traction-rich sneakers. At the door my heels caught the weave of the welcome mat, giving Lovecraft the seconds she needed to catch up. She nudged me with her microphone. I reached out for balance and escape, and grabbed Mrs. Woo's door. It opened.

I bolted the door. The reporter knocked urgently. "I want to help," she said. "We have to stick together." And on and on, invoking the ghost of sisterhood. "Please, just one good quote," she begged, "something women can get behind."

She continued to beg at the door. Then I heard her heels tick against the porch. She said something to the cameraman. I peeked past the blinds. He was positioned to shoot, waiting for Lovecraft to finish freshening her lips and fluffing her hair.

The camera's red light came on. She was doing the story without me; she was out on my porch saying what she pleased about me. What might spill from her mouth? She was an honest danger. But if I intervened, then that would become her story. I couldn't allow that.

I considered calling the police. But I remembered the police had taken Mrs. Woo away. They did the oppressors' bidding, and they'd arrest me for breaking and entering before they'd rid the property of Lovecraft. Tears were not far when I was rescued, miraculously. Like the cavalry on TV, my little terrorists had boarded the van, and one little Qaddafi after another sped away with chunks of high technology. From the porch Lovecraft chucked her TV voice and screamed, "Get back here, you little creeps!" The cameraman gave chase.

This new generation, how they love terror and mayhem. They stuff guns in their pants, knives inside socks, they wear high-tech helmets with spikes and dangerous lights. I remember a visionary piece of graffiti someone had scrawled in a library book:

Our future lies in the hands of our children.

But how could I explain my would-be murderers' rescue of me? Perhaps I was wrong about them, perhaps I'd been too far removed from children, perhaps where I read hardness and chaos I should've read lightheartedness and fun; the helmets were hats, the bullets spitting from their mouths laughter.

In the center of Mrs. Woo's living room there was a big TV set. So often I'd come home evenings and heard the set through the door. She couldn't see the picture or understand the words; it was simply a companion. On top of the set there was a bowl of plastic fruit and a vase of silk mums, white, violet, dusty. The couch and easy chairs were draped with brightly colored bedspreads that clashed with everything. In the air was the odor of food. I couldn't identify the particular foods, but I recognized the smell. It lived in our house in Queens and gradually dissipated after my mother died. Back in the days when the smell reigned, when she fried fish in a black wok, and the greasy steam climbed the walls and oils splattered the floor, our home was furnished with reconditioned junk. Edsel dragged home off the streets anything with a flat surface or legs. We had this musty old couch that I loved to sit on for hours, rubbing my fingernail into the upholstery until the fabric was just a few naked threads, and then I'd pick the batting out. Once, she caught me in the act, and my mother whipped me. Her job, one she did well. She slapped me across the face and then used a bamboo switch that whistled through the air and raised pretty red welts. We lived in junk, while my American friends' furniture was so soft and clean I was afraid to sit on it. All those years, milk crates for chairs, and she had that secret money squirreled away.

In Mrs. Woo's bedroom I found what I had expected. I knew she'd have things stored in boxes. Edsel found the money, wrapped in socks and rags, in my mother's boxes. The boxes were stacked high everywhere. My mother never threw anything away. Hers was a hoarding instinct, sharpened by encounters with flood, famine, and the Japanese invader. Mrs. Woo's boxes—piled in the closet and along the baseboards, the cardboard worn and soft—sagged into one another, melted by time. In one box I found letters, in another baseball cards, in a third baby clothes that were yellow and stained and brittle. I tried to imagine her son filling out these garments, the same son who'd kill his wife for a son of his own.

On the dresser, an elegant piece in ebony, she had a

picture of her son as a young man. A soft, womanish face, with slicked-back hair, an aggressive forehead, intense little eyes; a sardonic handsomeness. Next door in a fake gold frame was the sister, whose eyes were equally intense, who bore the same handsomeness, though hers was blunted by a helmet of tight curls that rose up from her forehead like an extravagant trifle designed to hide some secret fact. As far back as I could remember, Ellen had habitually permed her hair, while mine was forever Chinese-straight.

Mrs. Woo's grandchildren decorated the edges of the mirror attached to the dresser. The girls were cuties, though none of them were smiling. These were formal school photographs taken, I'd estimate, when each girl was in the second or third grade; I was struck by the sight—a family of daughters all the same age. I looked away and caught myself in the mirror. I had to pause. Was the face I saw there the face Ellen would've seen if she were standing in my shoes and had lived to be my age, thirty-four? I used to think I'd never be as old as Ellen. So much older and mature. Sometimes it seemed my parents couldn't wait for me to grow up, to stop being a kid and be more like Ellen. Once, a short time after Ellen and her family were killed, my mother dressed me in Ellen's clothes. Nothing fit; even her nylons were baggy on my legs. When Edsel saw this scene, he snapped a picture of me as Ellen.

He loved that photograph, and kept it on the mirror where he shaved. What were his thoughts in the makeshift darkroom he set up in the bathroom as he stared at the square of paper in the developing solution, and ever so slowly the fuzzy image came true? How many times did he blink his little eyes, adjusting them to the red safety light in the blackened room and to the girl in the photograph? Which one of us did he see? Whose photograph had he just taken?

In a red metal frame there was a photograph taken in

China. It was a portrait of six young women posed in three rows—three at the bottom, two in the middle, one at the top. The figures were rigid and dressed in black; their eyes were like pinholes—empty, unfocused. The photograph had been hand-tinted: the ladies had peach-pink cheeks and plum-red lips; they each stood behind a vase of pastel flowers and were separated, within their rows, by soft green potted plants. Was Mrs. Woo among these ladies? We had a hand-tinted photograph at home, only ours had men in it, and while the ladies were colored, the men were left as they were in the stern, no-nonsense world of black-and-white, their authority still intact. In the center of that photograph was my mother's mother, who was seated with her knees apart, a hand resting on each knee, and the hands were enormous and luminous things against her black clothing. Strange, like boxer's gloves cut from stone. My mother had big hands too; hers were menacing birds trapped inside a house, flying in your face, tangling in your hair—big clumsy unpredictable things. Perhaps if she hadn't lost her son, or if I had been born her second son, her hands might never have seemed so big or mean. But she had inherited the hands from her mother, and I was always worried I'd inherited mine from her too.

On my way out of the apartment I looked in on the kitchen. I thought of the night Mrs. Woo had prepared supper for us. How she raised all that noise and clatter, how the hot broth washed over her thumb and she never flinched, how she moved like a ghost, how the room filled with lovely food smells made by the hands of one whose children left her for dead. It was wonderful that she had developed such independence, but sad she was forced to do so.

I sat at the kitchen table. I almost saw Mrs. Woo moving from station to station. I wondered what it was like. I

studied the room, the placement of things; then I closed
my eyes. I got up and let go of the table and crossed the
kitchen to the counter. That was easy; I stepped on the rag
runner first, so I knew I was close. I felt for and opened
cabinets. I felt the insides of each cabinet, knocking jars
over, until I located a cup. I filled the cup with water and
drank. As I did so, I imagined Li was at the table, as he
had been that night, watching.

At the end of the counter I found the stove, its grooved
controls, its rough iron. I had watched Mrs. Woo cook
over what for her were invisible flames. She knew fire by
touch, by the heat it threw.

The matches were kept in the cabinet above the stove.
I struck one against the flint. I detected the light burst,
even through my lids. I steadied my hand, learning the
match. The moment I first sensed heat, I extinguished the
flame.

It wasn't until I tried the third of the stove's four burners
that I heard or smelled gas. I swept my hand over the stove
top to determine which burner was working. When I felt
the gas, the hairs on my arm stood on end. The gas was
cool and cut through to my bone. My joints stiffened. This
was my mother's hand as she lay in her coffin. At the wake,
a man I'd never seen before urged me to touch her, to kiss
her as he'd seen Americans kiss their dead on TV, but I
refused, and he nudged me, then pushed my arm forward.
Finally, I obeyed because the room was cold, the air heavy
with incense and smoke and flowers, the people crying
while I couldn't; and because I needed to make a good
daughterly show for Edsel, to give him face in front of his
friends. I was slightly out of my mind. I touched her hand.
My mother hit me because hers was a bitter life; she said
so; and I had always thought that she was right, that she
had every reason, that she had suffered most, her son and

daughter and grandchildren dead. I touched the hand that
hid the money. How poor and miserable she was in this
land! Poor woman, my mother. She hid thousands and
then hit me ("Don't tell your father," she said) when I
complained as she did. She turned her nose up to an American name because it was ugly and wrong, and I had to
call her Mother when I wanted to call her anything but
that. What I didn't know was this. Had I inherited my
mother's hand, which was warm only after she hit her
little girl, which for comfort reached for angry fistfuls of
her child's hair? How could I be sure that I'd tamed my
hand, that I'd taught it to be patient and soothing? For
years I feared my mother in myself, for things do run in
the family. We died young; who could guarantee the safety
of my children?

I was dizzy, as dizzy as I was that day with the incense
swirling, the paper burning, the refrigerated air, and I
touched my lips to her hard skin, an unforgettable chill.
The same man then led me away from the coffin, and I sat
beside Edsel, who told me, "Good girl, good girl," squeezing my fingers. I was dizzy now, the air was heavy and
strong. Tears came to my eyes. I opened them so the tears
could run freely. I pulled my hand away from the burner
and rubbed at the numbness.

All I wanted was warmth. One match now and I could
solve every problem.

I opened the window and breathed what seemed like
my first breath. I looked out at the yard, with the apple
tree before me, staring at what I believed were molecules
in the air—at the moment I believed my eyes were that
good. I massaged my hand, and as feeling returned, the
cold hardness at its core melted away. I looked out at the
yard again, but now, instead of the smallest things, I saw
over impossible distances: limestone mountains in mist,

birds in wooden cages, women in rice paddies whose legs were spread wide. Scenes of South China I knew from calendars Edsel hung in our home. This was the mystery wound in my DNA, this the very color of my genes, this my inheritance.

I went upstairs. I hadn't forgotten, but still was surprised. He was sitting up in bed, the covers lightly draped over his lap; the rest of the covers lay on the floor, kicked there in his sleep. He was wearing little white cotton socks, sagging around his ankles, yellowed at the toes. He was smacking his lips, tasting his mouth, making funny noises, as he rubbed his eyes with the backs of two small fists.

My father.

ACKNOWLEDGMENTS

I want to express my gratitude to the California Arts Council, the National Endowment for the Arts, and the W. K. Rose Fellowship/Vassar College for their encouragement and generous support, and to Barbara Grossman, Elaine Markson, and Bobbie Bristol for their help in turning these stories into a book.

And special thanks to Bruce Brooks.

And to Denny Hoberman Louie, who read these stories at the beginning, middle, and end, my deepest appreciation.

A NOTE ABOUT THE AUTHOR

David Wong Louie was born in Rockville Center, New York, in 1954. He attended Vassar College and the University of Iowa. His work has appeared in numerous magazines, including *The Iowa Review*, *Chicago Review*, *Ploughshares*, as well as *The Best American Short Stories 1989*. He has received fellowships from the National Endowment for the Arts, the California Arts Council, the Macdowell Colony, and Yaddo. He teaches at Vassar College.

A NOTE ON THE TYPE

This book has been set in a digitized version of the well-known Monotype face Bembo. The roman is a copy of a letter cut for the celebrated Venetian printer Aldus Manutius by Francesco Griffo, and first used in Pietro Cardinal Bembo's *De Aetna* of 1495. The companion italic is an adaption of the chancery script type designed by the Roman calligrapher and printer Lodovico degli Arrighi, called Vincentino, and used by him during the 1520s.

Composed by PennSet, Inc., Bloomsburg, Pennsylvania. Printed and bound by Arcata Graphics, Martinsburg, West Virginia.

Designed by Peter A. Andersen